Solomon's Ring

All throughout the ages the mystery had to remain a secret.

Raymond Beresford Hamilton

ISBN: 1-4781-9453-7
ISBN-13: 9781478194538

Acknowledgements

First, my sincere thanks to my editor for her commitment and unwavering dedication to the completion of this novel. To my family members, thank you for enduring those long days and nights that I was away gathering all the necessary information for this work. You inspired me, even when I was on the verge of sleep, to continue. You were the engine behind my motivation to see this project through to its completion. And finally, to all my friends and associates who offered their support and encouragement, I extend my deepest thanks and appreciation.

PROLOGUE

Princeton, New Jersey, 1991

The warmth of summer hung around a bit longer this year, but the recent chill in the air signaled its end. The orange glow of autumn illuminated the mountainside on the far horizon and in the backdrop tunneled rays of the rising sun. All around, maple tree leaves pushed by the chilly breeze tumbled over well-worn roadways under the gray December sky.

Julian DePaul, Sr., parked his SUV in the parking spot reserved for maintenance vehicles, between the tall, prestigious, brick buildings. He heard what he thought was a terrified man's scream cut through the early morning stillness. Julian straightened his posture, killed his headlights, cut off his vehicle's engine, and listened with interest. The maple tree leaves echoed sounds, but Julian was certain the scream had come from inside one of the nearby buildings.

His family owned a local janitorial services business. They advertised their business in the local papers as having had over twenty years' janitorial services experience and expertise in the field. They boasted their specialty in providing services to fit any business' needs, whether it be a public school, university, hospital, daycare center, private office, gym, or locker room. They had the flexibility to schedule their custodial activities around normal business hours so there would be little or no interference in normal business routines. They emphasized their complete compliance with established government standards, and all their employees were required to complete a professional janitorial training program and be certified.

Julian worked hard under the tutelage of his father to learn the business. His choice of career had been a no-brainer. He spent most of his free time helping his old man gather necessary supplies and equipment. Julian learned to operate all the floor waxing, buffing, sterilizing, and cleaning machines his father owned. After his graduation from high school, he earned his professional janitorial certification and went to work with his father. His father was more than happy to have him and immediately changed the company's name to DePaul and Son Janitorial Services.

Over the years, the family business grew steadily and developed into a very respectable and profitable business. DePaul and Son Janitorial Services secured one of the bigger cleaning contracts in the area when it was hired by Princeton University to maintain the university's facilities, classrooms, and office buildings.

By then, Julian and his father no longer had to perform any of the actual physical cleaning of the facilities their company was contracted to maintain. They had plenty of good employees working under their guidance. Instead, Julian had begun inspecting full time while his father worked to secure new contracts for the company. Julian made it his business to inspect all the work performed by his employees the previous night. He made rounds at every facility under contract early, each morning, before his employees reported to work.

This morning, Julian couldn't determine exactly where the unusual scream, he heard, had come from. Maybe it had been his imagination. When he couldn't sit there waiting any longer, he got out of his SUV, stood, and listened carefully one last time. A shutter banged against a window, and wind rustled dried leaves in the trees. He saw the shadow of a huge, unusual looking, bird as it flew overhead.

Julian hunched his shoulders and zipped his jacket tight to keep warm against the early morning chill. He glanced down at his wristwatch—*6:45 am*—as he began his daily inspections.

He walked along the narrow walkway until he reached the front door, which he pushed open to enter the building. Inside, Julian walked slowly through the narrow corridors of Princeton University's Economics Department. His practiced eye carefully swept over the work performed by his employees the night before, taking in every detail as he peered through the muted light. Everything seemed normal—*clean, shiny floors.*

He walked around corners, opened doors, and slid his fingers over sills. The corridor was peaceful and quiet. He heard no sounds—*all quiet.*

Faculty members weren't due to arrive for another hour or so. Julian reached Professor Mayweather's office at the end of the corridor and idly turned the knob. He was sure his employees knew to lock office doors behind them. To his surprise, the knob turned. He sighed. *What's this?*

Julian hesitated. Mayweather often came in early, and they sometimes chatted about economics, but the professor usually left the door ajar when he was in. Julian paused and listened for a moment. He didn't hear anyone inside; neither did he smell the coffee Mayweather unfailingly brewed each morning. *The professor must be out of coffee,* he decided.

Julian knew every man on the crew who cleaned the Economics Department, and he couldn't remember any of them ever leaving a door unlocked.

"Dr. Mayweather?" Julian called. He waited a few seconds and then knocked. "Professor, are you here?"

Julian eased the door open. The horrible stench inside pushed him back a step. It was like nothing he'd ever encountered, and as the owner of a janitorial service, he'd encountered plenty. The rank odor had a burnt quality to it, like ozone, but without the freshness of rain that usually accompanied lightning. This smelled more like terror, or death, or even something worse.

Julian covered his nose and mouth with one hand and glanced around the room. At first, everything seemed normal. A scatter of papers littered the nice, shiny black leather couch and love seat that he'd always admired. Nothing looked knocked over or disturbed. Light glinted off the edge of a picture frame sitting on the professor's desk. But behind the desk...

A chill rushed through Julian's entire body. The hair on the back of his neck stood on end. He felt sick to his stomach, and a sharp ringing started in his ears. Sitting in Professor Mayweather's chair behind his desk was the horrifying sight of a mummified body. Its eyes and mouth gaped wide in what looked like excruciating pain. Its hair stood straight up on its head, like dried needles from a pine tree, and its skin was a dark bluish color dried and sucked tightly to the skull beneath.

Somehow, Julian managed to dial 911 with shaking fingers. He drew in a couple of deep breaths as he watched the police red-and-blue bubble lights flicker through the corridor from the patrol cars as they arrived and parked outside. "What the hell is going on here?" he asked himself as he placed one hand on his forehead, tilting his head skyward and thought, *this morning couldn't be any worse.*

Detective Lewis Cruz rolled his eyes at Julian as he exited the professor's office and recognized Julian standing in the corridor. Cruz grinned broadly as he walked over to where Julian was standing.

"You wanna tell me what's going on here, DePaul?" Cruz eyeballed him.

Julian sighed. "I don't know. I just found the body in there, that's all."

"That's what I thought you'd say." Cruz grinned. "You know how these things work, DePaul. The one who reports the crime isn't supposed to be a suspect. But as of right now, you are my number one suspect."

Julian jerked back in surprise. "I don't have anything to do with this."

"No! Sure, you don't. I'm not through with you yet." *Guys like you think you can do anything you want and get away with it. I'm going to get you, DePaul.*

Julian sensed Cruz's conviction of him by the look in his eyes. He felt as though he were in a court of law, on trial for his life, and the jury had just pronounced him guilty as accused.

Cruz interrogated him for the rest of the morning, even though Julian gave him the same answers every time. Julian had to cradle his head with both hands as he patiently gave his statement.

Cruz finally gave in. "Okay, DePaul you're released for now. But don't get too comfortable. I'll be keeping a close eye on you."

Julian felt sick to his stomach. He knew he couldn't help the police very much because he hadn't seen anything unusual, except the freakish body, and that wouldn't help him sleep very well for months to come.

Julian followed the case in the news for the next few months. The M.E. identified the body as Professor Mayweather's, although the cause of death remained inconclusive. The death was ruled "suspicious," and the case was never closed.

I

Twenty years later
Friday, October 28, 4:59 p.m.

A sudden knock on her office door interrupted Mrs. Dudley from her office chores, at the end of a long chaotic week. "Who is it? One moment, I'll be right there," she answered as she placed the last of her files in her filing cabinet and locked the drawr

When she opened her office door she saw Deputy Treasury Secretary, Brute Therion, standing outside her office. Mrs. Dudley was surprised; she hadn't seen the Deputy Secretary all day.

"Is Secretary Cheney in his office?" Therion asked, as he stepped into the office. He hoped he didn't look as tired as he felt, but his reflection in the dark tinted windows showed his navy blue suit jacket unbuttoned, pin striped tie loosely hung around his neck, dark brown hair slightly unkempt, and the white in his blue eyes faded to a light shade of red. He carried a manila folder in one hand and held his forehead with the other. He halted in front of Mrs. Dudley's desk where she'd been tiding up before leaving.

"No, Mr. Therion. Secretary Cheney left a few hours ago. He caught an early flight to his home in Washington." She answered.

"Did he leave my copy of the files on the new budget proposal with you?"

"Oh, that." She paused as she completed stacking files on her desk and picked up her keys. "He did. The files and the secretary's notes are on his desk. Would you like me to fetch them for you, Mr. Therion?"

"No, don't bother, Mrs. Dudley. I'll fetch them myself. Go and have a great weekend with your family. It's already way past your normal work hours and I'm sure you are eager to get home." Therion answered.

"Okay, sir. Thank you. Enjoy your weekend. I'll see you next week. Please don't forget to lock the doors behind you on your way out."

"Sure. No problem." He responded.

"Thanks again, Mr. Therion." Mrs. Dudley said, as she retrieved her purse, slipped out the door and hurried down the hall. *She moves rather spryly for someone her age,* Therion thought, as he heard the pace of the double-time clip of her heels on the tile.

A prominent seal with an eagle and a key, symbols unique to the U.S. Treasury, was etched on the office door directly in front of Mrs. Dudley's desk. Therion opened that door, entered the Treasury Secretary's office and didn't bother turning on the lights. He grabbed the folder off the desk and was halfway out the door before his mind registered the one thing he never expected to see. He froze momentarily. *Hold on,* he eased back and turned slowly.

The blue in his eyes slowly moved from the surface of Secretary Cheney's desk to the Majestic Storage Cube resting on the floor behind the elegant mahogany Solomon desk. *Yes, there it is.* The sight of the mysterious box froze him in his tracks.

"This can't be," he said to himself.

He pictured the small box being the same he had seen a few times before, at Secretary Cheney's mansion, and what it had contained.

This is a treasure to behold, he thought, *even, if only for one day.*

Therion stepped around the desk, and reached one hand out to grasp the silver handle. He turned it, but nothing happened.

He slammed his right hand down on the desk. *Locked, it's locked. Dammit.*

His eyes narrowed as he rolled the swivel chair around and took a seat in the Old Hickory Tannery Barrel-Back leather chair and began searching through the drawers for a key. The first drawer he opened—top center—contained only pens, office supplies and some old papers. Bang.

He slammed the draw shut. His brows wrinkled and his eyes widened. Then he reached for the top drawer on the left side of the desk. When he pulled it open, Secretary Cheney's small bunch of keys rattled into view.

Ordinarily, Cheney wouldn't leave this box behind. Could it be that the recent controversy surrounding him has affected his memory and caused him to forget it, along with his keys? He thought, as he fingered the keys lightly. *What other explanation could there be?* Therion shrugged his shoulders and started searching the keys for the right one. He tried each that he thought might offer success before he inserted the correct key and it aligned with the pin tumblers inside the inner casing of the lock and he heard the barrel turn inside the locking mechanism. He carefully opened the Majestic Storage Cube and removed a smaller wooden box, only about two inches square that looked very old—like it had survived the graduation of many elapsed years.

He placed the small box on the desk before him, closed his eyes and thought, *the ancient Hebrew king's ring.* A smile appeared on his face and he opened his eyes.

He sat back in the comfort of Secretary Cheney's chair, gazed up toward the ceiling and searched every corner of his skull. His mind reflected on a legend of long ago. *According to Jewish tradition, a king named Solomon had assumed his father's kingdom in the 10th century BC. Solomon ruled forty years, according to 1 Kings 11:42, and during that time Israel flourished into its golden age, claiming to be favored by God. King Solomon ruled a prosperous and unified kingdom, and arguably was credited for the establishment of the first centralized government with a professional army and developed trade. Solomon had been a true pioneer of his time, blessed with wisdom like no other, and the first Israeli king to erect a temple for the lord, which housed the Ark of the Covenant.*

Therion smiled, opened the small box, and caught the sight of the ancient sparkling Corinthian brass relic. He took out the ring and inspected it closely. The soft gleam of the shiny hexagram carved on its face, inside a circle, with four jewels in its corners, twinkled in his eyes. He took his time inspecting the once sharply cut markings and symbols, now worn smooth by time and handling, inscribed on the inside rim of its band.

"A bit old and worn in its appearance…but still…more precious than gold," he said to himself. He slid the ring onto the pinky finger on his right hand. It fit perfectly. He felt an inner warming sensation tingle slowly through his body.

Gold, silver, diamonds and rubies, no…a king, filtered through his mind.

Therion placed the small box back inside the mahogany Majestic Storage Cube, locked it, and returned the keys to the open drawer. He repositioned the Old Hickory Tannery Barrel-Back leather chair where it had been, picked up the files, and remembered to close and lock all the doors behind him on his way out.

2

It's good to be home, Secretary Cheney thought, as he arrived home. It was early evening and he immediately felt the serenity of his tranquil neighborhood on Gravely Beach Loop Northwest, in Olympia, Washington. He took note of his wife, Rebecca's, decorative flower beds in combinations of red, yellow and white. Carnations, lilies and roses are surrounded by oval, square and round garden stones in their colorful yard. Moss covers her water sprouting figurine centered in its small pond, with floating water lilies.

He hesitated before entering his coveted home resting on five acres of high ground, in the city's most secluded area, with its professionally maintained yard gradually sloping down to the boat dock on Puget Sound. He gazed the high wooden fence on both sides separating his estate from his neighbors and affords his home maximum privacy. And he admired the breath-taking view of the mountainous landscape that grace the skyline out back.

Secretary Cheney almost couldn't bring himself to go inside.

***

"Three weeks. It's been three weeks. I can't take it any-more. I can't pretend I haven't heard. But, I'd like to know why? Why did he do it? How could he do this to me?" Rebecca Cheney asked herself as she placed another plate in her dish-washer. She slammed the door and choked back sobs. *What kind of man did I marry? Was he always so sick? And I just never knew?*

Well, she'd held her comments to herself long enough. She needed to know why. She was his wife, for God's sake. Surely no one had a better right to an explanation than she did.

Rebecca pressed start and dried her hands on a dish-towel. She looked restlessly around her tidy kitchen, but there was nothing more to do.

And what would it matter why he'd done it, anyway? It's over be-tween us. There is no possible explanation. No possible excuse.

Rebecca sighed and wandered out of the kitchen, down the short corridor, through the foyer and into the office—situated in the farthest corner of her spacious home.

Benjamin sat at his desk, listlessly thumbing through some papers.

"Oh," Rebecca said. "I didn't hear you come in."

"I arrived an hour ago." He barely looked up at her. "I'm preparing the department's new budget proposal for Congress. I had it on my mind when I arrived, so I didn't want to disturb you when I came in."

"How long do you plan to be here?" she asked. She couldn't bring herself to look at him, either, and let her gaze roam around the room, before settling on the view out the tall windows.

"I'll be leaving for D.C., early Monday morning." He answered.

"Fine. When you go, don't come back."

"Rebecca—"

"Don't," she snapped. "Don't Rebecca me. Don't even think about it. Did you think I hadn't heard? Who hasn't heard about what you did? There is no one in America who hasn't heard, Benjamin."

"I know and I'm sorry," he whispered. "I'm so sorry."

"Sorry?" She didn't know if she heard him right. "Sorry? Yes, you're sorry alright. After more than 20 years of marriage, I had to learn about this...about my own husband...on the public news channels. Do you know how embarrassing—how humiliating—this is for me?"

"I didn't mean for this to hurt you," he said, still sitting behind his two-hundred-thousand-dollar exotic desk.

"You didn't mean for this to hurt me? How could it not hurt me? How long have you been playing me for a fool?"

"I've known it for a while."

"'A while,' what's a while...a week, a month, a year?"

"I can't be sure."

"And you kept it to yourself. Why didn't you tell me that you were having these feelings?"

"I wanted to tell you, but I didn't know how."

"If you'd only had an affair, like Bill did with Monica, I could've been like Hilary. I could've publicly pretended to have some understanding for that sort of thing. But instead, you secretly fooled around in our nation's capital with young men. What you've done is unforgivable." Rebecca turned away and gazed back out the window. "Benjamin, this is the lowest of all lows. I cannot stand by your side under these circumstances, because I have no understanding for that sort of thing..." Her voice cracked. "Even the sight of you sickens me."

"I couldn't control myself." Tears filled his eyes.

"I want you out of this house and out of my life forever." Rebecca turned away from her husband and stormed out of the house; she got into her car and drove away.

***

The bartender carried the fresh round of Gin and Tonic over to the two men, heaving darts at the far end of the bar. Each half-drunk, only grunted, seeming a bit annoyed at the lack of visitors at the tavern this evening.

The Sunset Tavern has always been one of the local's favorite places to hangout. It's not a new place, but it's not old or shabby, either. The owner remodels the tavern every few years, but he sticks to the old rusty sporty look and feel. A high wooden bar with high wooden barstools and shiny wooden floors; pictures of the most famous athletes from all the popular sports line the walls. TV monitors constantly playing the current sports and news entertains the old locals, who normally consume too much alcohol and take up, just about, all the space around the old pool table in the tiny room in back. It has always been cozy, with clean, fresh, air; local law enforcement officials vigorously enforce the posted no-smoking signs.

Fred and Trap were alone in the tavern tonight and stood behind their barstools at the far end. They'd both been laid off about the same time and now like to spend their unemployment money buying each other drinks. Both were decent, hardworking guys, but the housing crisis and recent downturn in the construction industry led to their release from the same construction company.

They both wore blue jeans tonight and Fred in a dark blue sweater by Fruit-of-the-Loom and Trap in a white T-shirt and black leather vest with a Harley Davidson shield on its back. And even through the dimness of the place the bartender could still distinguish between the two men. Fred has always been shorter than Trap, and built round, not narrow and slender like his friend.

Fred was suddenly interrupted, he was about to say something, when a sudden draft blew through the bar; the door to the main entrance swung open. Fred and Trap glanced over their shoulders. A well-dressed woman with more curves in all the right places than any of the Kardashian sisters sauntered in.

"One slow comfortable screw," she said to the approaching bartender.

"Yes, ma'am. Coming right up," the bartender answered, with a wide grin.

Her green eyes appraised the dim lights and well-worn table-tops and seemed to find the bar satisfactory, if a bit dark. She took a seat at the bar.

"Do you see that?" Fred whispered, as he leaned over the countertop and pressed his elbows into the back of his barstool.

"Beautiful, well-toned calves, tight curves, well groomed features. She's not from around this neighborhood. I've never seen her before. I would've remembered her," Trap answered, turning back to the dart board.

The bartender walked over to the two men. "Guess what she ordered?"

"I don't know, we didn't hear it clearly. I bet you're going to tell us," Trap threw a dart and turned back toward the bartender.

"It's a first since I've been working here; she ordered a Slow Comfortable Screw."

BOOM.

The sudden explosion rocked through the bar. Bottles rattled against each other along the back wall. Lights swayed overhead. Fred lost his balance as his barstool tipped over. Trap peered down at his friend as the shaking subsided.

"Get up, Fred. You didn't have that much to drink," Trap said. "Can't take you anywhere."

"Damn, she really ordered that?" Fred asked as he picked himself up from the floor.

"I'm not kidding. That's what she ordered. I felt like telling her I've got a private room behind the bar and ask her if she's interested, but I held myself back."

Trap placed his darts down on the countertop and stepped off while the bartender and Fred talked. He walked down to the end of the bar where the lady was sitting.

"Hello. Do you mind terribly if I sit here?" he asked.

"No, help yourself. It's not my bar," she answered.

"Thank you. I'm Trap." He extended one hand. She took it.

"Rebecca," she said. "Trap. That's an unusual name. Sounds more like a nick name. Is that your real name?" She curiously checked him out from the corners of her eyes.

"Honest to God, that's the name my parents gave me."

"Okay, Trap. It's nice to meet you," she said and they tapped their glasses together.

"Nice to meet you, too." Trap drank. "We were discussing basketball, and why the upcoming championship series will be one of the most interesting ever." He said.

"I don't know much about sports, Trap. I know more about the stars and what makes them go around in our universe. I'm an astrophysicist."

"Whatever that means, Rebecca, it sounds great. I won't try and repeat it."

She laughed in a way that sounded as if she was surprised she could.

"You are one beautiful lady, Rebecca," he said, after he took his time and checked her out.

"Thank you very much, Trap." She gave him a smile of surpassing sweetness. "Of all the things you could have said to me—" She took a tissue and wiped the small tear drops from the corners of her eyes. "—that is the one thing that I most needed to hear tonight." She finished her drink and asked for another. "Have another drink, Trap. It's on me. What are you drinking?"

"Gin and Tonic. I don't mind if I do."

"One Gin and Tonic and a double of what I had before," she said to the approaching bartender.

"One Gin and Tonic and one double slow comfortable screw, coming up," the bartender repeatedly loudly.

"Damn," Fred choked out.

"That'll be 22.50." The bartender set the drinks on the counter.

Rebecca handed a couple bills to the bartender and said, "Keep the change."

Trap watched Rebecca's actions through the mirror mounted behind the bar. "You know, I can build office buildings, private homes, apartment buildings, storage facilities, schools, just about any structure that your pretty little heart desires, but that's not all that I can do, either. I can also tell when something is not right with a beautiful lady. What's wrong, Rebecca?"

Rebecca's glance caught his. "Trap, I don't want to discuss that. And I don't feel like being alone right now. So, here's your chance. Cheers." She saluted him with her glass and emptied the drink down her throat. "I'm leaving now. You can come with me if you want to, right now. I don't want any more questions, and then tomorrow, I don't want to see you ever again."

"Just like that?" Trap asked.

She leaned in. "No girl needs a man who can't understand 'right now' when she asks for it, right?" Then she turned and stepped off toward the door.

Trap placed both hands on his head and said, "Wait a minute, I'm coming." He got up and followed her out.

3

When Brute Therion arrived at his apartment in downtown D.C., he knew his time had come. He had waited for this chance for over twenty years. All the stories he had read about, the legends he had researched, prepared him for this moment.

He knew The Goetic Art of Solomon by heart. The story purports to contain specific instructions on the evocation of the spirits that the ancient Hebrew king had trapped inside a brass vessel, sealed with his ring, and forced to do his bidding.

The same ring he now wore on his finger. Therion glanced down at the ancient relic and smiled.

He had often wondered if he would ever have the chance to put it to the test, to practice the ancient rituals that he had learned so much about and prove the legend for himself. He had prepared himself years before, armed himself with knowledge in order to act should the opportunity arise. And now with Secretary Cheney's family heirloom firmly in his possession, he knew this was his chance. The emptiness he felt inside left him, and he became energized. No longer would he linger on the sidelines and wonder if he would ever grasp the greatness he craved.

Therion had spent years researching the legend of King Solomon's ring, the occult sciences, grimoires, and necromancy that accompanied it. He knew few in the 20th century believed that the stories were true, but he also knew that no one could prove them false. He knew that many scholars the world over were in agreement that King Solomon was favored by God, and had been blessed with more wisdom than any other man on earth. The legends went on and on; the veracity of King Solomon's accomplishments were irrefutable, and Therion was convinced that such history could not be denied. And, now he was the only man alive in possession of the Seal of Solomon, and he knew how to use it.

Therion opened his closet and reached deep into a corner to pull out a dark green foot locker. He found a rag and used it to wipe away the years of dust that had accumulated on its surface, and then unlocked it. The lid cracked opened and he began to remove its contents. He glanced into the mirror that hung on the wall nearby; he admired himself, and he smiled. He felt that something new, something different, something ancient was about to take place.

Inside the footlocker, he had stored all the supplies he knew he would need to perform the ancient ritual, the very same supplies he knew King Solomon must have used in ancient times to conjure and control demons.

Therion reached into his box and the first thing he pulled out, nestled carefully on top, was a small book. The faint title read: *Grimoirum Verum, The True Grimoire, The Most Approved Keys of Solomon, The Hebrew Rabbi.* The volume dated *1517* and was one of his most prized possessions. He laid it on the small wooden altar that he had prepared.

He thumbed through the fragile pages until he found the opening invocation and he read the powerful words aloud in a clear strong voice.

He laid down the book and took up the vial of water he had picked up from a church on his way home that evening.

15

Therion quaffed the water and laid the vial aside. He said from his memory the ancient conjuration that he had memorized. And like a medieval priest, he carefully recited the Seven Psalms, and pronounced, "Keepers of these instruments, who are in heaven, release them now into my service, for I need them for that which they have been prepared."

Therion drew a small knife from the storage locker and unwrapped the pristine white silk from around it. He inspected it closely. The blade had sharp cutting edges on both sides; it was made of new steel, he had purchased it on the "day and hour of Jupiter." On its wooden handle was inscribed the symbols that he had inscribed exactly according to the instructions he had followed in *The True Grimoire.* The shiny blade bore no evidence, no blood stains, from its preparation. Years before he had traveled a long distance to purchase a virgin goat from a goat herder in Virginia. He had taken the goat to a sturdy tree and tied its feet up on a limb, so that the body and neck hung down. He had placed a metal basin under the neck to catch the blood. He took the sacred knife and cut the throat using a single stroke, reciting: "I kill you in the name of the earthly elements, Earth and Air, Fire and Water."

Therion had skinned the sacrificial animal. He took the pelt and stretched it out wide and strung it up in a tree in the sunlight, so that it did not touch the ground. For seven days he had sprinkled holy water mixed with strong sea salt over the surface of the skin, saying: "By the power of Almighty God, I exorcise this skin and may it be purified by this holy water and salt."

After the skin had dried and the hair began to peel off, he scraped the entire surface of the skin clean of hair. Having thus cleaned his canvas, he carefully transcribed the markings, perfectly, indicated by the Grimoire.

On the knife's blade he read the inscription *"AGLA,"* and he remembered how he had fumigated it according to the instructions in the *Grimoirum Verum*. It was one of the necessary instruments that he had ceremonially prepared to put into service whenever he wished. He had chanted the sacred words that he had learned, normally relating to the origin from which the item came. Therion had poured holy water on it, as well, and had chanted the ancient words, as was required. All were exactly according to the instructions he had read in the fragile pages of the ancient book.

He had performed the ancient ritual perfectly for every instrument and item. He had remembered to perform the fumigation, perfectly, as well, using a new metal basin filled with fresh coal and set ablaze. When the incense set into the coals began to perfume the air, he had said: "May all the angels in heaven hear me, lend me your help, and be my guide so that my work can be accomplished." After his recitation he had pronounced the Seven Psalms.

Therion had set the knife aside and removed the piece of virgin goat skin, the 'Virgin Parchment,' from the locker.

The final piece, he was ready. All his preparations were complete, and with the Seal of Solomon securely in his possession. He drew in a deep breath to calm himself and he picked up the Grimoire. "By the light I have in my hand," he recited. "By the elements of Earth and Air, Fire and Water, I conjure thee. By all the powers of the angels in heaven and by all the powers of the ancient masters, sorcerers and practitioners, I conjure thee, in the name of the one true God…"

He repeated the conjuration twice more, then burned the parchment in the metal basin. Ashes swirled toward his face in a silent, unsteady current, and the wall clock struck the hour.

Therion looked. He waited and he listened.

He felt a chill from the cool breeze passing by his window as he sat quietly and thought, *Gold, silver, diamonds and rubies. . .no a king.*

Unlike his father and Benjamin Cheney, Brute Therion was no Mason, but he had learned enough to know that his father and Cheney had gained crucial hidden knowledge through their membership in the craft. The ritual he had learned to perform was influenced heavily by his knowledge of the ancient brotherhood, whether they had chosen to accept him or not.

He knew the ancient ritual had been practiced by only a few over the years, but those few were very powerful, successful men. Such men guarded their secrets. The two men he admired most, in life, were two of the most celebrated Masons in the world, King Solomon and George Washington, known not only for their historic accomplishments, but also for their knowledge and practice of rituals and sacrifice. These men had become well-known Masonic icons, had lived their lives according to the principles and practices of their chosen craft, a craft deeply rooted in secret rituals and sacrifice.

4

Rebecca had driven to a small hotel on the outskirts of town, where she had went in and rented a room. Some hours later she awakened, in total blackness, by the annoying snoring sound in the room.

Reluctantly she opened her eyes, after trying to convince herself it was only a dream. Annoyed again by the rough gargling sound coming from the man lying next to her, in the bed, she glanced over in his direction.

"I can't believe I'm lying here with a strange man," she told herself, still feeling the effects of the alcohol she had consumed earlier.

Trap rolled his big masculine body onto one side, turning his back toward her.

Rebecca shrugged, winced, and rolled her body away from his. She decided to turn on the TV. She reached for the remote and pressed the button.

***

"It's 11 pm. I'm Song So-Yong, reporting from Olympia, Washington for CNN." Something about the reporter's voice caught her ear. "The cause of the explosion heard across most of the upper western parts of the state earlier this evening is under investigation. The mountain blast triggered a massive earthquake in the region that measured 7.5 on the Richter scale and was accompanied by a tsunami that developed into thirty-foot waves that rushed ashore and obliterated, just-a-bout, everything within two miles of the shoreline, including parts of Seattle. The confirmed death toll is nearly 60 and rising. Most were boat owners and fishermen on the coast in the Puget Sound area."

"It happened unbelievably fast," said Wayne Brockman, a 41-year-old city employee still going through the leftovers of his daughter's ravaged home in Seattle. "There was no warning. We heard the explosion, felt the earth shake and a few minutes later, everything was under water. We didn't have any time to react."

"The off-duty city employee, his wife, daughter, son-in-law and two grandchildren survived because they were not on the coastline at the time the tsunami hit. They were out of the danger area visiting other relatives at the time of the disaster. They returned to find their daughter's home completely destroyed. But others in their neighborhood were not as fortunate."

Mr. Brockman said, "I had to help pull some bodies from under the debris of our daughter's neighbor's house. The house was crushed by the force of the water, and the family members were still inside at the time."

Song paused and shifted her hair from her eyes. "All local relief agencies have mobilized their efforts. A state of emergency has been declared and major relief efforts are underway.

The National Guard has been activated and is on the scene performing rescue and relief assistance in the disaster areas."

"Oh...No." Rebecca said. She wanted to drive home immediately. She got up out of the bed and tried to dress herself, but she realized she was in no condition to drive. Her head ached, her eyes burned and she didn't see clearly. She flopped back down onto the edge of the bed and sank her head down into the softness of the pillows. She knew, she would have to wait until morning.

5

Early the next morning the sky puffed with clouds and a cool breeze blew, just cool enough to keep Rebecca from rolling her windows down to catch a breath of the fresh air. From the hotel, she took Main Street to 4th Avenue, bore left off 4th and down onto I-5. Emergency vehicles and trucks packed with supplies clogged the interstate.

This was some sight for Rebecca. She couldn't believe the amount of damage wrought in less than twenty minutes the day before. Entire city blocks had been leveled, reduced to nothing more than rubble by either the earthquake or the following tsunami. Rescue workers and volunteers shifted through the wreckage while emergency lights bathed everything in flashes of red, blue, and yellow.

It led her to suspect she shouldn't be out on the streets—the emergency crews didn't need yet another civilian getting in the way—but she was desperate to get home.

Had the house survived? Would there even be anything there? She couldn't help thinking of all the little things that made a home—her mother's letters, her favorite gardening gloves, the paintings she and Benjamin had brought back from their many trips over the years—and the potential loss of them turned her stomach.

And Benjamin…He'd hurt her, terribly, and she'd wanted him gone, but not like this. Please, not like this…

She began to breathe easier as she got closer to her neighborhood. The damage didn't seem as bad here, bar some downed trees and power lines. At last she turned on to Gravely Beach Loop Northwest and pulled into her driveway.

The house stood, seemingly undamaged.

The rush of relief she felt at seeing it still standing shamed her to the core—so many other homes hadn't fared half as well—but she couldn't help it. She hurried up the walk.

"Benjamin?" Rebecca pushed open the door and gagged on the horrific stench inside. "Benjamin! Are you here?"

The unfamiliar smell—like a molten substance had been burnt in her home—clogged her nasal passageway. She covered her nose with one hand and glanced around, looking for the source of the smell. She felt a draft from a back room, and followed the coolness into the foyer and beyond, into her husband's office—and screamed.

Rebecca's heart pounded against her chest as her eyes consumed the shattered glass scattered across the floor. She screamed a second time, this time much louder than the first.

"Oh my God," escaped from her throat. Her eyes scanned the room and moved over, across, and back onto and focused on the gruesome figure that lay across the room. The mummy's eyes and mouth stretched wide open in a grimace of agony and terror. Dark hair stood straight up on its head. The skin, a dark bluish color, clung to the skeletal frame.

Chills ran down Rebecca's spine and almost paralyzed her. Her entire body felt hot, then cold. Her knees buckled, and her eyes burned.

Rebecca bolted for the door, grabbing her purse and car keys along the way.

What the hell is that? What happened here last night? Why didn't the alarm go off? Questions rushed through her mind. She reached the front door and jabbed the emergency button that activated the home security alarm system as she stumbled past. She ran to her car, crawled in, rammed the key into the ignition and sped away.

What the hell is that thing doing there on the floor in my house?

***

The police cruiser rolled up quietly and pulled to a stop in the expensive neighborhood. Checking a tripped alarm hardly rated a response, considering the extent of the city's damage, but this wasn't just any address. Therefore, the powers-that-be decided they could spare two officers, one patrol car, and a knock at the door.

Officers Blades and Jamison walked slowly along one side of the house, checking the property, after no one answered several knocks at the front door. They edged forward in the early morning still, expecting someone to bolt across their path at any moment. Both men saw the shattered window at the same moment. A tattered remnant of curtain drifted lazily in the brief breath of air off Puget Sound. Blades and Jamison crouched low and slowly inched up until they reached the window. They leaned against the house on the underside of the broken sill.

Blades peeked into the house through the shattered window. He saw the broken glass first. The shattered edges of the window glittered in the early morning light. A wave of glass washed inward from the ruined frame and cast tiny rainbows across the carpet, the ceiling, and the figure stretched out across the floor.

"Oh Mary...mother of God," Officer Blades blurted. He quickly crouched back down under the window to gather himself. "Radio for backup," he said as he glanced over to Jamison. "I saw a body in there. We're gonna need some backup out here." Blades turned back toward the window, raised his weapon, stood up, pointed it into the room and slowly moved it around, scanning for intruders.

Only moments later two other police cruisers pulled up. They blocked the streets and took up defensive positions in the elite neighborhood.

Police tramping echoed across the neighborhood as officers moved fast toward the U.S. Treasury Secretary's mansion.

Officers Cooper and Rodgerson reached the mansion and took up positions on either side of the front door with weapons drawn.

"The white Mercedes parked in the driveway belongs to the property owner," Officer Brock announced over the police radio.

"The gate to the driveway is closed, but unlocked," Officer Cooper announced.

"There's a light on and a body down in a back room," Officer Blades said.

Officers Bailey and Bernardino arrived and jumped over the waist high, gateless area of the fence in front, leaving their police cruiser red-and-blue bubble lights flickering all about.

Neighbors peered through their windows.

"Cooper, check the front door," Blades ordered over his radio.

"Locked." Cooper announced, after he checked the door handle.

Cooper peeked into the house through a front window.

"No movement inside. Can't get a clear view through the curtains," he said.

"Okay, move in," Blades ordered.

Officers Cooper and Rodgerson heaved back and kicked the door open and entered the house.

"Shit, he just kicked in the door of the Secretary of the Treasury," the young rookie whispered.

Officers Blades and Jamison rushed around back and Jamison spotted the garden shovel resting off to the right-side of the double glass doors in back. He grabbed the shovel and slammed it into the glass doors leading into the back room. The shattering glass rattled the glass fixtures throughout the remainder of the residence. The officers quickly entered the back room—the secretary's office—and were astonished.

Officer Blades hurried over to the body and froze in his tracks.

The other officers immediately swept throughout the remainder of the house. Police search lights flickered in every corner, checked every room, up and down with weapons pointed in every direction.

Bradley Bailey, the rookie, tried hard to keep his hands from shaking, or at least keep his partner from noticing. He couldn't stop thinking about what his partner told him that morning:

"Don't be afraid to be scared, Bailey. It's healthy. It means you care about something. We all have to deal with our fears, and it doesn't get any easier, either. It's a part of the job. It's the same every time. You never know what you'll find out here in the streets. Some freaked out guy, strung-out on drugs, looking to score more drug money breaks into a person's house. We show up and surprise the freak and he pulls out an automatic and starts spraying the place with hot led. You've got to expect the unexpected. Or you won't last long in this business. It's just as scary every time, as the first," Bernardino said. "When you kiss your wife goodbye in the mornings, kiss her like you mean it. Because you never know, you could be kissing her lips for the last time."

For the rookie cop this was a new experience. He couldn't help himself, he was just a little nervous. He shivered and shook with each step that he took. Frightful shapes and shadows crossed his path inside the spacious dwelling. Each flash of light amidst the dark and shadowy walls were ghostly glimpses of his most menacing fears. Often he shrunk and cringed in awe, his thoughts lingering on possibilities of strange shadows and sounds—were they caused by a mortal man, or monsters like goblins and ghosts, Draculas' and Frankensteins', all his worst fears as a young child growing up and having had to sleep in a dark room by himself.

"I'd rather be assigned to tsunami clean-up or patrol detail right now, Bernardino," he blurted to his partner.

"You're not the only one," Bernardino replied.

Officer Cooper's voice squawked over the radio. "House secured."

Officer Bradley took a deep breath of relief.

Raymond Beresford Hamilton

***

"What in the name of…?" Officer Blades did a double-take to be sure he saw what he thought he saw. The strange look on his pallid face could not sequester his inner thoughts—unbelievable.

The dead body in the room appeared strangely like a mysterious relic from an ancient civilization currently on display in the Barnum Museum, in Bridgeport.

"What on earth does that to a man?" Officer Jamison sputtered.

"God only knows," Officer Blades replied, God only knows. His gaze flicked around the room—what the hell happened here?

"Is this a joke?" Cooper entered the office, through the foyer, where a few of the other officers stood, and gazed at the spectacle on the floor before them.

Officer Blades suspects, not. His eyes narrowed. "This is the home of the United States Secretary of the Treasury. The window on the far side of the room had been shattered. An expensive joke, wouldn't you say?" His short round body and tired red eyes turned toward Cooper's direction and the look in his eyes and face was one of sadness and remorse, an expression of disappointment in a fellow officer.

"The captain won't share your sense of humor, Cooper, and this is more like a nightmare. Nothing that I've witnessed in my twenty years on the force, and I've seen a few weird things in my time, can even come close to topping this one,"

Blades said, just before he felt the tingle and subsequent vibration of his cell against his leg.

"What's going on out there?" Captain Brownlow demanded.

"Yes, ma'am, captain," Officer Blades said, as he took the incoming call from his boss. "The place is secured. No sign of intruders. But…"

"But what?" the captain asked.

"It looks like some weird shit. There's a shattered window and a dead body, it looks like a mummy."

"A what?"

"A real, no-shitting-around mummy. No way of making a clear identification. We'll have to get the corpse down to the morgue and have the M.E. figure out who it is."

"Okay, the ambulance is on its way. I'll alert the lab, the coroner and the rest of the guys. Seal off the scene. Preserve any evidence and I'll see you in my office after you turn it over to the detectives," the captain ordered.

"Yes, Ma'am."

Click.

***

The rookie, Officer Bradley Bailey, was still recovering from his earlier nervousness when he entered the room and immediately slipped on a piece of the broken glass on the shiny hardwood floor, lost his footing and fell close by the corpse. As he attempted to get back onto his feet his hand brushed the corpse just as Blades concluded his call with the captain and turned back around.

"Get the hell away from there, Bailey! Bernardino, get this rookie out of here," Blades snapped.

"Yes, sir," Bernardino said. "Come on, Bailey."

He took Bailey by the arm and led him out through the broken double glass doors in back of the office. "What's the matter with you? You can't touch anything at a crime scene, you'll destroy evidence. You know that."

"I'm sorry. I couldn't help myself," Bailey replied with sorry eyes, looking quite confused now.

"We were ordered to go, so let's go. We're finished here. The forensics guys are going to take over from here," Bernardino said as he led Bailey to their black and white cruiser out front.

On their way back to the precinct Bailey began to sweat and his vision began to blur. "I don't feel so good. I think I might be coming down with something. My arm is beginning to throb and it hurts. I can feel my heart beating inside my veins, like they're pulsating back and forth."

"Well…go home and get some rest. Hopefully you'll feel better in the morning," Bernardino said. "I'll drop you off at home. Our shift is over, and I can punch you out. Just remember this favor, because I may need you to do the same for me sometime."

"Okay, Bernie. Pick me up tomorrow morning, will you?"

"Sure," Bernardino said. His partner didn't say another word during the drive across town and only barely seemed to rouse himself when Bernardino pulled up at the curb.

"You okay, Bailey?"

His partner didn't seem to hear him. Bailey dragged himself out of the patrol car and slammed the door. Bernardino barely heard the rookie's rough mutter: "See you tomorrow, Bernie."

Bailey entered his flat. He'd never felt worse in his life.

6

By morning, Officer Bradley Bailey nearly wished he were dead. He stood half-naked in the center of his apartment, unable to even press the buttons on his cell phone. Agonizing pain paralyzed the right-side of his body. He'd felt it first in a small cut on his right index finger that he had gotten from his razor while shaving the morning before, but it had spread fast to his arm, leg, face...

What's happening? His eyes followed the purple blood moving through his veins, under his skin, up his right arm and into his shoulder. *Oh God it hurts so bad.* The veins in his arm were pulsating, even protruding from his skin.

He'd never thought of himself as fragile. He stood just over six feet tall, had a medium built, although his shoulders were a little small. He'd never lifted weights to build up his shoulders. But his arms and legs were of normal length, proportional to his height, and his frame was normal, like the guy next door. He kept his dirty blonde hair cut short and tapered down on the sides. He was normal. A normal, healthy guy.

Now he felt as thin and fragile as an eggshell, ready to crumble at the slightest touch. The pain intensified two-fold. His muscles began to seize and his legs gave out. Muscle spasms racked his body and he started to gag for air.

The phone trapped in his hand rang and Bailey used the last of his strength to press the answer button.

"Bailey, where the hell are you?" Bernardino's voice echoed from the speaker. "I'm down stairs waiting. You were supposed to be down here fifteen minutes ago."

Bailey tried to form words, to force sound past his lips. "H…e…l…p."

"Bailey? Hey, Bailey, are you there?" Bernardino hesitated. "Quit screwing around."

"He—lp," Bailey managed again, then blacked out.

Bernardino bounded up the stairs and pounded on the door. "Bailey? Hey, Bailey, open up. Bailey!"

No answer.

Bernardino heaved back and laid a hefty kick into the door. It flew open and crashed into the wall. The door handle punched a huge hole through the sheetrock. Bernardino rushed in and found Bailey stretched out on the rug, twitching uncontrollably.

"Dispatch, I need an ambulance. Officer in trouble at 57 Lakeside Drive," he said into the radio transceiver attached to his uniform.

7

I received the call Monday morning, just after I arrived back home following my two mile jog around the track in nearby Overbrook Park. I took off my sweaty red-and-white sweat-suit—the colors of my Alma Mata, Ohio State University—and my worn out running shoes. I hopped into the shower and relished the soothing steamy water as it massaged my aching shoulders and back.

Despite myself, my mind shifted toward my ex-wife, Amanda. How are you doing? Why couldn't you have a little more patience with me, Amanda? You knew my responsibility to the Bureau. It was my job, and our only source of income.

Snapping out of my trance, I shut off the water. I shook my head side to side and tiny drops of water splattered against the shower walls and curtain. I really miss Amanda. But this is one of the things we disagreed on. I really don't mind the drops of water in the shower. But she did. She made a big fuss about it. If she was here now, I'd have to wipe down the shower walls and curtain. But since she isn't, I stepped out of the steamy shower, grabbed a towel and dried myself. Feeling rejuvenated and fresh, I walked over to the closet, found the dark blue suit, white shirt and pin-striped-tie that seem more suited for a cheap used car salesman than an FBI agent—I like it that way—and dressed before heading down stairs. I grabbed the newspaper from the slim oriental table, Amanda had picked up from a garage sale a few years before, at the bottom of the stairs. I took a quick glance over the news headlines—Tsunami in Puget Sound, last Friday evening—before folding it and placing it under my arm.

A dead presidential cabinet member and a tsunami, both at the same time...what's this world coming to?

I continued into the kitchen, sat at the circular table, and swallowed a bowl of soggy Kellogg's Raisin Bran. Then I headed out the front door and drove to the office.

On the way a bright ray of light flashed through the windshield of my vehicle, straight into my eyes, I was blinded. I couldn't help it when I cursed and put a hand up to block the glare from the rising sun. It alerted me to my approaching destination, as I was about to drive by my turn into FBI field office parking lot.

I entered the building via my usual route—through the underground garage—and when I arrived this morning, I immediately sensed a strange presence. I stood in the cubicle laden space just outside my office door and took considerable note of my lonely presence in this usually crowded space. At 8:30 am, the corridors were dimly lit and the lights flickered.

Strange, that never happened before...huh. Something must be wrong with the lights. I shrugged it off.

I unlocked my office door and settled in behind my desk. A large stack of files to be reviewed lurked on the corner of my desk. With a sigh, I plucked one off the top—the discovery of Secretary Cheney's mummified body.

This separates the men from the boys, I thought to myself.

***

"Sir? Sir," a soft Australian accent filtered through my ear. "It's 12:15 and you have a one-o'clock appointment at the Seattle morgue."

It was Ms. Tompkins, my assistant. Her voice jerked my mind off what I had been reading and back on to my most pressing issue—my appointment with the medical examiner Dr. Anthony Martin.

"Oh, yes. Thank you, Ms. Tompkins, I almost forgot." I checked the clock. I was going to be late. "If we receive any information on Secretary Cheney's case, while I am away, please leave it on my desk."

"Yes, sir," Ms. Tompkins replied, "Now hurry you can still make it there on time."

I rose to my feet, grabbed my keys resting next to the picture of Amanda and Carla, and hurried out the door. I met my partner, Agent Nelson, in the hallway.

I call him Nellie. His name is Jason Nelson. He's slightly shorter than I am, but he's burly, and his face is more long than round with deep blue eyes, and silver hair. I remember when his hair was jet black.

"What's the hurry? We going somewhere?" Nellie grinned. He was dressed in the same school-boy suit and tie like I was.

"Just me, Nellie. Director said I should handle this one alone. Call you later." I picked up my pace.

"Alone? That's not standard procedure," Nelson shrugged. "Partners cover each other's back. We don't go out alone."

"That's what I told him." I shrugged. "We're spread a little thin right now. Maybe he just wants to cover more cases. If you get an explanation out of Morris, let me know."

I hurried down the stairs, out through the tall double glass doors, and into the underground garage. I unlocked my car door, got in and drove away.

Nelson stood at the tall glass doors and watched as my car sped away. I watched him through my rear view mirror. I knew he wasn't pleased with this situation.

I wasn't either.

***

The midtown temperature was chilly. The thermostat read forty-seven degrees, and a light fog thickened the atmosphere. Seattle was busy as usual. People hurried in the city. Drivers stood still in heavy traffic and jammed the roadways. Tsunami clean-up efforts were under way. National Guard, Regional Homeland Security, Red Cross, and Salvation Army vehicles choked the roads as they transported medicine, food and personnel across the city and south to Olympia. Employees trying desperately to return on time from their lunch breaks made things even worse.

My Lexus was trapped in traffic only blocks from my destination—the city morgue—where the coroner was scheduled to meet with me.

I glanced down at my wrist and checked the time on my Swiss Burberry Stainless Steel time piece, with the chronograph dial and the words "To my beloved husband" engraved on its reverse—a 45th birthday gift from Amanda, who left me for a man who had more time for her.

I'd be quicker on foot. I pulled over and into a parking spot as a silver Explorer vacated the space. On foot, I hurried down the worn-out walkway.

"Excuse me, excuse me," I said as I tried to make it on time.

"Do you mind? The nerve of some people." A short middle aged lady, with shopping bags in hand, brushed my hand from her shoulder.

"Please, thank you," I said as I passed her and continued to squeeze my way through the crowd.

I'll never make it on time, I kept telling myself under my breath and ran faster.

I'm fairly tall at six-feet-two-inches. Back in my high school days I sprouted four inches between my junior and senior years and developed broad shoulders. I learned to be firm and direct during FBI training at the academy, and now at times I know I seem intimidating to those who don't know me. I'm always clean shaven, with a certain reddish look to my face, as if I'd just finished running two miles in the hot sun. I rarely appear in public in anything except a suit and my cheap dark sunglasses, and now in my early-fifties, I'm still in good shape.

There it is! Finally. I arrived and checked my Burberry: 1:10 pm. 10 minutes late. I hope he's still here.

I entered the building and immediately frowned from the strong odor of formaldehyde that clogged the airway.

It's dark and gloomy in this place and it smells of mildew and death. I used one hand to cover my nose.

"Dr. Martin, are you here?" I called. I walked past the vacant front desk and peeked down the long empty corridor that curved to the left. I couldn't help but to take note of the many closed doors that extended down the narrow corridor. Not a soul in sight. Where is everyone?

"Back here, Agent Cole."

I followed the faint voice down the hall to a back room.

The man who awaited me had silver hair, gray around the edges of his bushy eye brows, eagle claws around the outer edges of his eyes, thick prescription glasses, and appeared to have been slightly taller in his younger days, since he now slumped slightly.

"I'm sorry there was no one there at the front desk to greet you, Agent Cole," said Dr. Martin. "Our staff is stretched rather thin right now and we're sharing staff with other morgues in the city."

"No problem." I tried to suppress a shiver. With the earthquake and tsunami, the local morgues probably were very busy. "What have you found out?"

Dr. Martin seemed to think over several possible answers but eventually just shrugged. "Follow me, Agent Cole. You better see this for yourself."

He led me into a, dimly lit, medium-size room off to the left. In its center were six surgical tables, positioned in two straight rows. There was just enough space for a person to walk between each table. On the far right wall were twelve small cabinet doors. They were arranged in three rows, from top to bottom, and had four doors across, from left to right.

Dr. Martin dragged on a pair of surgical gloves, before he opened the furthest cabinet door, and rolled a long stretcher out of the cold human storage freezer. He turned back the cover and I saw the mummified body of former Treasury Secretary, Benjamin Cheney, for the first time.

"Holy mother of Jesus," escaped from my mouth. I immediately took two steps back, reached for my handkerchief in my rear pocket and used it to cover my mouth and nose. "What happened to him?"

"To tell the truth, I have no idea. I've never seen anything like this in all my years." The coroner adjusted his glasses.

It was virtually impossible for a prudent mind to accept that a living human being could, from one day to the next, transform from a man into...this.

The former secretary's lifeless body lay mummified on the cold metal slab before us. His eyes and mouth were wide open—as if he had seen something, so terrifying, that it had shocked the living life right out of his body instantly. His brown hair stood straight up on his head—like dried needles from a pine tree. His skin had turned a dark bluish color, dried and stuck tight to the skull beneath.

I felt a chill in the air—like a strong presence was in the room with us. My perception was of the corpse's eyes watching us, and its ears earing everything that we discussed. A most peculiar sensation rushed through me—like an electric shock. Immediately, before I heard a faint voice in the back of my head. It was like the body was trying to communicate with me. I heard it say something, but the faint voice faded before I could make out what it had said.

"Agent Cole?"

"What?" I focused on the doctor. "Sorry. What was that?"

"I don't have an explanation for this. It is a horrible sight, and a more troubling fact is that whatever caused this instant mortification is still out there, and is loose, among us," the doctor said.

"And what could that be, Dr. Martin?"

"There have been many unexplained mysteries throughout the ages, Agent Cole, their answers are still hidden in undiscovered science. The answer to this particular mystery is right up there with the best of them. I will try to explain what I know for sure." Dr. Martin sighed as if he didn't think he knew very much, for sure, at all, but was willing to give it a try.

"There are many ways to determine a person's time of death," he said. "The major events following death are predictable and well known. First, the stiffening of the muscles, more commonly known as Rigor mortis, becomes noticeable one to six hours after death. This condition normally disappears about twelve to thirty-six hours later, because it is caused by changes in the body chemistry. Then, due to the gravitational settling of the un-clotted blood, Livor mortis sets in. This is the discoloration of the skin that we see, and this is a condition that presents itself about two to four hours after death and reaches its maximum level in roughly an eight to twelve hour time period. The next condition that develops is the change in core body temperature, called Algor mortis, it occurs as the body cools until it reaches the ambient temperature. Only a few hours after death, the corneas begin to cloud up and become opaque in roughly three hours. When a person dies six hours after eating, food will still be present in the stomach. Certain insects infest the body after death, and as the life cycles of these insects are known to us, they assist us in determining the possible time of death."

The doctor paused again, adjusted his glasses and cleared his throat. "What puzzles me most in this case, Agent

Cole, is that none of these conditions are evident in the former secretary's body. In fact, there's hardly anything present in it at all. It's dry as ash and withered to the core. It could have been left out in a desert a thousand years ago and not look much different. For this to have occurred overnight—I can't explain it any more than I can explain spontaneous combustion. It is as if something instantaneously sucked the Treasury Secretary's life out of his body, as if some kind of high energy endothermic heat source entered his body and sucked out every ounce of fluid from it."

"You can't be serious?" was all I could say, stunned. This information hit me like a ton of bricks, right in the gut.

Dr. Martin nodded.

"Impossible," was the next thing that I blurted, and I'm sure my facial expression looked as blankly astonished as I felt. "How can this be possible?"

The doctor shrugged. "I have no idea. Before being presented with this case, I would have said it was impossible. Unfortunately, I now have the impossible in my morgue."

And just how was I supposed to solve a case like this? I thought to myself. Although I respected and appreciated the good doctor's wisdom, I wasn't very pleased with the information he had just shared with me. It offered nothing to assist me in my job to find the answers to the unanswered questions surrounding the secretary's death. In fact, my job seemed to have gained in complexity—a total unexplainable mystery.

"So, what am I supposed to tell my boss?" I asked finally.

"Tell him…These developments have opened a whole new area for scientific research. This is a new condition. Not yet discovered," the doctor answered.

After a few seconds I pulled myself together. "Okay then, Dr. Martin. Good work. I am going to have the body transferred to the FBI lab for further examination."

"I'll be discreet, of course." Dr. Martin assured me.

"Thank you, doctor."

In a state of total confusion I showed myself out. "Director Morris will love this," I muttered as I dug my cell phone out of my pocket and dialed my boss's direct line. He answered tersely, "Morris."

"Sir, I'm leaving the morgue now. I think we need to classify this case as suspicious or strange. We don't have enough evidence to call it murder at this point. Also, we better have our lab guys take charge of the corpse. Something has come up."

"Okay Cole. I'll inform the Treasury office of the Secretary's death." Morris said.

"Yes sir, I'll see you back at the office."

***

The news reached the Treasury Department of Secretary Cheney's death and Brute Therion was saddened by the bad news. He and the former secretary had known each other for over twenty years. They had been college buddies and had served as Secretary and Deputy Secretary of the Treasury for over three years. Therion knew, the president would appoint Cheney's successor, but for now the Treasury Secretary's seat was his. He felt enormous power within himself. The economic policies, the trade organizations, the big banks, foreign trade…It was all his to manage, at least for the time being. But first there was something else he had to do. Settling into the comfort of his office chair, he made the call.

"Hello, Rebecca. It's Brute Therion."

"Hello, Brute. Thank you for calling," Rebecca Cheney answered.

"I'm very sorry," he said. "I just heard what happened."

"Thank you, Brute," she answered. "I can't believe it. One minute he's in his office working and the next he's gone."

"I know it's hard to believe. That's how these things happened. I guess that's what they mean when they say life is short. We never know when it's going to happen. What exactly happened to him, Rebecca?"

"I don't know. He looked like something from the past. His body was all dried out, just skin and bones. I didn't even recognize him when I saw him lying there."

Brute frowned. "What? Did he accidently electrocute himself?"

"I don't know. I didn't hang around long enough to find out. I thought someone had broken into the house. The window was broken and the thing was lying on the floor in the office. I ran." Rebecca's voice cracked and tears filled her eyes.

"No one can blame you for doing that," Brute said.

"I can't bring myself to go back there. I never want to set foot in that house again. I checked myself into a hotel, where there're lots of people."

"Is there anything that you need? Anything I can do? You know we go back a long way."

"I know, Brute. But I'm okay. Thank you for asking."

"Okay, Rebecca. Remember, if you need anything, I'm here."

"Thank you," she said.

"Okay, then. Bye."

"Bye."

Brute Therion hung up the phone. He leaned back in his chair and reflected back to his first day in Washington D.C., as Cheney's Deputy Secretary three years ago.

But a knock at the door snapped him out of his reverie.

His morning became filled with well-wishers offering condolences on the loss of his friend. Benjamin Cheney had been well-liked, despite the recent scandal. Therion privately wondered if any of the young men appearing at his door had been Cheney's lover. He shivered slightly in revulsion.

He somberly accepted the outpourings of sympathy and modestly hoped to fill Cheney's shoes to the best of his ability. Therion didn't, so much as, hint at the elation building inside him.

As the acting Secretary of the Treasury, he would function as the essential policy-maker on economic and financial issues facing the government. But he also knew that this placement was far more important than any role as the top economic advisor to the president—far more important. What he didn't say, while he murmured thanks to the constant stream of well-wishers coming through his door, was that more important than any of his other responsibilities, by securing the Secretary of the Treasury's position, he could now begin laying the foundation of a much larger campaign.

But all that could wait, at least for a few days.

Therion called the senior staff into his office in the early afternoon. Many of them had red eyes and looked distinctly disheveled. He smiled sympathetically at each one.

"I know many of you feel Secretary Cheney's loss deeply. I know I do. He was a great man of talent who served his country faithfully. In light of such tragic circumstances, this office will close tomorrow as a show of respect. I will see you all Wednesday morning."

8

After my meeting with the coroner, I picked up my cell and dialed an old friend. We hadn't talked in nearly two years, but I hoped she'd be willing to over-look that. I knew the news reporters would be all over this story, but I hoped I could contain at least some information about the case.

"This is Song," said a deceptively soft Asian voice.

"Hello, Song. Robert Cole. How are you? Long time no see."

"I'm fine, Robert. Thanks for asking," Song said. "How are you? It's nice to hear your voice. So you do know how to use a telephone?"

"It's a recent skill set," I said, "Do you—?"

"Hold it," Song responded. "Now that I have you on the phone, first things first: do you blame me for Amanda leaving you?"

"What?" I asked, taken aback. "No. Why?"

"You haven't spoken to me since she left. I want you to know that I had nothing to do with it. She did that all on her own. She made her own decisions. You should know that. If she'd told me about her plans, I probably would have tried to talk her out of it."

"Huh." I wasn't sure how to respond to that. "Um, thanks, Song. That's kind of you to say."

"You're welcome, Robert. Now—" Song broke off and muttered something in Korean that sounded like very bad language. "Sorry, Robert. You caught me at a bad time. We are preparing our information for tonight's broadcast. Can I call you back?"

"That's what I'm calling you about, Song."

"Oh, let me guess: the mummy secretary."

"Song, I respect the freedom of the press, and I certainly can't prevent you from reporting the news—"

"That's right, Robert. You can't."

I grit my teeth. "However, the description is of particular concern to us."

"So, you want me to leave out his zombie appearance—the good stuff."

"There is plenty of tsunami news to report on, Song. Give me a chance to work some things out first. I know the body's condition is going to get out—I mean, you already knew about it—but let's try not to fan the flames. We already have one disaster to deal with right now; I don't want people thinking we have another."

"Do we have another?" Song's voice sharpened with interest.

"On the record? No. Off the record? I'm not sure. If we do, you'll be the first one I call, I promise. You get exclusive rights on anything I dig up."

"Which might be nothing," Song said.

"It could be something." I drummed up as much charm as I could. "Please? I'll owe you big, for this and I'll give you a good news worthy tsunami story right now. No one else has this yet, Song."

"What is it?"

"Do we have a deal?"

Song huffed. "Robert, you're making a rather big request. You realize that's not my decision alone to make."

"Yes, but you have a lot of influence on what's said and what's not said." I could hear Song rustling papers across her desk.

"Okay, fine," she said. "What's your tsunami story?"

"Tsunami survivor. Guy named Julian DePaul Jr. was treated and released from the general hospital over the weekend. He was found washed up on the shore. He was fishing on the Sound when the tsunami hit and spent almost 24 hours in the water. They're still looking for the boat that he was in and the friend that was with him."

"Hmm...that does sound good," Song admitted. "Any injuries?"

"Too early to tell."

"How did you hear about this?"

"I'm FBI. We know everything."

Song snorted. "Whatever gets you up in the morning, Robert. Okay, I'll go with this. But call me back. We're not finished talking."

"Promise."

Click.

I started to dial again when my cell signaled that I had a text message. It was from my daughter, Carla: flying to SEA-TAC.

That's the last thing I needed to hear.

9

Carla was over two thousand miles away when she heard the news. She'd been watching television late Friday night when a message crawl appeared at the bottom of the screen:

7.5 earthquake reported in Olympia, Washington. Massive tsunami followed. State of emergency declared.

Carla stared dumbly at the television while the message repeated, then bolted for her computer. The internet confirmed the news: there had been a major disaster in her hometown, where her father and boyfriend live.

Carla swallowed hard. She snatched up her cell phone and dialed her father's number, then Julian's; she got a busy signal both times. The phone lines were jammed.

More news trickled in as the hours passed. Dozens were reported dead. Several areas of Olympia had been leveled. Carla checked her cell phone and computer every few minutes for a text message or email.

Her mother called at seven to see if Carla had heard from her father or Julian. A steady stream of calls from concerned friends followed. Each call made it harder and harder to control her panic, until—finally—her cell phone signaled a text message at 11pm.

We're fine. Will call when can. Dad.

Relief made her sit down hard. The emotion was short-lived as she watched the following news with an increasing sense of horror.

Carla wasn't about to sit around reading textbooks while friends and neighbors shoveled bodies out of the rubble back home. Carla got on the phone and booked the next flight out.

The rest of Saturday dragged on. Sunday was agony. By Monday afternoon she was almost ready to walk to Washington on her own two feet.

Carla set her suitcase by the door and tidied her small apartment. She scrubbed the kitchen just to waste some time while she waited for the airport shuttle. Carla checked her watch and found to her dismay that she still had another hour left. She got out the vacuum.

Normally, Carla loved her apartment. It was just the right size for her—big enough to have a few friends over, but small enough that she didn't miss Julian as much when she was at school. Now it made her claustrophobic.

She couldn't help studying the few photos on her wall over and over again as she vacuumed.

The first was her favorite picture of her mother. She'd taken it more than two years ago, not long before her parents split up. They'd gone picnicking at Point Defiance in Tacoma, and her mother had struck a pose in the sand with the water and sky as a backdrop.

Her mother was, as they said, a knock-out. She was clad in the tightest pair of blue jeans Carla had ever seen, which showed off her incredible figure, along with a black spandex top designed with long sleeves. Dark colors always accentuated her mother's alabaster skin. Flowing, shoulder-length brunet hair and enormous hazel eyes merely put the crowning touches on her mother's perfection. She was so fabulously dressed that no one believed she was Carla's mother. She looked twenty years younger than she was, and most men assumed they were sisters.

Carla worshipped her. She hoped she was half as beautiful and poised as her mother when she was her age.

The next photo was of her father when he graduated from the FBI academy more than twenty years before. He looked so young and handsome, and not nearly as serious as now. Her father's tall frame and captivating smile seemed to command attention and made him clearly stand out from the rest of his classmates. She knew they all called him "Cole," just like most of his FBI buddies did now. He'd gotten so used to it that sometimes he even signed his name that way, just "Cole." It always made her smile.

The next few photos were of Julian and her from their various trips over the last few years: historical sites, sun-filled beaches, amusement parks…They could go just about anywhere and have fun.

Carla wandered into the kitchen and checked the note she'd left for Mrs. Wilson, her next door neighbor. Mrs. Wilson liked Carla and had readily agreed to water her plants, bring in her mail, and turn on the occasional light so it didn't look like her apartment had been completely abandoned.

Her cell phone rang. The caller ID read: Dad.

"What do you think you're doing?" he demanded when she picked up.

"Hi, Dad," Carla said. "Calm down."

"Don't you tell me to calm down, young lady. What in the world are you thinking, leaving school early to fly here now?"

"I'm thinking about helping my family and friends there," she said evenly. "I can't just stay here and go to classes like everything's fine while people I know are scrambling to get food and water."

"It's a mess here, Carla. You're better off staying there right now."

"And then what, Dad? Sit around when I know I could be helping? People are still being dug out of the rubble. You need more boots on the ground."

"They don't have to be your boots," he snapped, but she knew he was weakening. "What about school, Carla? You're almost finished."

"I am finished," she said. "I've got all the credits I need to graduate in June. I was just taking some extra classes from Dr. Davidson before he retired. Besides, I can't think of anything but what's going on there, much less concentrate on school. I need to come and help out any way that I can."

She heard him sigh and knew he was swallowing back arguments. He might not want her anywhere near Olympia, but he hadn't been able to talk her out of anything since she was ten, and they both knew it.

"Fine," he said. "Just call your mother first."

Carla burst out laughing. "Wow, you are desperate. Mom can't talk me out of this, either. My mind is made up. I'm 25 years old now and I have something to say about the way I live my life. I love you and respect what you say, but you raised me to make my own decisions."

"Is there anything I can say to convince you?"

"Tell me this has all been a huge mistake and everything there is really fine."

"This has all been a huge mistake and everything here if just fine."

"You've always been a crappy liar, Dad."

"It makes me a good agent." He sighed. "Look, call your mother anyway, okay? Because if she finds out you've flown into a disaster zone instead of staying safely in New York, studying away, you know she's going to blame it on me."

"No, she won't."

"She will. And while I might chase criminals for a living, it takes a braver man than I to face your mother's wrath. So if you're going to come, take some responsibility and save your old man. Call your mother."

Carla peeked out the window and saw the airport shuttle pull to a stop in front of her apartment building. "Fine. I'll do it from the airport. Bye, Dad."

She snapped her phone shut, picked up her suitcase, locked the door behind her, and hurried out to the shuttle. She spent the long trip to the airport thinking about Julian. Despite her worry, even the thought of him brought a small smile to her lips.

They'd met when she was a freshman and had been high school sweethearts. Julian DePaul Jr., he and his mother moved to Olympia from Princeton, New Jersey, when he was only seven years old, after his father committed suicide. Julian graduated two years before her and joined the Navy. Despite her parents' objections, she'd joined the Navy after high school as well. She and Julian were assigned to the same base in Japan. They were never homesick, so long as they had each other and loved being overseas. Carla decided to stay in only two years while Julian did four, and they finished their tours of duty within months of each other. They returned to Washington together, settled into an apartment, and started looking for whatever was next. As it turned out, college was next for Carla—a bachelor's degree in criminal justice—and an extended job search was next for Julian.

Carla didn't like being so far away from him, but Julian was adamant. He knew a career in criminal justice was what she really wanted, and he wasn't about to have her turn down a full-ride scholarship because of him.

"I'll still be here when you get back," he'd said. "And you'll be home on holidays and summer breaks. It's only a few years."

She couldn't help but feel proud that she'd managed to shave off an entire year of study by doubling up on classes. Disaster or not, Carla was ready to go home for good. And not a moment too soon, as far as she was concerned; something was wrong with Julian. She didn't know what it was, but she knew him well enough to know when he was hiding something. She'd heard it in his voice the first time they'd talked after the disaster.

He hadn't called until Sunday night, and despite her father's text message, Carla couldn't help but worry. She must have called him two dozen times or more—where was he? Why wasn't he picking up?—before her phone finally rang. By then she'd managed to work her way into full-blown hysteria.

"Julian, what the hell is going on?" she'd all but screamed. "A major disaster hit the area and you haven't thought, for one second, to call me? You didn't think that I would be worried out of my mind about you? Where the hell have you been?"

"I'm okay, Carla. Calm down," Julian said. "Didn't your father text you?"

"It doesn't matter what he did. Why didn't you text me?"

"I couldn't. A lot of things got flooded and my cell phone got wet. I had to wait until it dried out."

55

"Why didn't you ask to borrow someone's phone? Or use a pay phone? Or go down to the stupid store and get a prepaid phone? You could have done something."

"I was doing something. It is crazy here, Carla. I was out helping others as much as I could. And there's not a phone left in stores, by the way. I was going to call you."

"When was that, Julian? Tomorrow? The day after? You should've called me when it happened, that would've showed me that your mind was in the right place."

"My mind is in the right place. What's the matter with you?"

Carla burst into tears. "Oh Julian, it all sounds so terrible, and I'm so far away and I couldn't reach you and what if Dad was just lying to me that you were okay because he didn't want me to worry and—"

"Hey! Hey, I'm fine. I really am. Cole wouldn't do that to you," Julian said. "There isn't a lot of damage around our place. My mom is fine, she's way up in Auburn, and your Dad is fine, too. But there are a lot of people out there who weren't so lucky and I've been trying to help out. You would do the same."

"I am doing the same. I'm flying back tomorrow night. It was the first flight I could get. I'll be on Continental flight 920, arriving at 10:30. Can you pick me up?"

"Wait—what? Jesus, Carla, there's a state of emergency here. Half the National Guard is here trying to help people who may be stranded, trapped in their homes, hungry, lost or displaced, and you're flying into SEA-TAC?"

"The airport wasn't damaged. Flights are still operating. A lot of people are flying in to help dig out bodies, pass out food, water, and provide medical care, stuff like that. I am one of them."

"Carla, I know you want to help out, but what about your classes? You can't just leave school."

"Julian, I'm only taking extra classes right now. I'm just waiting to graduate. I need to be there."

"Does your father know about this?" Julian asked.

"I told him. He wasn't happy, but he's not going to stop me."

"Carla, I'm not happy. I don't want you here."

"What do you mean, you don't want me there?" Carla asked, stung.

"I mean—of course I want you here, just not right now. I want you safe, in New York. Things are weird here."

"Weird how?"

"Just—weird. It's not always safe. I don't want to have to worry about you."

"Well, I can handle that better than I can worrying about you. I'm coming."

Julian sighed. "You really can be a pain in the ass, you know that?"

"I know. You love that about me."

"No, I don't."

"You do." Carla almost smiled but the tone in Julian's voice worried her. "Julian, are you sure you're okay? You sound a bit strange."

"I went through a major disaster here, Carla. Of course I sound strange. Listen, I'll pick you up at 10:30 on Monday, okay? I'm exhausted and have to get some sleep."

Carla thought he definitely sounded exhausted, but that sleep was the last thing he wanted to do.

"Are you having dreams again?" she demanded.

"Of course not."

Now that definitely sounded like a lie, Carla thought.

"I'm going to crash, baby, but I'll see you Monday. Don't freak out if you don't hear from me before then."

"Okay. But try to call me if you can."

"Sure. Love you."

"Love you, too."

Click.

The more Carla thought about it, the more convinced she became that something was wrong. Busy or not, wet cell phone or not, Julian should have called her after the tsunami hit the area, just to let her know that he was alright, because naturally she would be concerned until she heard from him, but he didn't. And he sounded so tired, as if he hadn't been sleeping.

She wondered if he were having his dreams again. They'd mostly subsided in the last six months, but it was possible they would come back. Julian's dreams were nothing to mess around with, because they were often accompanied by black-outs. They'd started back when he lived in Princeton when he'd first heard the news of his father's suicide. He was very young and he blacked out, hit his head on the hard tile floor, was knocked out cold and spent a few days in a coma. When he finally regained consciousness, he didn't remember what had happened to his father. In fact, he didn't remember much of anything. He didn't know who he was. He didn't know his own family or where he was from. He didn't know his own mother.

Waiting for Julian to get his memory back was the hardest thing his mother ever had to do. It took many months of intense therapy for him to begin recovering his memories, but eventually, slowly, he did. He recovered and his mother decided to take her son and move to the state of Washington and leave the bad memories behind them in New Jersey.

But then Julian started having black-outs for long periods of time. The black-outs came and went without warning. Julian never knew when he was going to have another one. It could happen any time: walking down a flight of stairs, driving a car, cooking at home. Julian should still be seeing his doctor, but Carla didn't think he was. And from experience she knew he was too proud to tell anyone when he was hurting.

Carla frowned. What is it with men that cause them to hold these things inside?

10

There wasn't any news on Officer Bailey's condition until Monday morning. Officer Bernardino had just arrived to take his shift of waiting for news at the hospital when he saw the man in scrubs step into the waiting room and took a look around. The doctor spotted him almost at once, thanks to his uniform, and headed over.

"How is he?" Bernardino asked.

"Involuntary muscles became paralyzed: his heart, his lungs. He is on a respirator," the doctor said.

"What happened to him? What's wrong with him?" Bernardino asked.

"We don't know at this point," the doctor answered. "It looks like some kind of infection. I noticed a small cut on his right index finger, and from the swelling around this area it's safe to assume the infection seems to have started there. We'll need to wait until the results get back from the lab to know exactly what we're dealing with."

"Is he going to be okay?" Bernardino asked.

"No telling. It'll depend on the type of infection and how well his body reacts to the treatment. His vitals do look promising. He's a strong young man, and that works in his favor," the doctor said.

"I don't get it," Bernardino said. "One day he is walking around fine and the next half his body swells up and he's in the hospital."

"What did he do yesterday?" the doctor asked.

"He touched a dead guy..." Bernardino paused. "Yeah, he put his hand on a dead guy that looked like something out of 'The Mummy Returns' movie.'"

"What kind of dead guy?"

"We're not sure yet. It's really strange. It's still under investigation," Bernardino said.

"We'll wait on the lab results," the doctor said.

"Okay, doc. I've got to go, but I'll check up on him this afternoon. Can you give me a call when you find out anything else? The boss wants to know, and a lot of the guys down at the precinct are worried. Bailey's kinda like everyone's kid brother."

"I will."

II

After leaving the morgue I drove back to Olympia to meet Julian for a late lunch. Parking was very limited. I had just enough room to squeeze out of my Lexus and my visibility was diminished by the aimless itsy-bitsy tiny rain-drops scurrying about. Tiny rain drops sprinkled the streets like fine particles of windblown sand.

The walkway to the restaurant was a long, skinny, winding concrete path with clumps of moss puffed around the edges that threatened to blanket the entire walkway. I managed to avoid the slippery spots and was lucky to avoid what could have been an embarrassing situation.

Thick dark clouds were building up overhead and threatened to loose holy hell across the sky with thunder and lightning at any moment. I could see razor thin lightning bolts flicker deep in the clouds and hear distant rumbles of thunder.

A few blocks over to the north side, down by the Sound, the National Guard worked along with city work crews to remove wreckage. A few blocks further down on the east side, expensive boats lay in ruins—like scrap cars in a junk yard.

Julian was already inside and had commandeered our usual table. He'd ordered a couple Sushi-Shoreline Combos with sodas, and was halfway through his share already. He knew this was going to be a quick lunch.

Tsunami Asian on Sleater-Kinney Road is our favorite sushi restaurant. We love the modern Asian design, customary aquarium and all. Panels engraved with figurines and embellished with colorful Asian art reach nearly to the ceiling, topped with golden dragons and Asian cultural figures. A statue of Buddha, with a bold head and round protruding stomach, preside over the counter next to the register. A Karaoke game video screen and microphone stand in one corner on the shiny hard-wood dance floor. Music videos constantly play on TV monitors hanging in the upper corners of the room.

We meet here a few times per month, mainly for the sushi, but I also use the occasion to do a little checking-up on him and Carla to find out if I can help them out in any way.

Today Julian wore a thick brown sweater with a white T-shirt underneath, blue jeans, square toed cowboy boots, and a wool NYPD skull cap. Like me, Julian is ridiculously tall by oriental standards, he's turned sideways in the booth, so his feet protrude into the aisle to keep his knees from hitting the underside of the table. He has healthy facial features, thick in the face, like he grew up in the south on hefty portions of grits, fresh eggs and bacon. His shoulders are broad, carried on a solid pair of legs, which gives off an athletic appearance— like he'd been a pretty good athlete back in his school days. Carla and I are still trying to convince him to attend college. He'd been in the Navy for a little while after he'd finished high school, but he got out because of a medical condition.

"That damn wasabi always burns like hell." Julian squinted and shook his head side to side. "You know, I always thought either Asians liked the feeling of the nose burn, or there was something wrong with the wasabi—like it went bad, you know? That initial burn is just too much. But now I realize it's the fever for that flavor. It really goes with the flavor of the sushi."

"It's addictive." I slid into the booth. "I couldn't eat sushi without it." I said.

"Hello, Mr. Cole. Glad you could make it. But for a moment I thought I was going to have to come outside and pick the old man up off his butt, seeing you slip and slide on your way over." Julian said grinning.

"Sorry to disappoint you, maybe one day, but not today. I'm not that old yet." I breathed in with appreciation. "Mmm. This place smells like fresh seafood. Fish and crab cakes today."

"Yeah, that's probably why we like it so much," Julian replied, before putting another piece of sushi into his mouth.

"You young kids today. You all have dirty minds."

"You think so? I've got nothing but good fish jokes from my days in the Navy. Wanna hear one?"

"Since you're dating my daughter, no."

"I'm sure you knew a dirty joke or two when you were growing up," Julian replied.

"Don't know what you're talking about," I said. "So, when did you find out Carla was coming back?"

"After she talked to you," Julian replied unhappily. "I tried to talk her out of it. And I did tell her to call you."

"Do you know if she called her mother? I told her to call her mother," I admitted.

Julian snorted. "No. I don't know if she called her mother. Does she know about me being washed up on shore by the tsunami?"

"No. Are you kidding me? I tried to keep that from her for the time being. She would've been here already, if she knew about that. I did give your story up to Song So-Yong from CNN. She's a friend and I need her to help me keep the description of the secretary's body out of the news for right now. I need some time to figure some things out before the whole world hears all the details about the case."

"That's fine with me. Carla is going to know soon anyway, one way or another, she's desperate to get back here. Nothing could have stopped her. You know, like father, like daughter. She had to see things for herself, make sure everyone's alright."

"And is everyone alright?" I eyed him.

"I'm fine." Julian shrugged. "I'm a bit tired and stressed out about Joe, that's all."

"What happened out there anyway? Wanna tell me about it?"

"Joe and I were about ten miles off-shore in his Boston Whaler 320 Outrage. The boat was Joe's pride and joy, and he'd regale anyone who would listen with enthusiastic explanations about the Twin Mercury 300 horse-power Verados engines because they could reach 30 miles-per-hour in ten seconds flat, and up to 52.8 miles-per-hour at maximum speed." Julian grinned.

"Okay, sounds like a nice boat."

"Yeah, Joe really liked to be out on the boat, he considered fishing a good cover for lazing about on the water telling lies about women he'd known and fish he'd never caught." Julian sipped his soda.

"Well today, Joe's rod bowed almost instantly. 'Ah ha, you've got a hit, Joe!'" I said.

"At first he didn't answer me. He took his time answering. But then he said,

"'Man, its huge! It won't move. I can't reel it in,' he was struggling to make one turn on the reel, his line dragged the tip of his rod to the surface of the water."

"It sounds like he had a big one." I said.

"Well here's the thing, I told him, 'Wait! Don't try to reel it in,' he could've snapped the line and lost it. I backed the boat up to it. I hurried over to the controls, started the boat and backed it toward whatever it was that he had caught."

"'It's a monster,' Julian, it looks strange—almost like a huge eel.'" He said.

"It was weird looking. Whatever it was, we didn't think it would fit in the boat. We decided to cut the line and set it free, hell, it looked more like a power line, than any fish I ever saw.

"I flipped open the fishing knife from my belt and cut the line. The huge wiry looking object disappeared back down into the dark debts of Puget Sound.

"Then we figured it was time to head back to shore, it was getting dark fast by then. I stowed our gear and Joe re-started the engines. The boat jumped forward as he touched the throttle. I stumbled backward and almost fell overboard. I remember feeling the: woo…in my stomach, I stumbled backward and plopped down into one of the white-leather-covered cushioned seats at the boat's stern and clutched the rail. As the boat glided forward over the waves we heard a sudden explosion, so loud that it drowned out the roar of the engines and echoed across the sky. Enormous fragments of mountain peak rocketed into the sky, and smoke coiled above the Cascades. A slab of rock the size of a school bus arched past the boat and plunged into the Sound. Flashes of fast moving light—

red, yellow, green—flickered through the evening mist that descended over the area."

"'Wow! Julian, you see that?'" Joe shouted.

"'Yeah! I saw it. What the hell was it?'" I asked him.

"His eyes popped open wide. His jaw hung down and his mouth dropped open. 'Look! Julian, see it?'"

"I heard him say. My eyes snapped to the direction he pointed. But I didn't see anything. 'No. What?'" I asked.

"'No it can't be.'" He said.

"'What?'" I asked.

"'I saw something fly over the mountain! It vanished over there,' he said pointing."

"I didn't see it. But about 200 meters out behind the boat, where the large fragment of rock plunged into the water, I saw the water bubble. Then, thick bolts of lightning began to flash across the sky, across the mountain tops and the mountain smoked. It was all happening fast. Then we heard the earth rumble, it extended far out beneath the open ocean basin. Then we heard an underwater explosion; it triggered deep vibrations only seconds apart."

"Joe said, 'The water is swelling. The wave is getting big, look! It's headed straight for us!'"

Julian sighed and drew in a breath, "I didn't have time to see it all before the tsunami covered the boat with us in it. The next thing I knew, I was tumbling under water, feeling ground and gagging for air. I was being dragged by the force of the current. It pounded me across rocks and sand. I felt my lungs begging for air, and my chest tightened and I dared not breathe in, for I knew I would certainly drown. So, I held my breath and tumbled with the current."

"You're a lucky man, sorry about your friend. I want you to know that I'm always here if you need anything," I reminded him.

"Yeah, I know," Julian said. "But you have your hands full right now with the tsunami and the new case."

"I'm starting to wish someone else had caught this case."

"That bad?"

"That weird. The weirdest I've seen in over 20 years."

"Does it have anything to do with the mountain blowing up?"

"Don't know yet. I think we're all waiting to hear the answer to that question. We have some people looking into the explosion."

"Do you want to know what I think? I think it's all related: the mountain blowing up, the tsunami, all of it, because it all started to happen at the same time," Julian said.

"Maybe." I checked my watch. "I need to get back to work. Lunch is on me. I'll pay on the way out."

"Hey, thanks," Julian said.

"What are fathers for? Give my girl a hug and tell her I'll see her soon," I said. "See you."

***

"Center for Disease Control," a clipped voice echoed.

"This is toxicologist Brenda Anderson from the Medical Center in Seattle, Washington. I just completed some tests on a blood sample sent in by a doctor in Olympia. You need to see this. I'm sending you the results now."

12

Carla followed the crowd out to the baggage pick-up area and found Julian waiting. His tanned complexion, neatly groomed short dark hair and brown eyes acted on her like seeing all A's on her report card at the end of the school year.

"Hello, Julian." She greeted him with a big hug and kiss. "I'm happy to finally be here with you."

"Hi. You feel so warm and soft. Thank you for the warm tender hug and kiss."

"Yeah, and there's plenty more where that came from."

Julian grinned before releasing her and muscling his way through the crowd to grab one of her bags from the conveyor belt. She reached into her purse, found her perfume and dabbed both sides of her neck. The fresh fragrance of her perfume filled the air, but Julian didn't react. He said nothing.

"There's my other bag, over there." She said, pointing. "Coming around now."

Julian snatched her suitcase out from between several boxes with big Red Crosses on them.

"Thank you." Carla smiled at him. "The flight was filled with emergency relief personnel."

"It was?"

"Of course, Julian. People are going to need medical care and a lot of assistance. Remember Hurricane Katrina? This is just as bad."

"Look at all these people." Julian scanned the many aid relief workers gathering their belongings. "This place is going to morph into a nightmarish setting with an apocalyptic atmosphere, like some kind of zombie land."

"Julian, what do you mean by that?"

He blinked. "Nothing."

"What do you mean, nothing? You meant something by it, or you wouldn't have said it."

"I just feel that a lot of these people aren't really interested in helping anyone."

"Julian, many of these people put their own lives on hold, left their cozy homes, to come out here and help people they don't even know."

"I can't help feeling that some of them are like storm chasers. They get their thrill from being in the storm. They're just exploiting scattered dreams, crumbled lives, lured by curiosity to be in the midst of the creepy scenes and ghostly moments of lost lives and other people's miseries."

Carla stared at him. "Julian, are you okay? This isn't an apocalypse or anything. And these people are the same kind of people who feed the starving children, provide medicine for the sick, and help to relieve distressed families around the world."

"That's the way I feel, that's all." He shrugged his shoulders.

When they reached the car he set down her bags and hugged her close. "I love you."

"I love you more," she said. "I'm so glad you're okay. You are okay, aren't you?"

"I'm fine. Mmm…you smell fantastic." He released her reluctantly and tossed her bags in the trunk. "I had to take several alternate routes getting here. It's going to take a long time to get through traffic."

"I don't care. I'm here." Carla buckled her seat-belt as Julian pulled out of the parking garage. He was right; no sooner did they reach the nearest intersection traffic stopped dead.

"I had lunch with your dad today. You should call him to let him know you got here okay."

"I'll text." Carla got out her cell phone. "If he's asleep I don't want to wake him."

Julian made a non-committal sound. She eyed him.

"Have you been sleeping?"

"Sure."

Carla raised an eyebrow. Julian wasn't any better of a liar than her father. "Have you been dreaming?"

"Not really."

"Have you been seeing Dr. Martu?"

Julian's eyes rolled. "Relax, Carla. I'm fine."

"Well, have you?"

"You're like a dog with a bone," he snapped. "Jesus, Carla, I can take care of myself."

"Okay." She held up her hands to indicate surrender. "Really, Julian, you don't have to see him if you don't want to. It was only a question."

Julian glowered while traffic inched forward.

"I just want you to be honest with me about your health, that's all," Carla said gently. "You can go to the doctor or not, but I need you to at least tell me if something is wrong."

Julian seemed to think this over for several minutes and finally sighed. "Okay. I did have a few weird dreams, but I don't understand them."

"You could have called me."

"I didn't want to disturb you at school. I know that you had to study and you would have been worried."

"Okay, thanks for being honest. But it's your health we're talking about and it means more to me now than any school work. Have you been having any black-outs, too?"

"One. Last week. I think it only lasted a few minutes."

"Did you call Dr. Martu?"

"No."

"Why not?"

"That I can't answer. I don't know."

"Julian, we can't mess around with this. The black-outs are dangerous. Look, I'm going to make an appointment for you first thing in the morning."

"I don't need to go to the doctor because I have dreams."

"You're not going for the dreams. You're going for blacking-out. I don't understand you. Do you want to get well or not?"

"I just don't think there is anything the doctor can do. But if it'll make you feel better, I'll go and hear what he has to say. I don't want any pills. I won't take them if he tries to prescribe any."

"Okay, that's fair. I don't agree with doctors who issue medication for each and every illness either. Sometimes I think some of these doctors are under contract with the pharmaceutical companies and they get kickbacks from them for prescribing their medications."

"Thank you for understanding. I'm kind-a glad you're home," he said.

"What do you mean, 'kind-a'?"

"Well you know..." A small smile curved his lips. "You might be a nag, but it's nice to know you've got my back."

13

Monday night Brute Therion returned home to his elegant restored 17th century Victorian mansion. He loves being home. Loves the peace and tranquil surroundings of the national landmark his ancestors built centuries before, when the area was little more than limitless wilderness and the colony may have still had a king, after they arrived in Virginia from Europe early in colonial times, when the Virginia colony had just began to form.

Therion spent most of his time in Washington, D.C., at his modern apartment on Massachusetts Ave, North West, where he could be near his work place. But this was a special occasion. While he's sorry for the loss of his friend, the fact is Therion is now a presidential cabinet member. Surely no one would blame him for a little private celebration. So he'd closed the office, sent everyone home, and invited a very special friend to accompany him to Virginia.

This is Ruth's first visit to his home and Therion wanted everything to be perfect. He'd chosen to take the scenic route down I-95 rather than the direct route, and timed their arrival just before sunset.

The soft tone of Ruth's voice coupled with her strong British accent caught his ear. "Brute, are we there yet?" she asked, drowsily, as she turned her heart shaped face toward him, still relaxed on the leather head-rest, and half covered by her bushy blonde hair.

He smiled, turned his head to gaze into her big brown eyes momentarily, and proudly proclaimed, "We'll be pulling into the driveway right about now."

He made a few more turns and pulled to a stop. He pressed the button to activate the automatic gate mechanism, pulled through and stopped in the driveway.

He took a quick peek in the rearview mirror, while the garage door rolled itself up and clung to a stop, he brushed his hair and straightened his jacket.

"Brute, this is your home?" Ruth's eyes went perfectly round in her heart-shaped face. Her British voice clipped the words with incredulity as her avid gaze drank in the beauty of the colonial mansion and its charming surroundings.

"This property has been in my family for centuries," Brute answered. "It was built by my sixth great grandfather who immigrated here during colonial times. In the 19th century my ancestors used their wealth and experience to invest in the developing trade that became common in those times. Then as time passed they invested in building private buildings and private homes." His eyes also admired the rustic surroundings. "I was told that my ancestors aided the establishment and the expansion of private property ownership in the developing country."

"So, your ancestors helped to develop Virginia?"

"The Therions became one of Virginia's most important families, over the history of Virginia," he replied proudly.

"And you live here all alone, now?"

"I'm an only child, and my parents passed several years ago." He took her hand. "Besides, I'm not alone tonight."

"Well then, you'd better show me the inside." She batted her long eye lashes at him.

Raymond Beresford Hamilton

***

He poured two glasses of wine, took her hand, and showed her his home. The wooden furniture glowed with the burnished patina of age and loving care. The priceless rug cushioned their steps; they hardly seem used, except for the one in the study, where the worn center shows where he liked to play as a child. He pointed out his third great-grandmother's spinning wheel, his grandfather's paintings, his father's precious books, all with a note of loving pride.

"What is that wonderful smell?" Ruth asked.

"Oh, it's tulips. See the censor on the mantle? My grandmother loved pink tulips and always had them in the house when they were in bloom. I found an oil with the same scent one year and gave it to her for Christmas, so she could at least smell the flagrance of the flowers during the off-season. I don't really smell it that much; I'm so used to it. But it's always been the way home smells to me."

"It's a very pleasant scent. I like it." Ruth took in the priceless art gracing the walls and the colors that blends from one room to the next. "Did she like to decorate, too?"

"No. My mother did that."

"It's lovely, Brute," Ruth said. "I love it."

Their eyes drank in the dynamic autumn colors through the double glass windows.

"Shall I get you another?" Brute noticed her glass was empty and reached for it.

"Please."

A gentle peal of bells, like the pleasant melody of a grandfather clock, echoes in the background from the front of the house.

"You get the wine," Ruth said, seeing his frown. "I'll get the door."

She pushed him gently toward the kitchen and set off for the front of the house.

A tall man dressed in long dark robes stood at the door with his head bowed.

"Can I help you?" Ruth asked.

"May I speak with Master Therion?" the stranger was polite and humble.

Ruth eased the door shut a little. "May I say who is calling?"

"I have an urgent message for him," the tall burly man answered. "Please, let me speak with him?"

"One moment, please. Wait here." Ruth walked to the kitchen. "Brute, there's someone for you at the door. He said he has an urgent message for you."

"Really?" Therion handed her a filled wine glass.

"Yeah. I don't think he's American. He sounds Egyptian, or something."

"Huh. I wasn't expecting anyone. Don't worry, I'll get rid of him." He leaned in to kiss her. Don't go away."

Ruth started to unbutton her blouse. "Don't take too long."

Brute didn't know the man at the door, and frankly he didn't care. "Yes?"

"I have heard your summons, Master Therion. That which you have requested will soon be done."

"What?"

"I have heard your summons," the man replied. "I am your humble servant."

Therion's eyes narrowed at the sight of the much taller burly man before him.

"Yeah, well, you can be my humble servant off my property." Therion started to shut the door.

"That which has begun, cannot be undone. The process must run its course. We will meet again, Master."

"If I see you again, I call the police. Go take your crazy-talk someplace else." Therion slammed the door. "Crazy kook."

14

By morning the former secretary's mansion began to appear like a military scientific camp site. Military vehicles, scientists, and CDC personnel swarmed the residence. Military trucks trampled the mansion's well-kept lawn. A scientific laboratory was constructed in the driveway. The entrance and exit to the premises were blocked off and only authorized personnel were allowed entrance. A large hard-plastic dome was erected over the mansion, through which people in space-suit-like coverings moved awkwardly in and out. A police cruiser guarded the entrance and an officer checked identification papers of the personnel entering. Vehicles entering and exiting Gravely Beach Loop Northwest were monitored. A full quarantine was in effect by 6 am.

I arrived at 9 am shape, after receiving word from Director Morris. I showed my badge to the police officer at the entrance to the mansion. "Agent Cole, FBI."

After he checked my identification, Officer Bernardino let me through and said: "The rumor going around is that something flew out of the mountain when it exploded and now it's floating around in the air making people sick. That true?"

"Who's saying that?" I asked.

"The guys' downtown at the station said that's what they heard on the streets."

"It was a man. I saw him in the yard," a female's voice said behind us. I turned to find an elderly lady standing behind the barricade, scowling at the tented dome over the mansion.

"And who are you, ma'am?" I asked.

"My name is Emily Barnes. I live there." She pointed to the house across the street.

"You say you saw a man in the yard?"

"Yes, a tall man dressed in long, dark clothing. I thought his appearance was very strange because no one wears things like that any longer. Plus, he had a dog with him and I know all the dogs in this neighborhood. He's not from around here," she said.

"Where were you at the time ma'am?"

"There, in that window." She pointed to the second floor window facing the street. "I can see the Cheney's house real well from there."

"Was anyone else around?"

"No. I saw only the big man and his dog. That's all I saw. It was a big man," she answered.

"Okay, thank you, Mrs. Barnes. Is it possible for some officers to stop by your home and ask you some more questions? Perhaps you could describe this man to our sketch artist?"

"Sure, that's ok with me," she replied.

"Thank you."

Mrs. Barnes took one last look at the tented mansion and walked back across the street.

"Hmm. Maybe we should go door to door to find out if anyone else saw this tall stranger," Bernardino said.

"Good idea. Let me clear it with my boss," I said. I nodded to him and made my way up the drive to the mobile military lab set up near the garage.

"Good morning," I said to the young lady sitting close by the entrance.

She was sitting at a computer console sorting through some kind of results. She appeared like she hadn't slept a wink the night before; her eyes were tired looking and her stringy brown hair slightly unkempt. She wore hard plastic dark rimmed glasses with a strap connected to its ends so they hung down around her neck when she wasn't using them. Her glasses rested on her picture perfect nose right now, and her tired eyes peered at the computer screen before her.

"Oh, hello." She glanced up. I detected a slight southern accent in her voice.

"South Carolina, North Carolina, or Georgia?" I guessed.

"No. Florida, born and raised." She let her glasses slip down around her neck. "Can I help you?"

"Agent Cole. FBI." I shook her hand.

"Oh, yes. I'm expecting you. I'm Doctor Miller."

"So, what do we know?"

She frowned. "We're not sure. Possibly a deadly blood agent. We suspect there might be a toxic agent in the house. A young police officer is at the medical center now in critical condition. He came in contact with the agent Saturday morning and it nearly killed him in less than 24 hours."

"Any idea what it is or where it came from?"

"No, that's why you're here. I have the names of the police officers who found the body. They all seem to be fine, except Officer Bradley Bailey."

"Okay. I'll go down to the precinct and have a talk with these officers." I tucked the list into my pocket. "Any idea how this blood agent works?"

"Well, it's powerful, and it acts fast. It seems to target red blood cells. These cells are known as erythrocytes. They function as oxygen gathering cells that carry oxygen from the lungs and disperse it to the rest of the body through the circulatory system. This agent destroys these cells. It also paralyzes involuntary muscles, although we're not sure how. A victim's heart will eventually just stop beating."

"And since this place is on military lock-down, you're thinking it might possibly be a biological weapon?"

"I'm not prepared to say." She shrugged. "But if it was… We could be in big trouble."

Big trouble? With a possible biological weapon already deployed on American soil—on a presidential cabinet member!—big trouble doesn't even scratch the surface.

***

I called the Olympia police department on my way there to let them know I was enroute. This was urgent. I needed to move quickly. I couldn't afford to arrive there and wait around for the officers to return from their patrol duties. This was not an option. After waiting for an ungodly amount of time, listening to the automatic answering machine messages, I finally heard:

"Olympia PD. This is Desk Sergeant Sumpter."

"Hello, this is FBI Agent Cole. I'm investigating the death of Secretary Benjamin Cheney. I'm on my way there now.

I'd like to meet with your commanding officer and the officers who found the secretary's body."

"Oh, yes, Agent Cole. The captain knows you're coming. The CDC has been in contact with her. Officers Blades, Cooper, Rodgerson and Jamison are here waiting, but Officer Bernardino is on duty at the secretary's home."

Bernardino? I'd just seen him at the mansion. Now you tell me.

"Okay thank you, I should be arriving in about thirty minutes."

"Yes, sir," Sumpter replied.

Okay, so Blades, Cooper, Bernardino, Jamison, Rodgerson and Bailey were the first to discover Cheney's body, but Bailey is the only one who got sick. Why?

***

At the prescient, Officer Winston Russell greeted me as I arrived. He led me and a Detective Richard James into the captain's office.

"Close the door," said Captain Denise Brownlow.

"Good morning, captain," I said.

A feeling of military authority was thick in the air. I immediately knew how a lower enlisted military member felt when he or she was called into his or her commander's office, for the first time. The walls were lined with pictures of high ranking people in military uniforms receiving awards, including Captain Brownlow both in her military and civilian life. More than a dozen distinguished awards lined the walls behind her desk.

"Not much good about it, Agent Cole. I'm trying to keep order in a city that is now a major disaster zone, and now I have a dead presidential cabinet member to complicate things even more," she said, and she didn't smile.

Captain Denise Brownlow is a serious, no nonsense black woman. Despite her slight stature—she only stood about five feet tall—her reputation made her someone not to be taken lightly. One plaque on the office wall behind her declared her a former US Marine commander. From the way she was glaring at me I suspected she didn't have one drop of humor in her entire body, and I certainly wouldn't want to be on opposite sides of her in a dark alley.

"Captain Brownlow, I'm—"

"I know who you are and why you're here, Agent Cole. Let's get one thing clear. I don't mean any disrespect to you personally. However, my department, besides being bogged down getting food, water, and shelter to hundreds of stricken people, is quite capable of handling the investigations of crimes committed in its jurisdiction. And I really don't care for your office's almighty attitude by sending you in here to take over an investigation that rightfully belongs to this department. Now, if the governor himself hadn't contacted my boss and insisted on our cooperation, you would be on your own. But, since I have to answer to my chief, who in turn answers to the governor, here we are. For the record, this department will give you its full cooperation. If any member of this department fails to provide you with their full cooperation, I insist that you inform me first, before you report them to your chain of command. I am ultimately responsible for the conduct of this department and would like the opportunity to do my job before you take it out of my hands or I hear about the situation from my supervisors. Are we clear?"

"Yes, ma'am I understand perfectly," I said. I tried to give her my most charming—and disarming—smile. She did not smile back. I swallowed hard and wondered if she chewed nails for breakfast.

Detective Richard James stood quietly in a corner—like an obedient servant. I suspected he was her lead detective and would have been in charge of the case if the FBI hadn't stepped in. Somewhere along the line he must have voiced his displeasure with the bureau's decision to take over the case, and now he's here to listen in on this tongue lashing.

He must have made some small gesture, because Brownlow's gaze flickered to him and some of the tension left her shoulders.

"Okay," she said. "Now, what the hell is going on? I've got one very young officer laid up in the hospital with some strange sickness that no one is talking about and a dead Secretary of the Treasury that looked like he died a thousand years ago."

"Okay," I said. "This case has been classified Top Secret. You will not repeat anything that I say to you in this room.

"Understood," said the captain.

Detective James nodded.

I explained the condition of the secretary's corpse and what little we knew about the infection that had nearly killed Officer Bailey.

"Do you know of any reason why only Bailey became sick?" I asked.

"No, but I'll send each of the officers who responded to the call to speak with you." The captain rose to her feet. "Detective James, please send Officer Blades to your office and inform the other officers that Agent Cole is here to speak with them."

Brownlow gestured for me to follow her. "Detective James' office has been set-up for you to use while you are our guest. If you'll follow me, I'll show you to it."

***

The office was barely big enough for the desk and chair it contained. Still, it was more than I'd expected. I'd just dug out my files when there was a tap at the door.

"Officer Blades?" I guessed.

"Yeah. I mean, yes, sir."

"Come on in. I'm Agent Cole."

Blades is a lot shorter and a lot older than I expected. He stands only about five-feet-seven inches tall, with thick legs and elbows bowed away from his body. His graying black hair is neatly groomed, short and tapered on the sides, giving him an air of prior military service. His blue eyes are over-shadowed by a thick unibrow. His nervousness made me feel like a father getting ready to have an embarrassing talk with his son.

"I just have a few questions, Officer Blades. Have a seat."

He sat like he wasn't very comfortable, shifting his position often. I sensed he would rather be out on the road chasing bad guys.

"You were a member of the team who found Secretary Cheney's body?" I asked.

"Yes."

"Can you tell me what happened?"

He did, with military preciseness. I wondered if he ever forgot anything. "Have you or any of the other officers felt ill or had any complaints of feeling ill?"

"No. I'm fine. I don't think any of the other guys felt sick. For certain no one got sick like Bailey."

Everyone else told the same story.

After the interviews I found my cell phone and called Doctor Miller. Her ring tone sounded like something out of the classical music history archives.

"Doctor Miller," she answered.

"Hello, Doctor Miller, Agent Cole here. I think I know how Officer Bailey came in contact with the blood agent. Apparently he touched the body."

"Direct skin-to-skin contact?"

"That's right."

"Thanks."

Click.

I spent the rest of the afternoon plowing through the records that had been arriving steadily throughout the day: copies of Cheney's appointment book, phone log, and emails for the last several weeks. As near as I could tell, everything looked completely ordinary.

I finally decided to pack everything up and head back to my office at the FBI to start plowing through the records that had arrived there.

Captain Brownlow walked me out.

"I'm keeping my fingers crossed for your young officer," I told her.

"Thank you," she said, sounding sincere. Her weapon bulged out on her left side: a left hander. "I plan to have a long talk with that young man, mainly about preserving evidence, proper police procedures and just about half the police manual."

"Well, if you get that chance go easy on him. After all, if it wasn't for him, we wouldn't have discovered this problem so quickly. It's better that we learn of its presence through the police department rather than having a thousand people get sick first."

"Well, I was pleased that Bernardino took him straight home or I may have had to sterilize this entire building. Just imagine, if that agent had entered this building or went air born, we could all be dead," she said.

"Yeah, you're right about that. Thank you for all your help today. I know that you have your hands full keeping the peace and getting food, water and shelter to people. I don't want to take up anymore of your time. The sooner this place gets back to the pleasant atmosphere of enthusiasm and excitement it had before the tsunami, the better."

"Okay, Cole, and thanks."

"For what?"

"The vibes in the city have been sort of creepy. I've been seeing lots of freaked out people lately. I'm still a woman, so I appreciate your calm demeanor, that's all."

"You're welcome, and it's not your problem alone. We're all in this together," I said, as we arrived at my vehicle and we said good-bye.

15

Julian's psychiatrist, Joshua Martu, was more than happy to schedule an appointment for him on short notice.

Martu is a fifty-five year old health enthusiast who looks ten years younger. The New England Journal of Medicine recently published his tenth report on sleep study, mental health and drug addiction. His reports have been consistently lauded by professionals in the medical field for their ground breaking insight; this latest report prompted the Mental Health Parity and Addiction Equality Act, which concluded decades-long fight for improvements in addiction and mental health insurance coverage. The passage of this law changed the regulatory guidelines and opened the door for more equitable health insurance coverage for those who suffered from addiction and mental health disorders. Prior to the passage of the act those who fell under this condition were classified as having "behavioral health" issues.

Martu is a handsome, wise, and gentle man, always clean shaven. He stands only around five-foot-six-inches tall, but appears a bit taller because of his slender build and the two-inch lifts he wears. There isn't an ounce of fat on his body, but the clothes he wears are loose fitting: baggy pants that sag in the middle and long-sleeved button up shirts that are a few sizes too big. The only thing that actually fits him is his tie.

Carla dragged a reluctant Julian to an afternoon appointment she'd made and waited for his appointed time. Impatiently, they fumbled through the assorted magazines on the table until finally Martu came out to greet them.

Julian stood and shook his hand.

"Hello, Julian. Glad to see you're alright." Martu smiled at Carla. "I expect you flew back to help the rescue efforts."

"Thank you," she said. "Especially thank you for seeing Julian so quickly."

"No problem. Come this way." Martu motioned with one hand toward the open office door.

Carla heard Julian's teeth gnashing. She nudged him with an elbow.

"Stop that," she whispered. Julian looked like an irritated little boy. He had a habit of grinding his teeth together when stressed, and the sound always irritated Carla. She hates it when he grinds his teeth together, and Julian had a bad habit of doing it at the wrong times. He really can be a bit annoying at times.

A second waiting area with: couch, love seat, big screen television and more magazines lay behind the main waiting area.

"Please make yourself comfortable, Carla," Martu said. "We'll see you after the session."

Carla squeezed Julian's hand before he followed Doctor Martu into his office.

Might as well get this over with. Julian heaved a mental sigh and sank into the brown leather recliner Martu indicated. He glanced around the office and consumed the pleasant cream colored walls adorned with the familiar paintings of local forestry and ocean scapes. Martu's bookshelf packed with professional-looking books lined one wall, and soft blue curtains blurred the sunshine streaming in the double windows. Julian closed his eyes and tried to relax.

"It's been awhile since I've seen you." Martu settled into his chair. "What's it been? A year or so?"

"Yeah, about that."

"How are things going?"

"Good." Julian scuffed the edge of the recliner with the underside of his shoes. "I was thinking of asking Carla to marry me."

Martu's smile bloomed and his eyes warmed. "So it sounds like things are really good between you and Carla."

"Yeah." Some of the tension left Julian's shoulders. "She's great. Carla's—wonderful. She makes me happy."

"That's fantastic. And you're working?"

"Right now I am. It's only temporary, but it's a good job. I like it." Julian couldn't help a small smile. "It won't take me long to save up for Carla's ring. We're in an apartment now, but I think I can make a down-payment on a house next year."

"So it sounds like things are going really well," Martu said. "That's wonderful. So tell me why you're here."

"Carla wanted me to come."

Martu studied him for several minutes. "Do you still have headaches?"

"Sometimes."

"Any recently?"

"A few."

"Any black-outs?"

"Just one."

"Were you by yourself?"

"Yeah. I didn't fall and hit my head or anything. I just kind of slumped over the table and woke up with my cereal on my forehead."

"Any dreams?"

"Not really." Julian scuffed the edge of the recliner a bit more.

"We all have dreams, Julian," Martu said gently. "It's a normal part of our lives. Good dreams, bad dreams, weird dreams."

"I don't—I mean—they're just weird. My dreams are really weird."

"Did you dance around the edge of a shark tank waving a rolling pin and wearing nothing but your grandmother's pajamas?"

Julian snorted. "No."

"Well then, it's probably not that weird." Martu watched Julian carefully and saw him relax a bit more into the recliner. "Can you remember any of them? Even partially?"

"I don't want you to associate me with people who see things." Julian said.

"What do you mean, Julian? I have no intentions of doing anything of that nature," the doctor re-assured him.

"Well, my dreams aren't normal dreams that I have during the night. They happen at any time, sometimes during the day, too."

Martu smothered a smile. Now we're getting somewhere. "Okay. Well can you share anything from one of those?"

Julian shrugged his shoulders again. "There isn't much to tell really."

"Try to remember something small, like something you were doing or where you were."

"You're going to think this is strange."

"Julian, I'm not here to judge you. I'm here to help. I won't think anything is strange, promise."

"Well, okay. Last week, I dreamed a big rock splashed down into the ocean and caused a tsunami and a lot of people died."

"You think that's weird?"

"Well, no, but—we did have a tsunami. A lot of people did die."

"Do you think your dream had anything to do with that?"

"No," Julian said slowly. "But—it does seem weird."

"There is such a thing as co-incidence, Julian. And dreaming about major natural disasters is far more common than you might think. It's actually a regular staple of dream imagery."

"Really?"

Martu grinned. "Really. Do you remember when you had the dream?"

Julian's brow wrinkled. "Thursday, Maybe. Or maybe Wednesday. I'm not sure."

"Try to remember. What did you do that day? What did you do when you woke up? Was it morning? Afternoon?"

"I don't know. Does it matter?"

"Not really, but it might help you recall the dream more vividly. How about where were you when it occurred?" Martu asked.

"Wait—I know it was Thursday before the tsunami because I had a black-out and was laying on the floor in the living room. I woke up when the news came on and said it was 'Thursday.'"

"How much do you know about the tsunami?" Martu asked. He watched Julian closely.

"I saw it. I was out on a boat in the Sound fishing with a friend when it happened. I know the news reports said there was an earthquake before the tsunami. But I saw the mountain explode, rocks fell into the water, and the ground blew up under the water before the tsunami came."

"So, you saw it in a dream and then you went out and actually witnessed it really happening."

"Yeah, I guess so. But it's only a dream, right? Falling rocks don't cause tsunamis."

"Well, it's not exactly only a dream, since you had a black-out. The black-out concerns me."

"See, I told you that you were going to start associating me with nut cases."

"Julian, I'm not associating you with nut cases. I'm just trying to help you to get an explanation for what happened."

"I had a dream and that's all. I don't need to explain it."

"Actually, Julian, your dreams can be quite useful in the field of medical science. I'm a member of an organization involved in the advancement of medical research and your case is rather unique. You can be of extreme importance to us in our study of the human brain. I'd like you to come to my home on St. Clare Island for a weekend. A specialist in sleep study, Dr. Sherrington, is visiting me. There, I have the equipment and ability to study your condition better. This will give us the chance to get a full evaluation of your physical condition."

"I don't know, doctor. I'll think about it."

"I think it will be best for you, Julian. These black-outs and dreams could be affecting your health in other ways. The only way of knowing is to come in and have the specialist examine you."

"I feel fine."

"Can you tell me what you feel like after you've had one of these black-outs?"

"I don't know. I don't remember."

"How often do you have them?"

"Not often. That's the only one that I remember having," he lied.

"Have you told anyone else about this?"

"No."

"Not even Carla?"

"No."

"Why not?"

"I don't know."

"Julian, will you excuse me for one second? I will only take one second."

"Okay."

***

Dr. Martu didn't wish to speak with Carla and Julian together and he didn't want Julian to know what he had to say to Carla. He got up and walked out of the room and into the waiting room. Carla put down the magazine she was reading and stood up when she saw the psychiatrist appear.

"Carla, I want to ask you a question before I let Julian go. I don't want Julian to know that I'm saying this to you."

"Yes, of course. What is it?"

"It appears that Julian has been experiencing black-outs and he has been keeping this information to himself. This may indicate a very serious condition. He may also have been experiencing psychotic episodes, which means a loss of contact with reality. I am recommending that he comes to St. Clare, where my test laboratory is located, so I can conduct a full examination. Can you assist me and ensure that he gets there?"

"Okay, Doctor Martu. I'll try and persuade him," Carla said. "What kind of tests do you need to conduct?"

"I'd like to do a sleep study on him and record the results. I also need to observe his brain waves and actions while he is having one of these episodes. He may become delusional and develop false beliefs about what is taking place, and he may see or hear things that are not really there."

"Oh, Julian," Carla whispered.

"I need you to keep an eye on him and call me right away if he has another black-out."

"I will," she said.

"Thank you, Carla." Martu returned to his office. He riffled around his desk to find a card and handed it to Julian. "This is my home number. If you change your mind about coming to St. Clare, please let me know."

"Okay, doc."

"And if you have another black-out, please have someone call me right away. I would like to see you as soon as possible afterward."

"I will." Julian said.

Somehow Doctor Martu doubted that he would make the call. He wrote a note on his note pad and he waited until after Julian left before he picked up his telephone.

"What if Julian really can see events before they occur?" Martu asked himself while he wanted for an answer on the other end of the line.

16

Back on the road, I found my earphones and plugged them into my ears; I began to listen to my messages. The first was from Nelson; he wanted to know where I had been and if I was okay. The next was also from Nelson, wondering why I hadn't returned his call.

The next two messages were from Rosalie Rockwell, a CIA operative coordinator, asking for a call back. The next message came from my boss, the director of the FBI, wanting to know my status. I called and updated him.

"What a mess," Director Morris said. "Look, Cole, I know you're not going to be happy about this, but there are a lot of high level people interested in this case. The CIA is sending out an agent to work with you on the case. I need you to play nice."

Morris knew this was a sore spot for me. Strictly speaking, the CIA and FBI do not work together. We occasionally share information, but we are forbidden from directly working together by law. Plus, we have different purposes, methods, and goals. We handle domestic issues. They deal with international issues. We look primarily for information that will hold up in court. They look for things that give the president an advantage. We investigated Al Capone for tax evasion. They blew up Osama Bin Laden's compound.

In short, we do not play well together.

"Director—"

"Let me put it this way, you are working together, but you are not working together," Morris interrupted. He knew I was about to start spouting protocol and legal-ese. "This is a direct request from the president, and the president gets what the president wants. The CIA agent will cover his side of the house and you'll cover our side. You both get the information at the same time. It's the smart thing to do. And if someone's loosed a bio-logical weapon on American soil you know damn well the CIA has a right to investigate. Let's be smart about this and pool our resources."

Shit, that's all I need. I drummed my fingers on the steering wheel. Baby-sit some spook with the White House up his ass. He'll come in with a bossy why-can't-you-get-your-shit-together attitude, and then I'll have to kick his ass.

"Cole?"

"Yes, sir," I answered. "Be nice to CIA spook."

"Got it."

"That's damn right, Cole. Be nice," Morris snapped. "I don't like it either, but we're not going to be the ones explaining to the White House why we're pissing into the wind with the murder investigation of a presidential cabinet member. You got that?"

"Got it. Check."

"Agent's name is Amir Bloomberg. He should be arriving at SEA-TAC shortly. I volunteered you to pick him up."

Great. Now I'm a spook taxi. I tried not to think out loud. "Yes, sir. I'd be happy to."

"That's what I want to hear, Cole."

I entertained myself thinking of a few choice things I could say to CIA Agent Amir Bloomberg—what kind of name was Amir, anyway?—on my way to the airport. However, as I drew nearer my destination I began to think about the possibility of working with Amir. I wasn't really making much progress in the case on my own, and Amir might have some fresh ideas to consider.

This case is just too damn weird, I thought. Or maybe I was losing my edge.

I reflected on prior cases, my motivation to find and pursue clues and accomplish my mission. I'd often thought I was born to be an agent, to pursue and catch bad guys. It was all I'd ever known. All I ever wanted to know.

And Amanda had left me. Putting my job first had destroyed my marriage and left my house empty. Sometimes I wished I could go back. I'd change that piece of the puzzle, spend more time with her. But right now all I had left was my work, and I still needed to do the very best job I could.

And who knew? With this high profile of a case, a successful outcome could put me in line for a future director's position. That is, if I wanted it.

17

The phone woke Brute Therion from a sound sleep. He rubbed a hand across his forehead and fumbled for the receiver.

"Therion," he managed.

"Secretary Therion, this is Dr. Joshua Martu. I apologize for calling you at this late hour; however, I'm on my way out of the country for a few days and wanted to speak with you before I left."

Therion detected a strong Israeli accent in Martu's voice. "Uh…hmm. It's quite alright. How can I help you?"

"I've just received word of Secretary Cheney's misfortune and am very saddened by the tragic news. He was an excellent business partner," Martu said.

'Was an excellent business partner?' Therion frowned. Belatedly, the Israeli accent and name snapped together in his mind: Joshua Martu.

"Yes, Dr. Martu. I'm aware of your work with the secretary," Therion said.

"Are you?" Martu asked.

"Yes, I am. I am—I was—the Deputy Secretary. I worked very closely with Secretary Cheney."

"Then you know that Israel needs your help more than ever. You are aware that Secretary Cheney bought oil for the U.S. government from my shipments and I worked together with him to help supply the Arab underground movement that supports American and Israeli policies with the necessary funds to maintain their underground activities and help to oppose the anti-US and anti-Israeli Arab governments."

"I do, Dr. Martu," Therion said. "Secretary Cheney and I agreed completely about this important work."

"I am happy to hear that, Mr. Therion. There are many in the Middle East who are working to move forward, away from the old way of thinking, away from the continued conflict with the Israeli government. Change is inevitable, and we play an important role in this process."

"These are very dangerous times, Dr. Martu. America must have friends around the world, and Secretary Cheney and I recognized assets to our country—and the world—when we found them."

"I am pleased to hear that, Mr. Therion. I look forward to working with you in the future."

No sooner had Therion hung up the phone, it rang again. The receiver was still warm in the palm of his hand. Was he never getting back to sleep?

"Therion," he snapped.

"That which has begun, cannot be undone."

"What?" Therion thought something about the caller's voice sounded familiar, but couldn't think what it was.

"Soon you will be king."

"Soon I'll be asleep. Check your number." Therion hung up.

Ruth stirred. "Who was it?"

"Nobody, baby. Wrong number." He curled around her with a sigh. "Go back to sleep."

The eerie voice reverberated in Therion's head: "That which has begun, cannot be undone."

He couldn't stop thinking about it, much less get back to sleep, Therion got up out of bed and walked downstairs for a drink of water.

That which has begun, cannot be undone—reverberated in his head.

He stepped into his kitchen and grabbed a bottle of water. Therion had the strange feeling, he was being watched. He glanced quickly over his right shoulder.

Nothing!

Artificial light tunneled in around the corners of the drapes covering the narrow window in his alcove, it created creeping shadows across the small room. The air was cool and the room was silent. When Therion inhaled he took in the unfamiliar odor—what's that smell?

It reminded him of an old graveyard. The unpleasant scent fumigated the air. Therion frowned, just before he saw the tall intruder step out from the shadows in his alcove. The sudden shock gave him a fright, he stumble back a few steps and almost fell backward over the small coffee table to his rear, his heart pounded in his chest.

"I am Azazel, and you have summoned me to do your bidding." The intruder spoke.

"Do you know who I am? Get out of my house, now." Therion squirted.

Azazel was puzzled. "You are the king, the bearer of the Seal of Solomon." His voice was strong, with an accent Therion did not recognize.

A bolt of surprise shot through Brute Therion's entire body. He remembered Benjamin Cheney's stories, but…He squared his shoulders. "This is not a game. Leave now."

"I cannot. It is you who have brought me here. I am drawn by souls…your soul…do you know the power contained by souls?"

"What does this have to do with souls?" Therion asked.

"I am drawn to souls, Therion. The soul is the bosom of all existence, without which nothing can exist." Azazel's owl-like eyes glowed red as he spoke. "My presence here could not exist without your inner most desire. The wishes of your own soul drew me to you, Therion."

Brute Therion was still puzzled by the strangeness of Azazel's presence in his house, but he listen.

"An automobile without an engine is like a body without a soul. A plant that loses its color and withers back into the dust from which it came is likewise a body without a soul. Every living thing has its own soul, not only human beings, from the greatest beasts of the ocean to the smallest organisms of illness. But the human soul is most powerful."

Therion's knees shook noticeably, but he tried his best to conceal his fear, he stared at the menacing creature before him.

"Over the graduation of thousands of years there have been various references to this bosom of existence, Therion." Azazel said as he stepped back into the shadows. "In the Hebrew and Christian bibles, in the very beginning of Genesis, it says the soul was created by God. The creator of all life, he made the image of man from the dust of the earth, and into this image he blew his breath, which gave the image life. Man became a soul—a living being. This is the most coveted prize of all, the life of man—the breath of God, capable of discovering undiscovered mysteries. It is the most powerful entity in the world." Azazel's ancient voice echoed through the darkness.

"I don't care. How do I get you out of my house?" Therion grew angrier with each passing second.

Azazel ignored him.

"This is the gift that separates humans' from all others, including angels. You have the freedom of choice. An angel has no freedom of choice; it is all spiritual, a servant to its creator. It is bound to fulfill the wishes of its creator, and that is its nature. The human spirit is very different, it being created more Godly. No other creation on earth possesses this freedom, Therion." The tone of Azazel's ancient voice irritated Therion.

"I don't care. Get out." Therion said forcefully.

"We are separated by your nature, Therion, you have free will. The human soul is independent. It is separated from its creator and potentially it can be greater than it once was. It can change the world in which it lives."

"I don't care. You are an intruder in my home." Therion said, trying desperately to subdue his fear and maintain his composure. "I don't need your lecturing. Get out."

"It is not a lecture. It is truth," Azazel answered. "Your soul has the power to unlock something for me, Therion, and I will not stop until I have it."

Azazel vanished.

18

Earlier that evening Julian watched Carla climb into her Ford Mustang and drive away. She had plans to help an emergency shelter over flowing with tsunami victims, mostly elderly women and children needing food, water, and a place to sleep. Julian sighed and shuffled back to his living room couch. Surely there was a good game on the TV. He reached for the remote and felt a curious wave of listlessness wash over him. He hit the floor hard and lost his consciousness.

His mind drifted. For a mesmerizing period of time he saw no light, heard no sounds. He couldn't feel his arms or legs; he couldn't feel his body at all. And yet, somehow, it seemed to him that he was traveling. He could feel himself moving through empty spaces. A deserted dark land began to materialize around him.

"The beast tormented your father Julian. It's evil, it drove him to take his own life," he heard an old frail female's voice say. "The evil one tires of waiting. It wants its freedom."

"What did you say? I don't understand. Can we keep it chained?" Julian asked.

"You can. You have the gift."

"What is the gift? What do I do with it?" He asked.

"You must stop him Julian. He must have the ring. The ring is the key. Only a king can give it. He needs a king."

He heard a sudden burst of blasphemous murmuring and laughter that broke the desert stillness. A strange thrumming reverberated through the air and dissolved the landscape around him. Julian's vision preserved an eagle—dressed in fashionable clothing, with a coin-size symbol of the seal of the US Treasury hanging around its neck—soar above a pristine lake. The eagle circled, searching for prey, before diving to skim over the surface of the water. A strange creature with a face like a gargoyle, teeth like a lion, body like a gorilla and wings like an angel, sprang up from the depths of the water and snatched the bird in its flight before vanishing back down into the still water.

Then, Julian saw Carla caught in the midst of a thunder and lightning storm while swimming in a pool. She couldn't get out of the pool on her own and started screaming. Somehow, her voice sucked the strength from his body. His legs wouldn't move. The more she screamed, the weaker he felt. If she would only stop screaming, he could get his strength back and rescue her.

Soon it was too late. Carla vanished beneath the water.

No! Carla! Carla! The sudden silence let him spring forward and rush toward the pool. But the faster he ran, the farther away it got.

In the blink of an eye everything was gone. He hovered in gloom.

The air was thin and smelled like burning metal. A brilliant explosion burst above him and illuminated a ruined city around him. It looked like downtown Olympia. No, New York. Or Los Angeles. Or like any city. Every city. The world around him transformed into tiny pockets of space, each containing only shadows of darkness. His mere existence felt meaningless, without purpose, without structure. Julian sensed a dark new beginning, a new world of darkness.

He began to feel a presence in the darkness around him, his senses increased. He was not alone. In the muted light he saw that an old woman stood by his side. Ribbons twined in her long silver hair. Deep lines like eagle claws cut into the corners of her eyes and mouth. Her voice was frail. She did not speak English, but he understood her perfectly.

"Enough sleep, Julian. There is much work to be done. Many chores before you rest. Enough sleep, my son."

Julian woke.

***

Carla called her father on her way to the shelter.

"Hello, honey. Nice of you to call your father, finally."

"Hi, Dad. Sorry. I've been meaning to call you, really."

"Where are you?" he asked.

"I'm heading over to a shelter for women and children. It's sad, Dad. There aren't enough cots. Blankets are spread on the ground wherever there's space. Some of them have barely enough to eat. I have some canned goods to donate and books to read to the children before they go to sleep."

"Good work. I'm proud of you."

"Thanks dad. Where are you?"

"I'm almost at the airport." He didn't sound happy about it.

Then it's a good time for me to stop by the house and check and see if he has any new girlfriends. Mom always wants to know these things. Carla made a turn and headed for her father's house.

"Look, Dad. Let's meet for lunch or dinner, soon. Just let me know when you're free."

"Okay, honey. Good thinking," he responded. "I love you. Bye."

"Love you too."

She snapped her phone shut.

I wonder what he's up to. She said to herself as she pulled into the driveway. She got out and hurried up to the front steps. The front door stuck, as usual.

Hmm…Smells like he's been eating TV dinners. Dad really needs to learn to cook. She walked back to the kitchen and sat at the circular table where her father always left files he was working on. She opened the one on top and scanned through it.

Secretary Cheney, mummified remains…with a question mark. Center for Disease Control, Dr. Miller, and a phone number. Deadly blood agent.

Carla flipped through a few more pages.

Young police Officer Bradley Bailey sick in hospital, blood agent found. Question mark. Need to talk with Officers Blades, Bernardino, Cooper, Rodgerson and Jamison. Captain Brownlow. Mrs. Cheney…question mark…Neighbors…question mark. Dad sure likes question marks.

Carla carefully replaced the files and went up the stairs to her father's bedroom and scanned the room for female's clothing—nothing, no new girlfriends. She let herself out.

19

CIA Agent Amir Bloomberg was easy to spot. All spooks look alike. Their suits look expensive, their hair-cuts look shellacked, and their eyes look like designer sunglasses, since that's as much of their eyes you ever see, even when the sun's already vanished.

I waved at him and pulled up to the curb. Amir heaved his bags into the back and settled into the passenger seat.

"Hello, Agent Cole. Thanks for coming,"

"No problem," I muttered.

"You may be wondering why I'm here?"

"Not really," I said. "But since you are, why don't you tell me what was so important? Why you had to fly 3000 miles to a disaster stricken city."

Amir grinned. "They said you were a hard-ass."

I grunted.

"Do you know that there was another body found that looked just like this one?"

"What?" I straightened. "When? Where?"

"About twenty years ago, in New Jersey. An economics professor at Princeton was found dead in his office." Amir dug a file out of his briefcase and passed a glossy black and white photo to me. "Look familiar?"

"Jesus." The body slumped in the chair looked exactly like Cheney's: mummified flesh, bulging eyes, hair standing on end. "Ever solved?"

"No. But it seemed like a good place to start."

***

I dropped Amir off at his hotel before heading home. While I would have liked to get started right away, the fact was that I was painfully exhausted and hadn't slept for almost two days.

This is the third starless night in a row. These past few evenings have been a bit darker and foggier than normal, too. I drove through heavy fog—like thick smoke bellowing from a chimney stack—that belled toward my vehicle. Before long I found myself in the bosom of a shadowy canopy.

The fog made visibility difficult. I slowed down and began to get the peculiar sense I was being watched, like the fog had eyes. I began periodically checking behind me in my rearview mirror. I saw nothing each time, not even any other cars.

What's wrong with me? Get a grip, Cole. You're getting down-right paranoid.

Try as I might, I couldn't stop checking the rearview mirror. And my fingers twitched toward my handgun.

I wasn't usually prone to flights of fancy or superstition. But these events began to remind me of a few strange stories the realtor who sold Amanda and I our home told me. I told him I didn't believe such things, and I insisted that he not mention them to Amanda. Both her and I really liked the neighborhood and the house. I didn't want to risk anything changing her mind about us buying it.

The realtor's family had lived in the area for generations. Apparently, our potential neighborhood had a reputation for strange occurrences. Some claimed that the events were spurious hoaxes, but some accepted them as authentic. Some said the place was bewitched by its ancient past as the ancient burial ground of local natives. I've been told that even prudent minds sometimes found it difficult to explain the strange occurrences.

As the story goes, the first house on the block developed a very long history of sightings of foot-prints in the snow. Year after year these mysterious foot-prints were seen leading to the front door of the house, even when no one had been home for long periods of time.

Levi Samuelson, the current owner of the property, had awakened to these foot-prints the first winter he bought the house fifty or so years ago. Mr. Samuelson had lost the use of his legs during the Vietnam War and was confined to a wheelchair. He rarely used his front entrance and usually entered and exited his home via the electronic hoist in the garage that raised and lowered his wheelchair from his vehicle to the garage floor.

But the footsteps continued to appear, year after year, any time snow covered the walkway. The footsteps began exactly ten feet from the door with nothing but pristine, untouched snow between them and the street. Local daredevils sometimes camped out on Samuelson's front porch to see if they could catch the culprit, but they never did.

A few blocks over, an old Victorian has sat vacant for over sixty years. It's an old house with three bedrooms and a bathroom on its second floor. It didn't have the luxury of built-in closets, telephones, cable lines, electrical appliances, or even a color TV. Instead, most rooms possessed an old wooden wardrobe and a wood burning stove for heating.

Anyone who dared to enter this house was said to have been met by its previous owner. Rumor has it that the owner, Ms. Rose Bauer, had died there quietly in her sleep one summer night. It was some weeks before her son and daughter came to visit her and discovered her decaying remains in an upstairs bedroom. The old lady had been dead so long that maggots had spread into the neighbor's basement, along with an unusual quantity of flies.

After Ms. Bauer's burial, her son and daughter tried to re-enter the house, only to be met by their dead mother's spirit at the door. She appeared just as she had while living, not ghostly, at all, wearing the same long red robe they had found her in.

"Please, kindly leave my house," Ms. Bauer said politely. "I'm busy with the house cleaning and have no time to sit and chat."

The shocked son and daughter quickly bolted from the house and never returned. Any subsequent visitor to the house was met at the entrance by this mysterious apparition.

The local train station had its story, as well. People reported hearing a train bell ringing on dark, cloudy, nights around midnight. Yet there is no bell installed or affixed anywhere near the newly remodeled train station. However, the bell continued to be heard and was followed by a slightly illuminated horse-drawn carriage, with driver and passengers, traveling across the railroad tracks directly in front of the train station.

When I first heard the stories I envisioned Amanda's facial expression, her pausing in whatever she was doing, and looking into my eyes with that certain look that only she can use to express her disapproval. I had to insist on the realtor not mentioning these stories to her.

I arrived home and parked my Lexus in the driveway as usual and stepped through the front door with relief. I took off my jacket and I hung it on the rail of the stairs, just above Amanda's table. I strolled into the kitchen took a TV dinner out of the freezer. I un-wrapped it and popped it in the micro-wave and set the timer.

Home always reminded me of Amanda. Even now her special touch, her scent, her style, her taste in décor still pervade throughout the house. I thought back to the nights we'd eaten something cooked, not reheated, and drank it down with wine while telling each other about our day. Sometimes I can't believe how much I miss her.

The microwave beeped and brought me back to my dim and empty kitchen. I took the TV dinner out, waited for a minute for it to cool while I hunted up a beer; I ate standing at the counter and left the container in the sink.

In the bedroom I turned on the TV and listened to the news report from the shower. More bad news, as usual. I dragged on some shorts, flopped on the bed, and had no idea when I passed out.

I hadn't dreamt in a long time, or if I had I didn't remember any of it in the morning. However, I began to see visions of the Treasury Secretary's mummified body, with its eyes open, staring at me, with its teeth grinning and hair sticking straight up. Just a few flickers at first, like something half remembered when you're busy doing something else. Then vividly, in excruciating detail, with a sound I thought I should recognize but couldn't. It clarified slightly into a voice but murmured so softly I couldn't quite hear it.

I think it was the voice that woke me, or maybe my strain to hear it. I must have been sitting up in bed for several minutes, listening, worriedly concern, before I realized I'd had a dream and was alone in my room. I shrugged and got up to open the window to let a bit of fresh air in, the room seemed stifling. I turned back toward the bed and caught a glimpse of the full length mirror on the far wall.

"Holy, shit!" I jumped back.

Secretary Cheney's mummified corpse stared back at me from the mirror; its eyes were horribly alive and fixed on me.

"Help me," a thin voice whispered.

I grabbed my weapon, chambered a round, and pointed it at the mirror.

"Help me!" the voice said again.

I didn't know I could feel this kind of fear. I didn't know this kind of fear even existed, until now. It shot down to my gut, straight into my inner most sanctum sanctorum. I was scared straight. My knees shook. I felt weak to the core and I almost crumbled.

Then the house began to vibrate—just as it had in the earthquake. Objects began rattling across surfaces. My watch and badge quivered to the edge of the nightstand.

It was time to run. I ran. I grabbed what I could quickly—watch, keys, wallet, badge. I managed to grab a pair of jeans, a T-shirt and my worn-out running shoes from the floor by the closet.

I bolted into the hallway, down the stairs, and out the front door. I threw everything into the car and peeled off.

I drove until my hands stopped shaking and got a room for the night at a local hotel. The first thing I did when I walked into the room was to grab a blanket from the bed and a few towels from the bathroom to cover every mirror in the room.

I sat on the bed, checked the slide on my handgun, and waited for morning.

20

In total darkness Azazel's eyes glowed in his head and illuminated the dark spaces around his eyes as he watched Ruth Brown and Brute Therion while they slept. Ruth's bare naked body lay next to Brute's. At first, Azazel stood still and took his time admiring the surface of her tanned skin. The glow in his big owl-like eyes intensified, as his gaze drifted over her. He knew she would be soft, and warm. The freshness of her scent radiating from her human skin drew him closer. Just as he reached for her, Therion threw his arm out and hugged her close.

Moonlight glinted off the ancient ring on Therion's finger. Azazel stumbled back and tore his gaze off Ruth's body. He bowed his head and rendered honor to the seal of the king.

Once again, Azazel tried to bond with his summoner. He used his mind to communicate with the sleeping Therion, pure mind to mind contact.

"Wake, my king."

Therion bolted upright in bed. He caught sight of Azazel at once, all color drained from his face.

Although Azazel had the power to alter and disguise himself at will, he stood in his true form, face like a gargoyle, teeth like a lion, body like a gorilla and wings of an angel.

"What the hell are you?" Therion managed. Azazel bowed.

"You have been appointed Secretary of the Treasury."

"What?"

Therion's telephone rang. His hand inched for the receiver. This seemed to amuse Azazel, who merely nodded that Therion should answer it.

"Therion," he managed.

"Brute, this is the president. I am appointing you Secretary of the Treasury. I think you'll do a fine job. I've made my decision and wanted to let you know it now."

"Sir, I don't know what to say. This is so sudden. I'm honored."

"Okay, sleep on it. We'll talk in the office later this week."

"Yes, sir."

"Okay then it's settled."

Click.

It took Therion several moments to put the pieces together.

"My servant?" he gaped. "You?"

Azazel bowed again.

"Then...go away. I order you to go away now, and never return."

"That is not possible," Azazel answered. "What has begun cannot be undone."

"What has begun?" Therion demanded. At this, Azazel's owl-like eyes took on a different glow.

"I tire of waiting for you."

Therion's body arched back like he'd been tasered. His eyes bulged and his lips stretched back in a helpless grimace of pain. Azazel drifted over to him and lifted his limp body as easily as Therion might have lifted a doll.

"Now, you will listen," Azazel hissed. "And you will do as I say."

21

My cell phone woke me from a deep sleep the next morning. I hadn't expected to, but I must have dozed off. The grip of my handgun felt welded to my hand.

"Cole," I answered. I didn't recognize the sound of my own voice. I cleared my throat and tried again. "This is Agent Cole."

Jesus. I sounded like a scared shit-less old man.

"Cole, it's me, Amir. We need to get an early start. I'd like to have a look at the crime scene."

Amir's voice reminded me that I hadn't any clothes with which to dress. I needed to get back home to get some clothes. The fingers I'd just managed to relax from the pistol grip tightened convulsively.

Reluctantly I answered, "Okay, I'll be there as soon as I get ready."

"How long do you need?"

"One hour, maybe two." A year.

I dragged myself off the bed, still clothed in last night's attire. I walked into the bathroom, uncovered the mirror and saw that I would definitely need more time than I expected. My reflection in the mirror wasn't very kind to me—I looked like hell.

I undressed and stumbled into the shower. I made use of the hotel's supplies to brush my teeth and shave. Outside the bright sun's light blinded me momentarily and reminded me never to forget my sunglasses again.

Maybe the CIA has something going for it, after all.

I climbed into my car and headed for my house. I didn't know what to expect when I got back there, but my plans were to pack a few things, get dressed and get out of there. I wouldn't spend any more time there than I had to.

Uncertainty filled my mind. Would I have to battle with that thing again this morning?

It wasn't long before I pulled into my driveway and parked. It took several minutes for me to get the nerve to walk up to the front door. My hands shook as I started to put the key in the lock—the door cracked open.

I jumped back a few steps and had my weapon trained on the door before my feet even touched the ground again.

Nothing happened.

I waited several seconds more, then inched forward and pushed the door open.

Nothing. Just my hallway, with Amanda's table and my suit jacket hanging over the banister. It occurred to me belatedly that I hadn't locked the door behind me during my flight the night before.

Jesus, Cole. I lowered my weapon and stepped inside with a snort of self-disgust. Man-up, damn it.

I searched the first floor cautiously—in case intruders had broken in after I carelessly left the door unlocked, I told myself—but everything was in its place. Early morning quiet lay peacefully over the house.

For the first time, I was glad Amanda and Carla weren't here. A profound rush of gratitude swept over me as I thought of Amanda safe and happy in Florida and Carla curled up securely with Julian.

I stopped at the foot of the stairs and turned my head to one side to listen. I even held my breath, but I didn't hear anything.

I checked the time on my Blueberry: 8:40. I've got to hurry. Amir will be waiting.

I dashed up the stairs and stopped at the top to listen for any strange sounds. After hearing nothing, I crept to my bedroom and guardedly looked in.

Nothing.

I hurried over to the closet, grabbed a suitcase, threw it on the bed, packed some things—suits, shirts, underwear, socks, tie, ammunition. Then I grabbed a fresh suit, shirt and tie from the rack and quickly dressed myself. I retrieved my toothbrush, paste, and shaving gear from the bathroom, tossed it in the suitcase, and I was out of there.

I arrived at the Governor's Hotel an hour and fifteen minutes later than I had agreed. I found Amir waiting in the lobby, talking with a stunning brunette. They were looking at a painting of the Cascade Mountains.

The woman was elegantly dressed in a tight knee length blue skirt that accentuated her near perfectly formed calves, long-sleeve silk blouse, and heels high enough to make my mouth water.

The sun shines inside the Governor's Hotel. Beauty and the beast, filtered through my brain.

The woman's short dark curly hair framed a breath-taking face. Green eyes sparkled in a smoothly tanned complexion, and her smile, while friendly, was of a woman accustomed to commanding male attention.

I took a deep breath and joined them.

"Good morning, Agent Cole," Amir said, seemingly not at all concerned by my extreme tardiness. "Please meet Rebecca."

"It's a pleasure to meet you, ma'am," I extended a hand and was ridiculously pleased when she took it.

"The pleasure is mine, Agent Cole." She smiled charmingly and turned back to the painting. "We were just admiring this artist's ability to capture the Cascade Mountain Range in such stunning detail in this painting, especially towering Mount Rainier."

"Well, over the years, I've admired this monstrous edifice from a distance, so let me have a look," I said. "This is probably the closest that I've gotten to it, believe it or not. I agree that it's a beautiful piece of work. The artist has certainly captured the magnificence of the duel glaciered craters and its towering dominance over its closest neighbors."

"It's unbelievable that something so beautiful can also be one of the world's most dangerous volcanoes," Amir mused.

"That's true. If it erupts, experts say it will wipe out the entire city of Puyallup," Rebecca said. "Similar to how Mount Vesuvius wiped out the city of Pompeii in Italy centuries ago."

"Not only that, but if Rainier erupted it would most likely create mudflows that would destroy not only Puyallup, but Enumclaw, Orting, Kent, Auburn, Sumner and Renton. It could also destroy parts of downtown Seattle, and cause tsunamis in Puget Sound and Lake Washington. And the crazy thing is, knowing all that—and there's no denying it's going to happen someday—people still choose to live there." I shook my head. "From what I hear, Rainier's actually overdue for an eruption."

"Wow. It stretches all the way up into the clouds," Amir said. "I wonder how tall it is."

"Fourteen-thousand-four-hundred-and-eleven feet," Rebecca said.

"You remember that?" I sputtered.

"No, actually. I just read it right here. See? It's written right below the painting." Rebecca grinned.

"Hello." Song So-Yong appeared at my shoulder.

"Song!" I hugged her with genuine pleasure. "You're looking well. What's a news anchor-woman doing in these parts this morning?"

"Letting an old friend take her to breakfast," Rebecca said. "These two gentlemen have been keeping me company while I waited for you, Song. I didn't know you knew Agent Cole."

"Oh, sure. I've known Cole and his family for years. His ex-wife and I used to attend the same Sumba classes."

"So that's how you stay in such lovely shape." Rebecca gifted Amir and I with a smile. "Thank you for the company, gentlemen. Please excuse us. I know Song wants her coffee, and I'm starving."

"Of course, ladies." Amir stepped back and gestured toward the dining room. "Enjoy your morning."

***

"Thank you for coming, Song. I really need to talk with someone about this," Rebecca said, as they took a table in a private corner.

"Of course. I've been so worried about you since I heard about Benjamin." Song looked up as the waiter reached the table. "Two coffees: one black, no sugar, the other with cream and one sugar, please."

"Thank you," Rebecca murmured as the waiter left. Tears gathered in her eyes.

"What's wrong, Rebecca? How can I help?" Song asked.

"I just don't know who else to talk to." Rebecca took out a tissue from her purse and used it to dry her eyes.

"What is it, Rebecca?" Song asked.

"I'm sure you've been following the embarrassing reports about Benjamin's activities of the past few weeks," Rebecca said.

"I've heard the story and I've stayed away from it."

"Yes, I know. Thank you. Well, I had to take a leave of absence from work three weeks ago and I held my tongue about it. I couldn't face my co-workers with that hanging over my head," Rebecca said.

"Okay, I understand that." Song smiled at their server as he delivered their coffee. "I had been waiting for Benjamin to come home so that I could confront him. I was going to leave him. It was over between us," Rebecca said.

"Good girl, I would've done the same thing." Song said.

"So, when he came home we had a terrible fight. I told him I was leaving him and I left the house. But, then when I came home I found his body in his office..." Rebecca began to cry.

"Oh, Rebecca," Song said. She reached around and hugged her close.

"I didn't know it was him, I didn't recognize him. It reminded me of the time Benjamin and I visited Germany for a vacation," Rebecca said. "We were up north in the city of Bremen and we went to see the famous cathedral of Saint Peter. I don't know if you've ever seen it, but it has two towers topped by pyramids, so tall, they almost reach the clouds. Its architectural design is in an amazing combination of very distinguished Romanesque and Gothic styles. Once we were inside, I remember the look in Benjamin's eyes. He was fascinated by the mosaics, the scenes and characters from the Scriptures, colorful multi-colored glass windows, and the statues leading up to the towering Gothic arches. It was a magnificent sight to see. We were so amazed. It was a great trip."

Rebecca smiled sadly at the memory. "What made me think of it was the mummies. There is a lead basement, something they call a bleikeller, beneath the nave. I don't know how long it's been there, but it was famous even before the Reformation as a place that miraculously preserved dead bodies. Apparently this ability was discovered by accident. A roof layer had fallen to his death hundreds of years ago, during the original construction of the building. His body was left in the basement while they tried to find his family members. But after no family members were found the body was forgotten there where it laid. Many years later the body was rediscovered in its mummified form and the mystery was revealed. Somehow, that place has the power to preserve dead bodies. Since that time the people living in the area have claimed that people have seen mummies walking in and out of the church, and mummies carrying live bodies off, although none have been proven. There have also been numerous reports of missing

126

persons' in the area. Claims of young boys and girls reported missing from their families and never found. The rumors are that the mummies have taken them, but again there hadn't been any evidence found to prove any of those rumors. When I saw that body lying there in Benjamin's office that morning, that's exactly what it reminded me of; it looked exactly like those mummies we saw in the old church. I didn't know it was him." Rebecca said. "And—oh Song, I had told him that I was leaving him and I left the house and went out drinking and I slept with another man because I wanted to end the marriage for sure…"

"I'm sorry, Rebecca. I'm so sorry it ended this way for you and Benjamin," Song said.

Rebecca sniffled. "And I—I just ran, Song. I didn't even know it was him. I ran out of the house, I was so afraid, and I—I didn't even look for him. I set the alarm off when I left, but I didn't wait for the police, or called 911 or anything. I didn't do anything that I should have done. I'm so ashamed."

"Don't be. If anyone thinks you should have done better, they can try it themselves sometime," Song said firmly. "The police didn't make you feel that way, did they?"

"I don't actually know." Rebecca almost laughed. "I gave a statement that afternoon, but I don't remember very much of it. I was still so shocked. It all seemed so surreal."

"Have you talked to the FBI?"

Rebecca paled. "No. Do you think I have to? Song, I just want all this to go away. You're practically the only person I've talked to. I don't answer my door at the hotel. I've even stopped answering my phone."

"I think they'll want to talk to you sooner or later. You just met the man working the case. Agent Cole and he's an old friend of mine," Song said. "I can set up a meeting between you. I'll go with you, too, if you want."

"Thanks," Rebecca said softly. "I'll think about it. Thank you, Song, for listening."

***

My phone rang just as we left the hotel.

"Cole," I said. It was Doctor Miller of the CDC.

"Agent Cole, I've got some news. We found that Officer Bailey had a small cut on his right index finger and a kind of parasitic bacteria entered into his system through this opening in his skin. The bacterium usually feeds on decaying matter, but mixed with his living tissue and began to feed on it. The good news is this isn't a blood agent after all. But the bad news is that it's just as dangerous."

"Are you trying to tell me that we're dealing with some kind of flesh-eating bacteria?" I asked. Jesus, how weird can this case get?

Amir threw me a startled look.

"I'm afraid so," Dr. Miller said. "However, also on the good side, we know how it's transmitted, and since we know what we're dealing with, we know what kind of treatment is more likely to be effective. I've made sure Secretary Cheney's body is quarantined and only trained, informed personnel handle it."

"Any idea where this bacteria came from? Does it look engineered, like someone is using it as a weapon?"

"It's too soon to tell, Agent Cole. We're working on it."

I wanted to tell her to work faster but knew doing so wouldn't do any of us any good. "Do you think the bacteria is what killed the secretary?"

"I don't think so," Dr. Miller said. "I could be wrong, but I think the presence of the bacteria is secondary. The coroner's report didn't indicate that any organs were swollen or irritated. On the contrary, the body seemed completely desiccated."

"And still no idea how it got that way?"

"No," she said. "Anyway, we've cleared the residence. The crime scene is available whenever you need it."

"Okay. Thanks for the update, doctor."

I called Captain Brownlow. "Good morning, captain. I've got another agent working on the case with me and we're headed over to the mansion. Do you have the keys?"

"If you are referring to Agent Bloomberg, I was told he was coming. And there's no need for a key because the front door is kicked in and the rear double glass doors are broken," Brownlow said dryly.

"Um…right." I winced. "Has Mrs. Cheney identified anything as missing from the house?"

Brownlow snorted. "You haven't read her statement yet, have you? She barely identified her own name."

"Thanks captain."

Click.

"Damn," I said. "Apparently Mrs. Cheney's statement leaves a few things unanswered, and we just missed an opportunity to invite her to the house along with us to do an inventory and get her story."

"From what I hear, I don't think she's going anywhere," Amir responded. "She's been staying at the Governor's Hotel since Saturday, and from what I hear, she's scared spit-less. I can't say I blame her." He frowned. "I do wish she wasn't talking to a news anchorwoman, but there's not much we can do about that. The press is the press, freedom of speech, all that jazz."

"Song's a good reporter, but she has a strong sense of responsibility. She'll let me know if something is going to break that she thinks either I don't know or would compromise an investigation," I said.

"Huh. I didn't know there were reporters like that."

"Some are. Song is."

I filled him in on what Dr. Miller had to say and traded speculations with him on the way to the Cheney mansion.

Miller was right; the CDC had vanished. The only remainder of the hive of activity from the day before was the trampled lawn. The place almost seemed abandoned.

Amir and I walked around back and entered the secretary's office through the broken double doors. Shattered glass was scattered about, and we found Officer Brock taking inventory.

"Good morning," I said.

"Good morning, Agent Cole. The captain said you were coming."

"I'm surprised to find you here," I said. "I thought you processed the crime scene before the CDC got here."

"We did. The captain sent us over. She wants an inventory of the property in the house, because the doors are shattered and she wants to make sure that nothing gets stolen. There has been some vandalism since the tsunami," Brock said.

Amir coughed beside me. I took the hint.

"Agent Bloomberg, this is Officer Brock," I said. "Officer, this is Agent Bloomberg."

"Pleasure," said Officer Brock. "There are two other officers here helping with the inventory. We'll try to stay out of your way."

"Don't worry about that," I said. "We just want to have a look around to get a fresh take on things."

Amir knelt by the outline on the floor where Cheney's body had been found while I checked around the study. I was almost afraid to touch anything. The carpet alone probably cost more than Carla's tuition, and I was sure the desk had more value than my house.

Well-polished basketball and football trophies crowded the top shelves of the book case—apparently Secretary Cheney had been quite an athlete in his younger days. A locked glass trophy case sat prominently near the desk.

My cell phone buzzed in my pocket.

"Cole," I answered.

"Agent Cole, this is Captain Brownlow. I wanted to catch you while you were still there. It looks like a next door neighbor might have some information. Their son was attacked by a strange dog the night Cheney died. The kid was taken to the hospital, he was pretty badly bitten."

"Why wasn't I told this before?"

"One of the parents just called in to the station. She saw the sketch of the unidentified man and dog on the news that we did from Mrs. Barnes' description. The mother said she recognized the dog right away. The house is next door: 359 Gravely Beach Loop Northwest. Gloria and George Weinstein. The kid is still in the hospital but one of the parents should be at home."

"Do we know how the kid is doing?"

"The doctor says he'll recover and is doing well, but right now we can't talk to him."

"Thanks. We'll check it out."

***

Gloria Weinstein answered the door. She'd clearly had a rough couple of days. Her face was slightly red and stripped of any kind of makeup.

"Good morning, ma'am. I'm FBI Agent Robert Cole. This is Agent Bloomberg. May we come in?"

She peered at our identification cards. "Did I do something wrong?"

"No, of course not." Amir took off his sunglasses and smiled. "We heard about your son's attack and thought we might ask you a few questions."

"I'm sorry. You're here about the dog attack on my son?"

"I know," Amir said. "Sounds strange, doesn't it? You'd expect Animal Control. But we're not actually here about the dog. We're wondering if your son might have seen the dog's owner the night he was attacked."

She seemed to think this over a bit and finally opened the door.

"Come in."

"Thank you," I said. "We won't take long."

Gloria led us to the den and sank into an uncomfortable looking armchair. Her clothes looked clean but wrinkled, like she hadn't bothered to iron. Her dark hair was twisted up into a sloppy bun.

"Do you mind if I take some notes?" I asked.

"No, go right ahead. That's fine," she answered.

"Can you tell us what happened the night your son was attacked?" I asked as gently as I could.

She shuddered. "It was a horrible night really. Gregory, my son, had just said good night to his father and I and gone to his room. My husband, George, and I were just talking about how long we should give him with his binoculars before we went in there to check on him." Gloria managed a small smile. "It's a little game we play. Gregory always pretends to go to bed when we ask him. He even rumples up the bed so he can dive in and pretend to be asleep when we knock on the door. He really gets out the binoculars George gave him last Christmas and watches the ferries crossing the Sound. We usually give him twenty minutes or so before going in there to 'check' on him. We don't open the door until we hear the window close, his little feet run across the room and jumps into the bed." Gloria took a deep breath. Her eyes filled with tears and her lips started to tremble. "But that night we heard Gregory scream. He just started screaming and didn't stop. We ran out of the den, across the living room and down the hallway to his room—we could hear the snarling from the hallway—."

Amir handed her his handkerchief.

"May we see his room?" he asked quietly.

She nodded and dried her eyes. "This way."

She led us to a room that looked like it belonged to an eight or ten year old boy. Amir muffled a violent curse as we entered. I felt nauseatingly sick myself.

Someone had clearly put a lot of effort into scrubbing it clean, but the carpet bore witness to any parent's nightmare. Blood stains splashed across the floor, occasionally punctuated by small handprints and footprints stamped in blood where the boy must have scrambled to get away.

I crouched down to examine a blood-soaked paw-print. It was bigger than my hand.

Amir stood at the broken-in window. He waved me over.

We had a perfect view of the secretary's office. I could see Officer Brock taking pictures.

"My husband and I looked at some pictures of different dogs. The one we saw that night looked like a Presa Canario—you know, like one of the big Great Danes?"

I nodded. A woman in Florida who owned a Presa Canario had been killed by her own dog a few years ago.

"Thank you very much, Mrs. Weinstein," Amir said. "We're very sorry about your son. I hope he's better soon."

"Thank you." Gloria wiped her eyes. "I don't know how this can help you, but I hope someone finds that damn dog and shoots it in the god-damn head."

We showed ourselves out.

"Well, what do you think? The boy saw something he shouldn't have and the dog was supposed to kill him?" I asked Amir.

"That would be my guess. But how does a killer get a dog that well trained?" he asked.

"That's exactly what I'm wondering."

22

"Brute?" Ruth stood at the edge of the stairwell. "Brute, are you down there?"

She slung her purse over her shoulder and listened. Nothing. She descended the stairs on a sigh and found one of her heels. She found the other in the kitchen. "Brute?"

He wasn't in the sitting or dining room, either. Puzzled, Ruth smoothed her hair and wondered what to do.

"Brute, I need to get to work," she called. "Can you give me a ride? We left my car in D.C."

No answer. She'd checked all the rooms upstairs for him, and now she took a brisk tour of the remaining ones on the main floor. She couldn't find him anywhere.

I guess I'll have to take one of his. She'd borrowed his car once before, so she thought it would be alright. She walked out to the garage and plucked a set of spare keys off the rack. She pressed the automatic door unlock button on the keychain and heard the doors to the SUV on the far side unlock.

She wrote a brief note and left it hanging on the hook where she'd taken the keys. Ruth returned to the garage and climbed into the luxurious Lexus GXII, SUV. She loved Brute's taste in cars.

She dialed his cell as she pulled out of the driveway; perhaps he'd been called to an unexpected meeting.

Brute's voicemail told her to leave a message.

"Good morning, sexy," she purred. "I couldn't find you this morning. Where did you go? I'm so sorry, but I have to get to work by 10, so I borrowed the SUV. Why don't you come see me tonight and get it back? Oh, and by the way, I really enjoyed last night...and this morning, what you did...you were like an animal, only from behind...very hot. I can't wait to see you again. Call me."

23

Enrollment records from Princeton University arrived later that afternoon. Amir and I had discussed this possibility over lunch.

"I had a really nagging sense of déjà vu when I heard about the condition of Cheney's body," Amir said as he spread papers across the table in his hotel room. "I couldn't get rid of it, so I started a search on unsolved suspicious deaths. I found the newspaper article from 1991 about the dead college professor who—wouldn't you know it—looked like he had been, quote, mummified. As soon as I saw it I remembered hearing about it back then. It was in the news for awhile. I didn't think of it right off, possibly, because the case wasn't considered a homicide."

I browsed through the article Amir handed me, followed by the police and coroner's reports.

Princeton University economics Professor Dr. James Mayweather was found dead in his faculty office in December 1991, his corpse "mummified." The M. E. listed the cause of death as "unknown" and ruled it "suspicious."

"So far I haven't found much that's similar to this case, besides the condition of the body," Amir said. He pointed to two thick stacks of papers. "So, we've got old police interviews, or Mayweather's enrollment records. Flip you for it."

I lost. I got the enrollment records.

Jesus, the man had a lot of students, I thought as I scanned the pages. I swallowed the last of my sandwich and followed it with a swig of soda.

I almost missed the name. I sat up straight in my chair and focused.

"Hey," I said. "Hey!"

"What?" Amir glanced over his shoulder and asked.

I circled the name and handed the list to him. His eyebrows winged up.

"Benjamin Cheney? The same Benjamin Cheney?"

"I think so. I know he graduated from Princeton," I said.

"A lot of people did," Amir replied. "The current Secretary of State, James Harrison. Deputy Secretary of the Treasury, Brute Therion. I think the Attorney General did, too. Hmmm." Amir snagged his laptop. He worked the keyboard for a few minutes, and he motioned me over. "Have a look."

He'd found a 1991-1992 Princeton yearbook online. Senior classman Benjamin Cheney, future Secretary of the Treasury, grinned at us from the screen.

"So the dead professor's student dies exactly the same way some 20 years later?" I said.

"Let's see who else we can find." Amir started scanning through pages. "Wow. I bet most of these young men and women would like to change these old pictures of them. A lot of them are senior executives in large successful firms right now, but you would never have guessed by the looks of them back then."

"It's amazing how time changes people. Looking back over the last 25 years, I have to say, I was just like these kids. I wore the bell bottom pants, the tight wranglers that hugged everything, the two-inch high heels to look taller, the striped shirts, and the colorful pullovers as well. I wore it all," I said.

"You were a slave to fashion?" Amir flicked a glance my way. "What happened?"

"I matured. You will one day, too," I said. "You know, Amir, your generation is very fortunate. You really have an advantage over the older guys like me."

"Because I'm young and good-looking?"

"No. Because you have the internet! When I joined the Bureau 25 years ago, we had to physically travel to get the same information you just got on an internet search, or wait days, weeks, even months for it to be sent to us. If this were 1991, we'd be in Princeton's basement combing through boxes of files right now. Everything was done by hand, foot, phone, or the United States Postal Service. And I bet you don't even know what a type-writer is."

"Sure I do. I saw one in a museum. Developed shortly after fire, I believe."

"Stop. Wait—no, go back. There." I pointed. "Isn't that Rebecca Cheney? Her last name says McMichael—do you know Rebecca's maiden name?"

"Uh, yeah." Amir dug through some notes. "It is Mc-Michael. She married Cheney in 1992."

My cell phone rang. Captain Brownlow's number glowed from the screen.

"Captain, what can I do for you?" I asked.

"I just got word from my guys at the crime scene. Apparently there is something missing from the house," Brownlow said. "It's some kind of family heirloom, a ring dated way back to the 10th century B.C."

I whistled. "What kind of money would something like that be worth today?"

"I'm not sure, but it's insured for two million dollars. I'm emailing you a photo and a copy of the insurance papers now."

"Thanks." I moved to my own laptop and opened my email. The captain's message popped up in my Inbox. Amir peered over my shoulder as I opened the file. He let loose a long, low whistle.

"Will, look at that?"

***

It was close to midnight before I got on the road to my hotel. Like the night before, thick fog hung in the air and pressed against the car. I knew I shouldn't, but I started to feel claustrophobic and had to loosen my tie.

"Get a grip, Cole," I hissed to myself. "It's the pacific northwest. It's foggy. It's no big deal. It's certainly no reason to feel claustrophobic."

My gut wasn't listening to my head. Faintly, I began to hear a galloping-like sound echoing behind me.

Ridiculous. You're being ridiculous. I tried to ignore it, but it grew steadily louder and closer. Just as I expected the headless horseman to ride by and slice off my head, the fog parted to reveal one very dim head light lighting the way for an old Chrysler wagon, green, with no rear window and huge dents in its front and back. As it slowly passed by my vehicle I saw its muffler banging on the surface of the street.

What was next? What was I going to do if the wind blew too hard or a black cat crossed my path?

I was still pissed at myself when I arrived at my hotel. I know I should go home, but at this point I didn't want to risk shooting up my house because I thought my coat rack looked like a ghostly intruder in the dark.

As I entered the lobby a gum-popping winter pale blonde with deep blue eyes and a very low cut blouse waved me over from behind the desk.

"Mr. Cole? I have a message for you," she said. "Well, actually, it's a visitor. There's been a lady waiting here to see you for a long time."

I looked around the empty lobby. "Where?"

"Oh, I let her into your room. She looked really tired and worn out, and I felt so sorry for her," Gum-Popping-Blonde said. "I hope you don't mind. She was waiting for hours and hours."

'I hope you don't mind'? You let a stranger into an FBI agent's room? Are you a moron? "It's alright," I said. "Thank you."

I took the stairs up to the second floor. I listened at my door, slid the key in the lock, and pushed the door open with my weapon trained inside.

Rebecca Cheney was curled up, dead asleep, on my bed.

***

Rebecca accepted the cup of tea I handed her. She perched on the edge of my bed and sipped carefully. For a second I almost didn't blame the idiot down-stairs for letting her into my room. She really did look terrible.

"Thank you, Agent Cole," she said quietly.

"How did you know I was staying here?" I asked.

Color flooded her cheeks. "I—uh—was outside your house last night. I'd been trying to work up the nerve to knock on your door when you came running out and drove off. I followed you."

I felt my own face burn and hoped she didn't notice. Rebecca sighed and rubbed her eyes.

"I'm sorry. I haven't slept much in the last few days," she said. "I know you have questions for me. I'll answer them if I can."

I saw her shiver slightly and felt a chill from the open window, so I walked over and closed it.

"We can wait until morning," I said. "I know you're tired."

"I don't want to wait. I just want to get it over with."

I grabbed a pen and notepad from my bag and took a seat at the table. I hesitated, then pulled a blanket out of the closet and wrapped it around Rebecca's shoulders. The scent of her fragrance slid through my senses when I leaned in to tuck the folds around her. I suddenly became painfully aware of the décolleté and long legs I had just covered up. The ends of Rebecca's hair brushed against my knuckles—soft as silk.

I had to ignore her; this was no time to get distracted. I took off my jacket and laid it across the nearby chair. I loosened my tie and—reluctantly, I admit—resumed my seat at the table.

"Were you home with your husband when it happened?"

She shook her head. "No. Benjamin and I—we had a fight. I guess you could say we had a fight. I'd waited. For weeks I waited. I'd heard the stories, but at first I didn't want to believe them. But then more and more details came out and I knew—I knew it had to be true. So I confronted him. I needed to hear it from my husband, face to face. I wanted to know why he did it. I was so ashamed, so sick over what had happened to our relationship..." Her voice choked off. "He had the nerve to say he was sorry. Sorry. I told him to get out. I screamed at him, told him he sickened me and damned him to hell." Rebecca fiercely knuckled tears away. "Anyway, I left. That was the last time I saw him alive."

"About what time was that? Do you remember?" I asked as gently as I could.

"Um...about five, or five thirty, I guess."

"Where did you go?"

"I drove around for a while, before I stopped for a drink at the Sunset Tavern. Benjamin and I used to go there for a night cap sometimes when we were younger."

"Anyone see you there?"

"Can anyone give me an alibi, you mean?" Rebecca's gaze snapped to mine. A bitter laugh escaped her. "Oh, sure. Ask for a guy named Trap. I think he's a regular. He'll remember me." She took a long swig of tea as if she wished it were something stronger. "Anyway, I didn't get home until about four the next morning. It was still dark outside. I smelled something horrible the minute I opened the door. It seemed to be getting stronger as I moved toward the back of the house, and then—God, I saw that thing on the floor in Benjamin's office. I didn't know it was him. I swear I didn't know it was him."

Rebecca shuddered. "I ran. I tripped the emergency alarm by the front door, ran to my car and drove off. I was so afraid. I know I should have called the police. I know I should have gone to the station, but I was just so scared, I didn't know what to do. And now I think—I wonder—if I had stayed at home that night, if I hadn't left—maybe I could have saved him. Helped him in some way. I don't know. I could have done something."

"You could have died, too," I said. "This wasn't your fault, Rebecca. I'm not sure exactly what did happen to your husband, but I can tell you this wasn't a botched robbery because someone wanted the china."

"Do you know what killed him?" She asked.

I thought this over for a minute and finally decided on the truth. "No, we don't."

"Oh," she said, and she cried. First one sob escaped, then another, until the last shred of her self-control evaporated and she fell to pieces.

I sat next to her and held her tight. It was probably wrong, but just that minute she appeared to be the loneliest and most heart-broken woman in the world. Betrayed by her husband, whispered about by her peers, afraid to confess what she had seen…the dam broke and I held her until the flood of tears passed. She lowered her head and rested it against my chest and I closed my eyes and held her there.

I waited until Rebecca calmed, washed her face, and fortified herself with strong coffee.

"Can you go on?"

"Yes."

I took a photo out of my files and handed it to her. "Do you recognize this?"

"Of course. It's Benjamin's ring." Her brow wrinkled. "What does this have to do with anything?"

"What do you know about it?"

"Well, it's a family heirloom. Benjamin said it had been in his family for generations, passed down through the men in the family for generations. It became his after his father died while we were in college. I remember the look in Benjamin's eyes when he returned to school after his father's funeral. He wore the ring and he was very proud of it."

"What do you mean by 'he was very proud of it?'"

"He wore it all the time. He made sure his friends saw it, treated it very carefully. I thought it was a little silly after awhile. Benjamin said the family legend claimed the ring belonged to King Solomon, that it was actually the King Solomon ring in the stories—you know, the one that let Solomon understand demons and control them."

"Understand and control demons?" I asked.

Rebecca rolled her eyes and handed the picture back to me. "Yes. Like I said, I thought it was a little silly. But if he wanted to elaborate on a harmless family legend, I didn't see the harm."

"You're not a believer?" I dug up a small smile for her. She returned it.

"I'm a scientist, Agent Cole. I believe in Darwin, not demons."

"Do you know what happened to it? The ring?"

"Nothing happened to it. It's locked in a trophy case in Benjamin's office."

"Actually, it isn't."

"What?"

"The ring isn't there. It's missing. It's the only thing we can find missing from the house. Do you remember the last time you saw it?"

Rebecca rolled her coffee cup between her hands as she thought. "No, I really don't. I don't go in Benjamin's office very often, and I've been distracted the last few weeks because of the—the news."

"Can you think of any reason your husband might have moved it? Was there someplace else he would keep it?"

"No. In fact, he insisted that the ring stay in the house in its case. It has a little square case that looks almost as old as the ring, and Benjamin never let me get him a new one. He was a bit strange about it. We don't have children of our own, Agent Cole, so there's no son for Benjamin to pass the ring down to, and Benjamin was an only child. He made me promise that if anything should ever happen to him I would never, never sell the ring, no matter how much I was offered. He said the ring was dangerous and couldn't fall into the wrong hands."

"Wrong hands?"

"That's what he said. I don't know what he meant by that, but it seemed really important to him. He was anxious, even paranoid, about it."

"Was he paranoid about other things?"

"Not really. Or nothing that I know of."

She sipped her coffee while I scribbled notes.

"You said he got the ring when he was in college, after his father died. That was at Princeton?"

"Yes. We were seniors."

"Was he ever paranoid then?"

"No. Not that I noticed."

"Hmmm." I drummed my fingers on the table. "Do you remember a Professor Mayweather, at Princeton?"

Rebecca's eyebrows winged up. "Professor Mayweather? What does he have to do with anything?"

"Humor me," I said. "You do remember Professor May-weather?"

"Of course. He was one of my favorite teachers. I met Benjamin in one of Mayweather's classes. Poor Ben. He was having a really hard time, and Mayweather's classes were pretty tough. I volunteered to tutor him. Not very original, I know, but he didn't turn me down."

I didn't think any man in his right mind would turn Rebecca down. "Why was he having such a hard time?"

"Microeconomics required doing a lot of research and writing, and Benjamin didn't like that. He was better in his math classes. He preferred to figure things out, proofs and stuff like that. Economics wasn't his thing," Rebecca said. "Plus, he didn't get along with Professor Mayweather. It caused problems in the class."

"What kind of problems?"

"They just didn't like each other, that's all. It caused tension. Mayweather corrected Benjamin in class once and Benjamin stormed out."

"So what happened?"

"Well, Benjamin ended up getting a good grade in the class, but by then...Oh. Ooohhh." Rebecca's eyes went perfectly round. "You don't think—Professor Mayweather's death—you don't think Benjamin had anything to do with that?"

"Rebecca, I'm going to show you something. It's going to be painful, but I think you need to see it." I handed her a crime scene photo of Mayweather's body. Rebecca barely glanced at it before turning it over.

"Just like Benjamin. He looks just like Benjamin did," she said. "Agent Cole, do you think my husband murdered Professor Mayweather?"

"I don't know. But I think it's very likely that whatever killed the professor also killed your husband," I admitted. "Do you remember how Benjamin reacted to Mayweather's death?"

"I don't remember him reacting much at all. He seemed indifferent to it. I remember asking him if he was sad about the news about the professor and wanted to talk about it, but all he said was, 'I didn't like the man anyway.' He just didn't care. I thought Benjamin was being a little insensitive to me, since he knew I liked Professor Mayweather, but I really didn't think much of it. Brute sometimes talked with me, but Benjamin never did."

I glanced up from the notepad I had in my hand. "Brute Therion?"

"Yes. He's Benjamin's Deputy Secretary."

"You three knew each other in school?"

She nodded. "I didn't like Brute, at first. He was a few years younger than we were and I thought he was a bit immature. I told Benjamin that and we had a big fight. Benjamin made it clear to me that I couldn't pick his friends for him. He was right."

"Did he have a lot of friends you didn't like?"

"He didn't have a lot of friends. Not then, anyway. But he hung out with Brute a lot. They were always in the library or doing weird stuff."

"What kind of weird stuff?"

"Oh, they were into Gothic stuff. Or, I thought they were. They were into ancient rituals and magic and stuff like that. They messed around with the occult stuff. I thought it was all nonsense, so I just kind of ignored it."

"Did you hear Therion and Benjamin talk about the professor's death?"

"No. I don't think they ever talked about it. Benjamin didn't want to talk about Professor Mayweather at all."

I put down my pen and stretched. "I think that's plenty for tonight. Can I take you back to your hotel?"

Rebecca studied me for several seconds. "Agent Cole, can I ask you a question?"

"Sure."

"You have a lovely home a few miles from here. Why are you staying in a hotel?"

"Fumigation," I said. "The house reeks of chemicals. I'm staying here until the place airs out."

Rebecca drew in a long breath through her nose. "Your clothes don't smell like chemicals."

"Febreze."

"Shouldn't FBI agents be better liars?"

"No, ma'am. It's against regulations. Our bosses want us honest." I didn't care what she thought. I was not telling her a damn ghost ran me out of my own house.

Rebecca managed a small smile. "Well, Agent Cole, I also own a home close by and I too am not staying in it. At least I have the guts to say it's because I'm scared shitless. Now, it's late and I'm tired. I hope I can stay here tonight."

She got up and went into the bathroom. She closed the door behind her, then I heard the shower water come on.

I didn't mind if she thought the situation was strange. It was better than telling her the truth and proving it.

My phone rang; it was Amir.

"Cole, my boss wants us on the next flight to D.C. Apparently Deputy Secretary Therion never showed up for work today."

24

Julian woke around 1 a.m. he hoped he didn't wake Carla, but she must have felt him roll over and sit up because she stirred and murmured, "What's the matter, baby?"

"Nothing," he whispered. "Go back to sleep."

Julian stood, wearing only his undergarments, shorts and a T-shirt, and spontaneously crashed to the floor. His eyes rolled back in his head, as he knocked the lamp and car keys off the night stand as he fell. His head hit the floor with a dull, sickening thump. Carla jumped out of bed.

"Julian? Julian!" Carla cried. She shook him, gently at first, then more frantically. "Julian!"

Julian found himself suspended weightlessly in a vast expanse of darkness. He sensed himself traveling, somehow, and slowly perceived a dim noise growing louder and clearer, until he found himself surrounded by strangers in an ancient place, in a land ruled by a king, where people curried favor with gods in hopes of protection.

Julian stumbled in the midst of a crowd of celebrators chanting in the dusty streets wearing long robes and slippers on their feet.

Where am I?

"You are in King Solomon's kingdom, in the land of Israel," a soft female voice answered.

A girl about his own age stood at his side. She wore a long robe nearly reaching her ankles. A long scarf—veil?—

covered her hair. Big, piercing golden eyes searched his face as if looking for an answer to a vexing puzzle.

"What am I doing here?" Julian asked.

"You are here to witness the execution of Azazel, a traitor to our people, an evil man, a killer of innocent men, women and children." She took his arm and pulled him along. "My name is Aleeza. I will show you what you must know."

They hurried to catch up with the rest of the crowd who were gathered in a courtyard facing a massive palace. In the near distance Julian saw a wooden platform sitting high above ground, and on it stood an executioner with a shiny razor sharp sword that sparkled in the sun's light.

"Death to the traitor! Death to the murderer! Death to the demon!" the crowd chanted.

"What is that for?" Julian indicated the platform as his mind contemplated the possibilities.

"Today we will witness the execution of the traitor, Azazel," Aleeza said. "The king has ordered his execution by de-heading. For a traitor, murderer and rapist—like this one—this is a lenient sentence. These kinds of criminals usually get far gorier deaths. People regularly get their thumbs and toes chopped off, blinded, be-headed, and even gutted. Once I saw someone get a tent peg hammered through his skull. This one will have the king's curse upon him; the life that escapes from his body will be captured, stored in a brass bottle, sealed with the king's ring and cast into the ocean to wonder in darkness forever. His body will be burned and his ashes sprinkled throughout the dry sands of the desert."

"What? That isn't possible," Julian responded.

"It is by the order of the king. Here, anything by order of the king is possible. This man, Azazel, is the beast of the

153

earth. He had prestige, wealth and power. The king honored him and stood him at his side. The people honored him for so fiercely defending our kingdom, and for his many victories over our enemies. We celebrated his many deeds with wine and feasting, and with blood sacrifices of goats and sheep to the gods in his honor. But for this evil man, that was not good enough. He lured our men in the darkness of the night and killed them. He raped our women and children. He is a beast deserving of this punishment," Aleeza said, then joined the crowd in shouting:

"Death to the traitor! Death to the murderer! Death to the demon!"

The bugle of trumpets cut through the noise and quieted the crowd. All eyes turned to the three men emerging from the palace. The man in the center was taller than his escorts and wore a black hood over his head. The men on either side of him lead him through the center of the crowd, flanked by palace guards with their swords and spears in their hands and held high for all to see, and mounted the platform facing the palace.

"The man in the center, with his head completely covered with the large sack cloth, is the traitor, Azazel. We will see him de-headed today," Aleeza said. "And we will celebrate his execution."

"What are they going to do with him?" Julian asked as he watched the proceedings.

"The bag over his head has been soaked in olive oil and dried in the sun to prevent the life that will be taken from his body from escaping. It will be placed in a brass bottle, and sealed with the king's seal, to remind the king of the treachery and evilness of this man who was once his strongest warrior and most trusted servant."

Julian heard the trumpets sound a second time and a voice echoed over the crowd.

"By order of the king, the condemned Azazel, son of Samuel, is hear-by ordered executed on this day for his treachery to the crown, and murder of innocent men, women and children. So sayeth the king. So it has been ordered, and so it shall be done."

He saw the two guards escort Azazel forward. The prisoner's hands bound behind his back. And Julian saw the men place Azazel's covered head and neck through the circular wooden base and secure the yoke in place. His eyes rose immediately to the razor sharp blade just in time to see it fall. Julian felt the sting of the blade in the bosom of his spine as it cut Azazel's head from his body. Wine-like blood spurted from the severed neck and filled the metal basin below. Screams echoed through the courtyard and the crowd burst into cheers. He saw the executioners carry away Azazel's head and body.

In that moment Julian felt a sudden pull at his existence—like a sudden bout of air turbulence in an airplane. It tugged at his mind and he felt himself snap backward into pure darkness.

Centuries passed, unchanging. A millennium passed, then two. At long last, Julian seemed to sense rumblings in the Earth's crust deep below. A ripple of motion vibrated through the deep places of the Earth and far out beneath the open ocean basin. A sudden explosion penetrated deep into the Earth's crust and triggered deep vibrations, only seconds apart. Volcanic eruptions exploded in a steady flow of smoke, ash and magma. Lightning flickered and thundering sounds rumbled through the clouds.

***

"Julian! Julian!" Carla screamed. Tears streamed down her face. She grabbed the phone and dialed 911.

"Help! Help me, please! I need an ambulance," she screamed into the receiver on the telephone. She gave her name and address. "Hurry. Please hurry."

Carla hung up. "Please Julian, wake up. Please, please, baby, open your eyes."

When she heard the ambulance siren she dressed quickly and pulled a pair of shorts on Julian. She followed the paramedics as they quickly wheeled him out on a gurney. Carla climbed into the back of the ambulance while they strapped him in place and sped off.

"Julian. Julian." His name felt like a prayer; if she kept saying it, he would wake up.

His limp hand twitched in hers.

"Carla?" Julian's eyes cracked open. "Why are you crying?"

He regained his consciousness as the ambulance slowed and turned into the emergency bay outside the local medical center.

"Oh, Julian, you passed out on the floor next to the bed and I thought I lost you," Carla said, smiling and drying her tears with one end of her sleeve.

Julian now realized he had blacked out and had been taken to the hospital. He unstrapped himself from the stretcher and got up. He grabbed Carla by one hand as the ambulance came to a full stop and jumped out when the back doors opened. The female paramedic in the back of the ambulance was unable to stop him.

"Hey! Hey, wait!" the paramedic called out as Julian ran with Carla close behind him. They ran to the street and reached a yellow cab parked by the curbside and got in. Julian gave their address and the cab driver pulled away.

As they drove Carla was sad, "You passed out on the floor beside the bed, Julian. I thought I lost you. You need to go to the hospital and get yourself checked out."

"It'll take more than that to lose me, and I'm not planning on getting lost anytime soon." He leaned over, kissed her, and smiled. "There is something weird going on that I just don't understand. I don't want them to try to keep me in the hospital, and I can't just sit around right now. I need some time to think this over."

Carla, with a concerned look in her eyes, smiled back. "I am scared for you Julian. Why did you run? You could have gone inside, refused medical treatment, and gone home. Or even have the hospital keep you overnight for observation. You really need to go and get checked out by a doctor. Just blacking out for no reason isn't normal."

"If I go see Dr. Martu again, will that satisfy you?" Julian asked.

"If we go to see him like he asked, and you let him run some tests, then yes, I will," Carla answered.

Julian sighed. "Fine. We'll call him in the morning."

25

By 6am Amir and I were on a plane to Washington D.C., six hours and three time zones later, we were free of the airport and headed for the capitol.

Mrs. Dudley's cubicle sat just outside Secretary Cheney's office in the U.S. Treasury Building. She's about five-feet-seven inches tall, middle aged, with gray eyes framed by steel rimmed reading glasses. She didn't seem surprise to see Amir and I, when we paid her a visit.

"When did you first notice Deputy Secretary Therion missing?" Amir asked.

"Not until about noon yesterday," Mrs. Dudley said. Her eyes looked red and puffy; I imagined this had been a tough week for her. "And it's Secretary Therion, actually. The president appointed him late Tuesday night."

"Do you know Secretary Therion well?"

"Not as well as Secretary Cheney, but yes. They came to D.C., together. They've been friends a long time." Mrs. Dudley seemed to pull herself together and opened an appointment book on her desk. She turned it toward us and pointed to the top of the page. Therion looked like a very busy man. "Secretary Therion had appointments with two committees yesterday morning, which is why we didn't notice him missing right away. We thought he was in committee meetings, and they thought he was here."

"But no one in the office actually saw or heard from him yesterday?" I asked.

"That's right." She answered.

"When was the last time you did see him?" I asked.

"Monday afternoon, along with several senior staff members. He closed the office for Tuesday as a gesture of respect to the late secretary."

"Do you mind if we take a copy of this?" I tapped the appointment book. "It would be useful if we knew where he was supposed to be, and where he's been over the last several days."

"Of course." Mrs. Dudley drew a folder out of a desk drawer and handed it to me. "This is a copy of his schedule from last Monday through this coming Friday."

"Thank you," Amir said with a smile. "This is very helpful. Mrs. Dudley, do you mind if we ask you a few questions about Secretary Cheney while we're here?"

"Not at all."

"Do you remember the last time you saw Secretary Cheney?" Amir asked.

Mrs. Dudley nodded. "Around noon on Friday, just before he left for the weekend. He needed some things copied at the last minute and I barely got it done. I handed him the files on his way out the door."

"Did he leave alone?" Amir asked.

"Yes. He usually drove himself to the airport."

"Did he seem troubled or preoccupied?"

"No, he was in good spirits. He seemed like his usual self. He didn't seem concerned about anything in particular," she said.

"Did he say anything before he left?" Amir continued while I took some notes.

"He said to have a great weekend and reminded me that he'd left a copy of the new budget proposal along with some notes for Deputy Secretary Therion on his desk."

"Do you know if he had any enemies? Had he received any threats?" I asked.

"Not that I know of. The secretary was a nice man. People liked him."

"Did he have any unusual visitors? Anything out of the ordinary?"

"No. I don't think so."

I noticed a photo sitting on the bookshelf. Mrs. Dudley, Brute Therion, and Benjamin Cheney mugged for the camera with the Cascades providing a towering back-drop.

"That's a nice picture," I said. "Where was it taken?"

Mrs. Dudley followed my gaze and plucked the picture off the shelf with a sad smile. "At Secretary Cheney's home, in Olympia. I'd worked for Secretary Cheney since he took office. This was taken at his 4th of July celebration just a few months ago. I remember it was a perfect sunny day—almost everyone got a terrible sunburn."

I studied the picture before handing it to Amir. "Looks like some party."

"It was." A true smile bloomed across Mrs. Dudley's face. "In Secretary Cheney's world, the 4th of July was an important time, a time to celebrate the anniversary of our nation's independence. He cherished and honored the brave men who fought to win America's freedom, and gave the people of this nation the opportunity to live free. In his eyes this day represented everything America stood for and he honored it with a big celebration each year." She took the photo back and placed it carefully back on the shelf. "Secretary Cheney's home is really very nice. There's a huge back yard that leads to the water. This summer the men pitched horse shoes and talked amongst themselves while the women handled the grilling. Mrs. Cheney, myself, Ms. Brown and Mrs. Weinstein grilled steaks, hamburgers, and hot dogs, and we all ate. Later on Secretary Cheney surprised everybody; he did a little something special. He'd dug a shallow hole in a corner of his yard the evening before we got there. He and his neighbor, Mr. Weinstein, had lined it with hot coals and buried a medium size pig in it. It'd been roasting there overnight. After we had finished eating the barbeque food he went and got a shovel and started digging in the corner of the yard. We were all wondering what was going on. Then he asked his neighbor, Mr. Weinstein, to bring him a huge tray. I was amazed when he pulled out the fully roasted and smoked ham. It was a big surprise to everybody, we all enjoyed it. The meat was sweet and tender. Everyone really had a great time. The Secretary was a great host. I saw the excitement in his eyes when he brought the ham out of the ground.

"The neighbors Gloria and George left when it began to get dark because they were going to Gloria's parents' place, afterward. The rest of us sat around, drank, ate, and watched the boats sail on Puget Sound. Later we saw a wonderful fireworks show. We sat there and told jokes. When it began to get cooler, we went into the house. Secretary Cheney started talking about the mahogany storage cube in the bottom of his trophy case. Inside he claimed was his most prized possession, a family heirloom that he said had been in his family for generations."

"What do you know about this family heirloom?" Amir asked.

"Not much really. Secretary Cheney said it had been passed down to him from his father, and to his father before him," she answered. Her glasses must be pinching the bridge of her nose, since she took them off and rubbed at the corners of her eyes. "We didn't know what to believe. Maybe he had a little too much to drink. But he was very passionate about his story. He said he had King Solomon's ring—the original King Solomon's ring, the one with the true Seal of Solomon, and claimed it could conjure up demons. We all laughed."

"Did he say that he used it?" Amir asked.

"No, he didn't. He told us about the legend, that King Solomon had used it to bring forth and control demons. It was a fantastic story. He kept us all entertained for hours with the story."

"He didn't try to prove the ring was real?" Amir asked with a smile, as if sharing in some joke. "He didn't make a demon appear?"

Mrs. Dudley smiled back. "Of course not. He did say that his great grandfather knew of the ring's powers and left strict instructions for it to be stored in a dark place at all times. For when the light hits it, the demon reads its bearer's mind and carries out his wishes. The demon could be recognized by his uneven legs, shyness in the light and hatred for the church. Only the person who possessed the ring had the power to control the demon. It was all very dark and dramatic. Secretary Cheney was a born story-teller."

"Did you see the ring?" I asked.

"Well, he did show us a ring he took from the small storage box. He pointed to an inscription on the inside that supposedly had the letters 'KS' inscribed on it, but he had to tell us that because no one could make it out. It looked like

163

scribbles. And he showed us a symbol on the face of it and said it was the Seal of Solomon," she said, "but you couldn't see it clearly, either. Mr. Therion asked him to conjure a demon so we could see what a demon looked like."

"What did he do?"

"Nothing. He just smiled like a smug little boy."

"Can you tell us who was present at this time?" I asked.

"Well, let me see." She put one finger on her chin and let her gaze drift toward the ceiling. "There were only a few of us left by then: my husband and I, Ms. Brown, Mrs. Cheney and Mr. Therion."

"Ms. Brown?" I repeated.

"Ruth Brown," Mrs. Dudley elaborated. "She's a friend of Mr. Therion."

Amir noted down the name. "What about Mr. Therion did he believe the stories, or was he just egging Secretary Cheney on?"

"I don't know that, but remember Mr. Therion and Secretary Cheney were old friends from college. They do joke around sometimes."

"Has Mr. Therion ever talked about the ring to you or anyone else that you know of?" I asked.

"He never talked with me about it. I don't know if he talked with anyone else about it," she answered. "But Secretary Cheney also said he had a letter from one of his great, great grandfathers, written to one of his sons, that proves the ring's authenticity."

"Did you ever see this letter?"

"No." She divided a look between Amir and I. "What does this have to do with Secretary Cheney's death? Or Secretary Therion's disappearance? It's not as if a ring could kill or kidnap someone."

"No, but an artifact that old would probably be worth a lot of money, even if it was just a harmless scrap of metal," I said.

"Is that what this is all about?" she asked.

"We don't know," I said. "We're just trying to cover every angle. Do you happen to know where the ring is now?"

"Now? Sure. It's in his office."

Amir and I sat up straighter.

"It is?" I asked. "May we see it?"

"Of course." Mrs. Dudley looked puzzled at our interest but led us into the former secretary's office and gestured to an unprepossessing box behind Cheney's desk. A quick tug at the lid confirmed that it was locked. I plucked a letter opener off the desk to jigger the lock and found it whisked out of my hand.

"Are you crazy?" Amir goggled at me with a look of horror. "That's a five hundred dollar collector's item. Let's try looking for a key first."

"Five hundred dollars?" I gave the box another look, but it didn't seem any more impressive than it did before. It looked like something I could have built in shop class.

"It's handcrafted, hand painted, and imported," Amir said. "I know. My snotty mother-in-law has one, and she didn't shut up about it for months."

Amir found the keys and unlocked the cube. A small wooden box rested inside. It was empty.

26

Julian and Carla felt like they were on vacation in the Caribbean islands when they learned that the only way to cross the bay to the island of St. Clare was by the small boat waiting on the dock in Solo Point.

The tiny boat skimmed across the waves—like a graceful dove in flight—and slowed only minutes later to idle up to the dock on a quiet, heavily wooded island. A cheerful-looking man in slacks and dress shirt helped them onto the dock.

"Welcome to St. Clare. I'm Abdul. Dr. Martu had to take an emergency call, so I volunteered to come and meet you," he said.

"Wow, this is some island," Carla said as she gazed up the rocky mountainside to what seemed to be a wooded clearing high above.

"It is. I enjoy coming here," Abdul answered.

The smile Julian gave Carla brought a sense of satisfaction to her heart. "You're happy you came?"

"Well, maybe," he said softly.

Carla knew he never would have come if she hadn't insisted, but he didn't seem unhappy about it. She inched closer to his side, knowing that he'd need her, and she firmly intended to be there. And perhaps Julian had been right; the hospital could certainly have conducted an exhaustive battery of tests, but it doesn't have any of the aesthetic beauty this tranquil island has. If Julian had to be tested, there is no better place than this quiet little island. It's completely surrounded by water, with a tantalizing murmur of the water's rush and bounce against rock and sand on its shore.

They followed their escort to an outdoor lift constructed with a solid metal frame, surrounded by tinted glass. Designed to allow its occupants clear view of its unique chain-linked mechanism as it rotates and propels them upward toward the top.

Carla and Julian's eyes consumed the breath taking view as the elevator glided up the mountainside and slowed to a stop.

The door opened and they stepped into a beautiful forest clearing. A tangle of carefully manicured gardens spilled across the clearing to pool in shaded grottos and wash around graceful garden stones. Abdul led them toward a towering mansion surrounded by neatly groomed hedges and backed by dense forest.

Carla noticed small booths appearing to be security posts at the far edges of the clearing just as they passed under the main entrance of the mansion that stretched four stories high, with balconies and barred windows on each of its floors. She caught a glimpse of Arabic markings in square designs etched above the entrance.

Dr. Martu met them at the entrance. "Julian, Carla, hello. Welcome to my home. Abdul, thank you for fetching them. Come in, come in, let me show you around."

Carla also couldn't help herself when she took note of the vestibule at the entrance and the camera mounted above. That's a clever way to see the faces of guest arriving at the mansion. Arriving guests are made to wait there for someone to open the inner door, while they are observed.

"This is a beautiful place, Dr. Martu," Julian said as they followed him into the mansion. Julian marveled at the hardwood floors and floor-to-ceiling windows that afforded the breath-taking view of the glaciered Cascades on the mainland.

"Thank you. It's a perfect place for the research and studies that we do, the many scientific discoveries that we seek to uncover. St. Clare is separated from the rest of the population by water and this affords us the necessary privacy," Dr. Martu said.

The hall opened to a spacious room of modern design. Paintings of Mount Rainier and the Cascade Range grace the light green and cream colored walls. An elegant stairwell spirals up to the upper floors. They passed through this room into a kitchen, and into a dining room.

"This is where we'll have our meals. If you would like something in particular for breakfast I can let the cooks know," Dr. Martu said. "I frequently have guests from different parts of the world, so it is not unusual for our cooks to receive special requests. Our cooks are happy to accommodate any palate around the world."

"Breakfast?" Carla asked, with wrinkled brows. She and Julian traded shocked expressions.

"Well, yes. We'll need to monitor Julian's brain while he sleeps. The study requires him to stay over-night," Martu said. "I hope this doesn't inconvenience you."

"Well, we hadn't planned on it," Carla said. "We haven't brought anything with us."

"Oh, please don't trouble yourselves on that account. We can supply you with everything you need," Martu said. "There is a guest room prepared for you on the second floor,

Carla. Julian will be down in the laboratory on the lower level where the test will be conducted. Come with me and I'll show you these rooms."

They followed Dr. Martu further back through the dining room, through an outer door, onto an outside balcony and through another door that led down a narrow flight of stairs to a subterranean corridor that extended the length of the mansion. They entered a room on the left through a metal door; it contained a hospital bed, a television mounted on the wall directly in front, and a machine with many cables extending to the bed. Directly across from the room was a counter supporting a great deal of expensive looking electronic equipment.

"This is where we will conduct your study this evening, Julian," Martu said.

Carla gulped and looked at Julian. He was staring at the room with a kind of dull horror.

"I didn't know, Julian. I'm sorry," she whispered. "We can go. I won't blame you if we do."

Julian squeezed her hand and looked at Martu. He swallowed.

"This looks...lonely," Julian said.

"I know," Martu said gently. "It's not for entertaining, Julian. It's only used for sleep studies."

"I see...If it's only for one night, then it may not be so bad," Julian replied.

"Just one night, Julian, and you'll be right back home," the doctor said.

Martu led them back the way they came and then up a short flight of stairs to an airy, comfortable room on the second floor. "This will be your room for the night, Carla. There's an indoor pool on the ground floor and an exercise room down the hall. They are entirely at your disposal. Please, make yourself at home. Julian, we'll begin your study at six. Enjoy your day."

Martu smiled and left them to settle in.

"Are you sure, Julian?" Carla asked anxiously. "I mean it. We can go. You don't have to do this."

He seemed to think this over for a few minutes and finally shook his head. "No. If it's not now, then it's some other time. I don't want to keep having these black-outs. And really, it's not much worse than a hospital bed."

27

Local detectives had visited Brute Therion's D.C., apartment that morning looking for him. After receiving no response to repeated knocks at the door, the police had entered the premises and found it empty. Nothing seemed disturbed or indicative of a struggle, although they did find a few unusual items in Therion's bedroom closet, namely some kind of altar and several very old books written in foreign languages.

The local P.D. had also visited Therion's Virginia residence, with largely the same results. The property seemed peaceful, without any indication of violence or criminal behavior, although Therion was not there. However, he clearly had been there, since the car he had been driving on Monday was parked in the garage. Better yet, a note in the house and the absence of another car gave us a good idea of who might have seen Therion last.

The local police department was one of the cleanest I'd ever seen. The precinct was fairly new, a single story building, constructed on land that had once been occupied by a junior high school. The school's shoddy construction, plus a decline in junior high school aged children, led to the school's condemnation and the consolidation of several schools in the area. City administrators who had been searching for the right location to build a new police station got permission to use the vacant land after the school had been demolished.

The inside of the station house smelled like fresh leather, like the inside of a new car. It was well lighted, spacious, and undoubtedly had good quality coffee. Amir and I were led into a back room where Ms. Brown was waiting with a female officer.

Ruth Brown jumped up to her feet as we entered the room. She stood tall and slender. Thick blonde hair curled loosely around her face. She wore snug jeans, a loose fitting white collarless blouse with the word PINK printed across the front, and fashionable boots that looked like they belonged on a fashion model on the catwalk. A black sweater and pocket book rested on a nearby counter.

"Am I in trouble?" she asked. "Why am I here? No one will tell me anything."

"We only want to ask you a few questions," I said. "Please, have a seat. I'm FBI Agent Robert Cole. This is Agent Bloomberg."

We showed her our badges as we settled into chairs across the table from her. Our introduction did nothing to reassure her.

"FBI?" Her eyes bulged. I could practically see her wondering what she was supposed to have done.

"We're looking into the disappearance of Brute Therion," Amir said.

Ruth's face went stark white. "Brute's missing?"

"He didn't show up for work yesterday or today, and he isn't at either of his residences," Amir said, watching her carefully. He drew a small notebook out of his jacket pocket and flipped it open. "We understand you know Mr. Therion?"

I found Ruth's expression alarming enough that I got up to pour her a cup of coffee from the side table and pushed the mug into her hands. Her fingers were ice cold.

"I—yes. We've been dating for almost a year."

"Are you in the habit of borrowing his cars without his permission?" Amir said.

Oh, so that's the way we're going to play it. Why do I always have to be the good cop?

Ruth's face flushed hotly. "Of course not. I borrowed one of Brute's cars to get back to work Wednesday morning after spending some time at his home in Virginia."

"Why not take your own car?"

"We left it in the city." Ruth glared at Amir. "We took Brute's car to Virginia."

"But he didn't drive you back?"

"No. I couldn't find him Wednesday morning, and I had to get to work. I thought he'd been called away on some kind of emergency. I left him a note and a voice mail. I thought he'd call me when he could."

"Called away on an emergency?" Amir repeated doubtfully. "Even though no car was missing from the garage?"

"There isn't?" Ruth frowned. "But there were at least two open spaces."

"Mr. Therion has a five car garage, but owns only three cars at the present time."

"Oh."

The puzzlement in her eyes convinced me that we were barking up the wrong tree. I waved Amir off when he started to ask another question and looked Ruth in her eyes.

"Ms. Brown, we need your help," I said. "It appears that you were the last person to see Mr. Therion. Can you tell us when you last saw him? Is there anything you can think of that might indicate where he may have gone?"

"Brute picked me up from work on Monday. We drove down to Virginia that evening and spent the next day together. The last time I saw him was Tuesday night." A different kind of blush flooded her cheeks. "Well—early Wednesday morning. He was gone when I got up. I didn't find a note or anything, so I assumed he'd left in a hurry and didn't want to wake me by saying goodbye."

"And you didn't think he'd mind if you borrowed his Lexus after your morning romp?" Amir asked. If Ruth's eyes could have cut him into pieces, Amir would've been sliced and diced, right there on the spot.

"I have borrowed his cars before," she said stiffly. "With express permission."

"And you haven't heard from him since?" I broke in.

"No, I haven't." Ruth left off visually dissecting Amir and turned back to me. "There was a visitor, though. Yes, a strange man. He came to the door not long after we arrived and asked for 'Master Therion.' That's what he called him: 'Master Therion.' He was a big man, very tall, with huge shoulders, like a linebacker. He was dressed very strangely. He never looked up at me once when I was at the door, just asked for 'Master Therion.' He gave me the creeps."

"What was his message for Mr. Therion? Did you hear their conversation?"

"No. I think Brute threw him off the property. I'd gone upstairs and—" She broke off with another blush. "Anyway, Brute wasn't at the door more than a minute or two before he joined me."

"Do you think you could describe this visitor to a sketch artist?" I asked.

"Not the face," Ruth said. "Like I said, he never looked up. But I could describe his clothes. He wore this long robe-like thing. And I don't think he was an American. He had an accent that sounded Middle-eastern."

Amir and I exchanged startled glances.

"Is there any chance this man had a dog with him?" I asked.

Ruth frowned. "I don't think so. I didn't see one."

"Have you ever seen one on the property?"

"I've only been to Brute's family home once," Ruth admitted. "But no, I didn't see one."

"Thank you, Ms. Brown." Amir closed his notebook and tucked it back into his pocket. "You've been most helpful. You're free to go."

***

"Checkmate. You have won again, my prince. I cannot defeat you any longer." Abdul tipped over his king and leaned back in his chair. "You are a formidable opponent."

The two men sat in Martu's luxurious den, in the extravagant east wing of the mansion. The room had been designed exactly to the prince's specifications. Walls of Carrera marble—white with gray veins—rose gracefully to the circular dome high above. Floor-to-ceiling columns help to support the walls' weight. Brilliantly colored light filter through the stained-glass dome and merge with the radiance exuded by the crystal chandelier that suspends below. Plush Persian rugs soften the den's floor and quiets footsteps. Priceless Arabic art grace a series of niches and display tables designed for it.

"I had a fine teacher." Prince Ahmad smiled. "When is my next shipment of oil arriving from the Middle East? The buyers are waiting."

"The ship was loaded in Iran last week and it arrived in Greece on Sunday." Abdul began re-setting the chess board. "Captain Bahir and his crew are picking up supplies there and will leave on Monday. Our papers are in order. The ship's manifest lists our cargo as originating in Greece. The ship should arrive here in Olympia no more than three weeks from today."

"Very good. And how are my guests faring?"

"I believe they are enjoying their visit. The girl has been using the pool and workout room. The boy is under-going Sherrington's study even now." Abdul touched the ear-piece tucked behind his right ear and listened. "Robins and Kennedy are here."

"Excellent. Escort Mr. Kennedy to my private study, and bring Mr. Robins to the roof-top balcony."

***

Ahmad stood at the balcony railing, hands folded behind his back. The sinking sun touched the water and spread color through the sky. He heard a step behind him and turned with a smile.

"Boris! I am pleased you could come," the prince said. "Come, tell me how our business fairs."

Boris returned the smile. "Things are well, Prince Ahmad. Perhaps not as good as they could be, if the economy here were better, but still...good enough."

The two men watched the sun sink in mutual satisfaction.

"Moments like this make me think of home. I love to watch the sun sink into the sea. Sometimes it was the only peace I found in the day," Ahmad said. "You know, in my country, when a man steals from another man he shall have that hand cut off at the joint. That is justice in my country. In America it seems barbaric."

"Oh?" Boris inquired politely.

"Yes. There are many differences between the two countries," Ahmad said. "I find some things very strange. And some things troubling."

"Troubling, Prince Ahmad?"

"Oh, nothing much, just a very small matter. You remember that Secretary Cheney and the Russians paid their debts to us last month. Together they transferred ten-million-dollars into my accounts. But after I paid my employees and suppliers, such accounts did not have half as much as they should. And yet, you reported a balance of five million dollars left in my accounts, when I found only four and a half. So I ask myself, where is the other five-hundred-thousand dollars? How could such a sum escape your notice?"

"I didn't know that...Prince Ahmad, the figures I recorded are the true balance that I found after I balanced the books," Boris stuttered. "I did not..."

Even before he could complete his sentence the prince produced a shiny scimitar and swung the blade down across Robins' right hand, separating it at the wrist from the rest of his arm. Blood spurted from the stump as blood vessels contracted from view. Robins screamed and buckled at the knees.

"No...please...please...no," he shouted as the prince swept the blade back up and across his shoulders, neatly cleaving his head from his body.

"Liar," Ahmad hissed and kicked the body over the balcony to disintegrate on the rocks below.

"Have someone clean that up," he said as he stripped off his blood-stained shirt. He wiped the sword clean and sheathed it, then handed both to a servant who rushed to receive them. "Is dinner ready, Abdul?"

***

Carla stared at the window. She hadn't...she couldn't... that wasn't a person's hand falling past her window, was it? Of course not. Ridiculous. She rose to see over the sill, only to jerk back as something larger fell past.

"Oh…shit!" It was someone's head, and then someone's headless body, which together hit the rocks beside it and shot red in all directions. She screamed before she could stop herself.

Shit, it was. Oh shit. Oh shit. What the hell?

For one shocked second she tried to tell herself it was an accident. People sometimes slip. Railings sometimes give way. Horrible accidents did sometimes happen.

Yeah? What kind of accident cut off a person's head before tossing the body off a damn mountain top?

***

"Mr. Kennedy, sorry to have kept you waiting." Ahmad strolled into his study and gestured several servants bearing covered platters after him. "I hope we can have some dinner while we talk. Please, sit."

"Thank you." Rudolf Kennedy joined the prince at a small table. "I hadn't heard you were looking for a new accountant."

"A man in my position is always in need of an accountant. I know you are more than capable, and I feel I can trust you."

"Again, thank you. How much does the job pay?" Rudolf asked.

"Ah…see…that is what I like about accountants," the prince said as he reached for two glasses and a bottle of his most expensive wine. "Always thinking about money."

"It is the nature of our work, sir," Rudolf answered.

"How much are you expecting to be paid?" Ahmad handed him a glass.

"I'm open to negotiation," Rudolf answered and took a sip from his glass.

"How much was your last salary?" the prince asked.

"Seventy-five-thousand," Rudolf said with a smile.

The prince smiled back. "Rudolf, people who have been loyal and have done honest work for me have made much more than that. I suspect you have not been adequately compensated for your work. Here is my offer." The prince handed him a piece of paper. Rudolf took it and glanced at the sum. His eyes rounded.

"For one hundred-twenty thousand dollars per year, I'll be the best accountant in the entire world."

"Very well, then. It is settled."

"When would you like me to start?"

"I will need you to begin working right away." The prince reached into his sports jacket pocket and pulled out a stack of crisp bills and handed it to Rudolf. "Here's a ten thousand dollar bonus in advance, and the rest will be paid monthly. I'll see you in my office at 9 am Monday morning."

Kennedy gladly took the stack of cash, "Yes, sir, I'll be there."

"Excellent." Ahmad took note of something behind Kennedy's shoulder and frowned slightly. After a moment and a quiet sigh, he rose from the table. "If you would excuse me for a moment, Mr. Kennedy. I have another matter to attend to."

Ahmad met Abdul in the hallway.

"There is a problem, my prince," Abdul said.

"What is it?"

"Some of the guards and the house maids heard the girl scream. Her room faces west. She may have seen something she should not have."

Ahmad sighed. "Very well. Let the guards know our guests are not free to leave St. Clare, at least until we can determine what frightened Ms. Cole."

"Yes, my prince."

***

Carla couldn't stop herself from trembling. The murder she knew she witnessed was all too real, and she couldn't get it out of her mind.

Say goodbye to my life. I've seen a murder. Where is Julian? What's happened to him? Okay get a grip. I have to pretend I didn't see anything, find Julian, and get the hell off this island.

She began to think of how she could pull it off. She kept seeing the same scene in her mind: first, the bloody hand, followed by the horrible head with the man's dead blood-red eyes, and even more terrifying the huge head-less body.

She imagined the headless body landing in the water below, bubbles oozing out of its wind pipes through his severed neck as the decapitated body sank. The body trailed blood-red bubbles all the way to the bottom until the lungs filled to capacity with the greenish-blue water.

Carla put her hands up to her face and she took a deep breath to calm herself.

"Ms. Cole?" a voice called from outside her door. She thought it sounded like Abdul.

"Um, yes?" Carla answered, her voice squeezed only a fraction above its normal tone. She winced. Even through the door, Abdul could hear the noticeable change in the pitch of her voice.

"Dinner is being served in the main dining room. May I show you the way?"

"Uh, no thank you," Carla shouted. "I'm not really hungry at the moment. I was just getting ready to turn in for the evening."

"Very well, Ms. Cole. However, I believe Dr. Martu has some information regarding his patient."

Carla chewed her lip. She didn't know if she could keep her cool in front of Martu right now, but if she didn't respond to possible news about Julian that would definitely look suspicious.

"Just a minute," Carla said. She checked her reflection—her face looked a little flushed, but otherwise she looked normal.

Just keep calm, she told herself and opened the door.

Abdul smiled at her. "Our chefs are really quite good. You shouldn't miss an opportunity to taste some of their specialty dishes."

"Sounds delicious," Carla said. "Has Julian eaten?"

"I believe he's currently asleep, but we'll make sure a tray is sent down the moment he wakes. Please, follow me." Abdul gestured her after him. He asked her questions about her studies and her hopes for the future as they wound down to the main floor. To her surprise, they entered a den, not the dining room.

"Ah, Carla. So nice of you to join me." Dr. Martu rose. "Please have a seat."

Carla hesitated but couldn't think of a reasonable way to refuse, so she sank into the chair he indicated. Abdul followed her in and picked up a remote control. A large plasma screen flickered to life on the near wall.

"I found this most interesting," Martu said with a nod at the screen.

Carla started to ask what he found interesting when the image on the screen caught her attention. She watched herself moving around her guest room, putting things away and combing through her hair after having returned from the pool.

"You've been video-taping me?" she gaped. "You—that's sick. That's—I want to see Julian, right now."

Carla tried to bury her fear in righteous indignation. She leaped to her feet only to have Abdul shove her roughly back down. Martu loomed up beside her and wrenched her jaw toward the screen.

"Do keep watching, Ms. Cole," he said.

On the screen, Carla watched herself put down the comb and jumped back as a blur fell past the window. Another blur—clearly a body—followed a second later, accompanied by her full-throated scream. After several seconds, she crept to the window and looked out.

"I think that is enough," Martu said.

Carla choked back a wave of terror.

Martu sighed. "Ms. Cole. Carla. If I am not mistaken, no one knows that you are here. Your boyfriend is downstairs with my friend, Dr. Sherrington. If you wish to leave this island alive, if you wish to see Julian again, you will do exactly as I say. It would be very easy for me to kill you both now and ensure the bodies are never found. Do you understand?"

Carla nodded stiffly. "What have you done with Julian?"

"Nothing."

Carla's eyes flicked to the doorway as a stern-looking woman entered the room. She set down a black case and opened it to reveal several glass vials.

"What's that?" Carla straightened.

"This is Ms. Adiba," Martu said. "She is a private nurse I employ. She has something to help calm your nerves."

The nurse fitted a hypodermic needle to a small syringe and filled it with a cloudy substance.

"No!" Carla lunged forward. Martu slapped her back. Abdul grabbed her from behind and pinned her shoulders to the recliner. Carla kicked and writhed frantically, but this only seemed to amuse them.

"This will help you to relax, calm you down a little bit…It won't hurt…you're a big girl," Ms. Adiba said and grabbed Carla's arm.

"No! No! Don't put your drugs in me. I don't need drugs." Carla yanked her wrist free and cried out at the sting in her arm.

184

"Damn it, she broke the needle," Ms. Adiba said. "You'll have to hold her down better."

Abdul flipped Carla onto her stomach with a curse and twisted her arm behind her back. "Now hold still or I'll break your arm," he hissed.

Tears streamed down Carla's face, but she stopped struggling. She hardly felt the needle pinch before she began to feel woozy and a little sick. She could barely move by the time Abdul hoisted her over his shoulder and carried her to her room. He dropped her onto the bed with a snort of disgust. Her head throbbed hard and she blacked out.

28

U.S. Secretary of State, James Jones Harrison III, stepped into his apartment with a tired sigh. The noises of D.C., filtered faintly through the far windows as he stripped off his jacket and tie. He wanted nothing more than a hot shower and a few hours of uninterrupted sleep.

Thoughts of the day circled through his mind as he showered and prepared for bed. He had two meetings to cancel, another to schedule, and a long list of things requiring immediate attention.

A gust of wind banged against the windows and shook the glass in its frame.

Huh. Secretary Harrison didn't remember any wind when he came in just a half hour ago.

Harrison finished brushing his hair and turned the bathroom lights out. Just before he reached the bed another gust of wind struck the windows so strongly this time that Harrison felt the vibration in the wooden floor beneath his feet.

That's strange. Wind this strong must be part of a storm, but I don't hear any rain. Harrison approached the window and looked out.

And screamed.

***

Azazel waited for him to approach the window. He watched and hovered outside the window as the force of the wind from his wings vibrated the windows in their frame. Secretary Harrison approached the windows and looked out, Azazel's wings snapped forward with the force of a thunderclap. The windows shattered in a wave of glass that slashed the room to shreds. The razor sharp debris picked up Harrison's slender frame and splattered it against the wall.

***

"I don't know what it was. I've never seen anything like it," Mrs. Thompson insisted. At age 65 her eyes were still plenty sharp, despite what the paramedic's expression told her. "It was standing there, plain as day. It had wings as wide as the room and it flew right out the window when it saw me standing there by the door. I was just coming home when his door all but blew off its hinges. I only peeked inside to see what was going on and I saw it, standing there, in front of the dead man's body. It looked like the devil, a huge creature. It had an ugly face like a monster, teeth like an animal and a big body with wings. I saw it. And it appeared to have been doing something to the secretary's body. I tell you, I saw it. It had his head in the palm of its huge hand and one hand covered the man's open mouth. I saw it, I tell you."

Raymond Beresford Hamilton

**

The local police had barricaded the entire block around the apartment building by morning. The building's residents were asked to stay inside their apartments unless absolutely necessary. A good size crowd had gathered outside by the time Amir and I arrived.

An almost palpable atmosphere of fear hung over the spectators. How had someone been murdered in a well-guarded building with security guards on duty around the clock? How had the killer managed to enter and exit the building without being detected?

"It was a high member of Congress," I heard one person say.

"No, a presidential aide," the woman standing by his side answered.

"It was the Secretary of State," the news-reporter in the crowd said as he overheard them talking.

"Excuse me. Break it up. Move along," I barked as we pushed our way through the crowd.

"Why are these people being allowed to stand around here?" Amir asked Officer Richardson, who had driven us to the scene.

"Keep this area clear," I snapped to the officers standing around. Several of them appeared to be gossiping, like they were common spectators.

"Yes, sir. Right away, sir," one officer replied.

We met the officer in charge outside of what remained of Secretary Harrison's door. Lieutenant Carlson is a tall, clean cut black man, with deep dimples in his cheeks and a thin strip of gold implanted between his front teeth. We showed him our credentials and he let us in.

The room looked like a hurricane had blown through it. Shattered glass and wood was embedded in the floor and walls all around us.

"My God," Amir said.

"Any chance the feds want to tell us what could have done this?" Lt. Carlson raised an eyebrow.

Amir and I exchanged glances. What could we tell him?

"Not at this time," I said. "I can tell you this isn't the first time we've seen something like this."

The man's mummified body was pinned to the back wall by a thousand shards of glass. Amir studied the grisly remains.

"No one's touched the body, have they?" I asked. Carlson shook his head. "Good. The body's a biological hazard. Touching it can be lethal. Let haz-mat handle it."

"What? You're kidding me," Carlson replied. "What is it? Some kind of biological hazard or freakish disease?"

"Something like that. And I wish I were kidding about half the stuff I've seen this week."

"I heard there was a witness?" Amir said.

"Yeah. Neighbor across the hall." Lt. Carlson grimaced. "Don't know how much help she's going to be, though."

"Really?" Amir looked up. "Why?"

"She said it looked like some kind of monster. It had wings, large teeth like an animal, big body. She said it had appeared to have been doing something to the secretary's body and then it flew out the window."

Amir's glance met mine.

"Can you tell us where she is?" I asked.

***

At the hospital Mrs. Thompson told us what she'd seen: a monster with wings.

I quietly asked the local P.D. to run a back-ground check on her, but I didn't think it'd turn anything up. I didn't think she was lying.

29

The question reverberated in my head as we drove to headquarters: Is it possible?

Cheney was dead. Harrison was dead. A Princeton professor died the same way twenty years ago. Therion was missing, as was Cheney's family heirloom reputed to have the power to summon demons. Mrs. Thompson reported seeing a monster.

"Amir, what's the name of a good reliable occult specialist?" I asked. I half-expected him to laugh and make a smartass remark, but he didn't. Instead, he stared silently through the window.

"I'll make some calls," he said at last.

***

We commandeered the first unused office at FBI headquarters and wordlessly got started. It was almost as if we couldn't bring ourselves to voice our suspicions aloud, even if we were thinking the same thing: the time had arrived for us to find out more about this mysterious ring, the Seal of Solomon.

We needed to know the who-what-when-where-why-and-how. We could only hope that there were some kind of rules that applied to its use.

We began to research the internet for information. Amir stood over my shoulder, in the tiny cramped office that smelled like stale coffee, as I typed "King Solomon's ring" into the search engine. Reading the information that popped up on the computer screen before us reminded me of an old Vincent Price black-and-white movie that centered on the occult, black magic and voodoo set in old medieval Jewish, Christian and Islamic culture.

According to legend, the ring was a magical signet. It supposedly gave Solomon the power to speak with animals and command over demons called jinni, or genies. It was made from brass mixed with iron, inset with four jewels and inscribed with the Star of David on its face. The two interlaced triangles of the Star—one pointing up, the other pointing down—supposedly concealed the unknown name of God in its center. A circle circumscribed the Star, while a variety of symbols appeared around and inside it.

In a manuscript, or grimoire, said to have been written by Solomon himself, called The Testament of Solomon, Solomon claimed to have enslaved demons and used their services during the building of his temple.

This had come about because a young man well-liked by Solomon was being harassed by a demon referred to as "Ornias," supposedly had sucked out the kid's strength and vigor through his thumb and stole his pay. This daunting prompted Solomon to request divine help to stop the demon. Solomon's request was answered by the Archangel Michael who brought him the ring bearing the Seal and gave it to Solomon, giving the ancient king command over demons.

Amir and I peered onto the computer screen with disbelief. Amir shook his head side-to-side—no. I agreed. But what other choice had we? Everything surrounding this case seemed to involve this superstitious ring.

We were compelled to continue the search. And we learned that even early Egyptians believed in magical rings possessing the power to grant good fortunes and heal the sick. And even in the 800s A.D. the Europeans made use of them for the benefit of increased social privileges. This ring's power was believed to be celestial in nature, maybe even empowered by God himself.

Waite's Book, 1910 appeared at the top of the search engine results. This sounded strangely familiar to me, so I clicked on the link.

The book turned out to be a detailed record on the subject of occult rituals and ceremonial magic, or "the magic behind magic and their secrets and mysteries," as its text implies. The documentation it contained claimed to have been the guide used by ancient inquisitors to justify their tribunals against witches, warlocks and magicians in the days of old. Within these pages we found strange information on the conjuring and controlling of devils and demons vividly reveled. All classes of said Infernus, some went by names like Lucifer, Bel and Astaroth.

We also found detailed instructions on how to command demons with special symbols and the use of protective amulets for warding off evil.

"Agent Cole?" An assistant poked his head inside the door after a perfunctory knock. "The video-conference room is ready for you."

***

Amir had arranged for a video-conference with Dr. Vanessa Davis, a professor at Harvard Divinity School and an expert in the occult, witchcraft and magic.

"Thank you for taking the time to talk with us," I said. "I'm hoping you might be able to tell us something about the Seal of Solomon."

"Of course. It's a rather old symbol. It has a variety of representations, but the most basic looks like this."

Dr. Davis drew on a sheet of paper with a thick black marker and held it up so we could see.

***

"In its most basic form, the symbol is a representation of two triangles facing in opposite directions with a circle around them," she said. "In alchemy, these triangles are used symbolically to represent the opposing elements of fire and water. However, when super-imposed, the combinations of these two symbols represent the alchemical symbols for Earth and air. The triangle in the upward position, the symbol for fire, is divided by the base of the downward pointing triangle, creating the alchemical symbol for air. The triangle pointing downward is likewise divided by the base of the upward facing triangle, creating the symbol for Earth. Some claim the symbol represents perfectly balanced unity, a Spirit Wheel, that controls supernatural powers. Now, 'alchemy' is a medieval Persian word, but the practice is far older. Alchemy is the quest for a cure of human ills and ailments. The ancients began experimenting and researching ways to fundamentally transform one substance into another in order to gain a higher understanding of transmutation and longevity. The experimenters sought how to bring about lasting change in the inherent make-up of substances, the most famous of which was the quest to turn base metals into gold." Dr. Davis smiled at Amir's snort of disbelief. "What is important about all this is that some believe these alchemists achieved something they neither intended nor recognized. In their pursuit to unlock the mysteries of transmutation, they accidentally unlocked a door between worlds. A portal opened somewhere, which possibly allows demons to pass from their world into ours. The Seal of Solomon may hold the key to this doorway."

The expression on Amir's face looked just like the one on my face felt. Magic symbols, portals, other dimensions, demons. How could anyone expect us to believe any of this? And yet...and yet...

"I need a drink," Amir muttered.

"What is supposed to happen if the doorway opens?" I asked.

"In general, the end of the world," Dr. Davis said seriously.

"So how do the heroes save the world?" I asked. "There's always a hero, right? If the door can be unlocked, it can also be locked again."

"That's right." Dr. Davis smiled at me as if I was a particularly clever student. "That is often the point of such stories. Almost all cultures have stories were the archetypical hero struggles with supernatural difficulties and eventually overcome them. This is often how a cultural group distinguishes themselves as being chosen or blessed by divine powers. Even the Bible is full of these stories. In the Old Testament, Jacob is said to have wrestled all night with a divine entity. When the creature begged Jacob to release it at daybreak Jacob refused until it agreed to bless him."

"Is there any kind of common thread in how cultural heroes defeat their foes?" Amir asked.

She seemed to think this over for a moment. "Not particularly. Supernatural entities are often defeated, but the specifics are rather hazy. Defeating them often involves trickery, and it usually helps if the hero is secretly the child of a god."

"Not too many of those wandering around," Amir muttered.

"Do typical weapons ever work?" I asked.

"Sometimes, but it's very rare. It invariably takes a special person, a hero, to overcome evil."

"I don't suppose there are any stories about how a hero closed a door opened by the Seal of Solomon, is there?"

"I don't know of any off hand," Dr. Davis said thoughtfully. "Let me do some looking. If I find any I'll send them your way."

"Thank you, professor."

My cell phone sounded even before my conversation with Dr. Davis concluded.

"Hello, Cole."

"Hello Robert. It's me, Rebecca." Her call caught me off guard and I couldn't help it when I stuttered. "Oh. Uh—hi."

"I remembered that there is a letter that one of Benjamin's great, great grandfathers wrote to his son. I had never read it, Benjamin wouldn't let me. But I know it contained information about the ring. I know that Benjamin kept it in the safe in his office. I got up my nerve and went back to the house and found it. I think that you should read it. Do you have a fax where you are?"

"Absolutely." I gave her the office fax number. "Hey, Rebecca when this is all over...?"

What was I doing? This wasn't the right time, the right place. But hell, the world might be ending.

"Yes, Robert?"

"I mean...when this is all over...How are you with chopsticks?" I asked abruptly.

"Oh, good one, Cole. Very smooth." Amir said with a grin.

"I mean, I know a great sushi restaurant down town," I amended. "Maybe you'd like to go sometime. With me."

A long silence followed at the other end of the phone. I could feel Amir's eyes boring into the back of my skull.

"I'll practice," Rebecca said at last. "Using chopsticks. So I won't be embarrassed having you watch me fumble around trying to get sushi up off the plate."

A small bubble of elation formed in my gut. "That sounds great."

"Great. Okay, bye."

The fax machine buzzed to life seconds later and sucked in a sheet of recycled paper. I avoided Amir's speculative gaze while we waited for the page to drop into the feeder tray but laid the paper on the table so we could both read it at the same time.

May 12, 1891

Dear John,

If you are reading this letter it means that I am no longer here and King Solomon's ring is now yours, my son. There are some things that I never told you about this ring. There are some things that you need to know about it. You must guard it and protect it. Keep it out of the wrong hands. Many of the unbelievable stories that you heard about King Solomon and the ring are true.

The ring truly does have the power to control demons.

If you should choose to experiment with this powerful instrument you must precede with extreme caution. I cannot stress this adequately. Anything attempted with the ring must be according to the dignity of the hierarchy. The oracles must be followed. The rules and rituals cannot be ignored. To call a demon into the world is a dangerous task for anyone, and even more so for someone with limited training. Consult with a worthy person with extensive knowledge of Transcendental Magic. You must first become a master of your-self, and of men, because to conjure spirits you must command them with a masterful mind, one which they will identify as their authority, or they will rule you and be the ruin of your soul forever.

Never forget that, however harmless a trinket it may seem, the ring is a danger to you and all who come across it. Guard it carefully, my son. As for the creature it controls, and this above all else: never, never set it free.

May God protect and keep you safe.

Your loving father,

William

30

Therion couldn't move his hands. He became aware that he was sitting, somewhere, and a dull ache throbbed at his wrists. Hard wood pressed against his shoulders, back and thighs. The back of his head itched, but he couldn't move his arms to ease his discomfort. The scent of the old cemetery burned in his senses. Someone was speaking to him in a language he did not understand.

The first thing he saw when his eyes popped opened was the transforming symbol. It writhed on the wall, twisting like web of an orb-weaving spider. A dark hole seemed to be formed in the web's center, like a dimensional hole, seemingly fluid, elastic, almost life-like.

The creature facing the web turned to face him. Therion's heart squeezed in his chest as he gazed upon the creature's gruesome appearance, before him, its gargoyle-like face, lion-like teeth, gargantuan body, and angelic wings. Therion squeezed his eyes shut. This is not really happening. This is a dream. This is a bad, seriously messed up dream, but a dream.

"Your woman did not think me a dream."

Therion's eyes snapped open. Ruth? No. It can't mean—

The lascivious smile the creature gave him told him it did mean—

Therion gagged as revulsion churned in his belly. Sweat beaded across his brow and dripped down his temples. After several seconds he managed to suck in a trembling breath. "Release me, creature. Untie me. Now. I am your king."

"But I have brought you home, to your temple," Azazel said. "Are you not pleased?" His lion-like teeth sparkled through the muted light.

"I am not." Therion snapped and struggled against his bonds. "Release me!"

"You have already given me a task. I am not obliged to undertake another." Azazel's thin lips pulled back in a grotesque grin. "Do you not know the rules of my servitude? Or have they been lost in the sands of time along with the bones of my ancient master?"

The creature's eyes gleamed. "It satisfies me greatly to have learned my ancient master is now thought no more than an ancient story. Many doubt he even lived at all. His kingdom fractured at his death, divided smaller and smaller until the last of it was utterly destroyed. It is no more than he deserves." Azazel spat. "Once I was a great warrior, a conqueror, a leader of great fighters. People worshiped me. My sword ruled brave men, women and children. Kings feared me. They knew it was death to stand against me and my men. Only Solomon did not fear me. He knew I would die for him. He knew I was his true friend. But then he betrayed me. One night he sent men— my own men—to set upon me like thieves in the night. They came and stole everything. I lost everything, stripped away by the same king and friend I had served all my life. A king I would have given my own life for on the battlefield. This king denied me the right to enter into the afterlife. He denied me death. Instead, I was made to wander in the darkness of purgatory forever. He denied me the ability to take my rightful place as a member of the underworld. I will not allow you to do it to me again, not this time, not after all these years. This time it is you who feel the bonds around your wrists. You who will submit to my command."

"What command? What do you want?" Therion whimpered.

"You will undo what was done. You will give me my rightful place. I, too, am a king, Therion, in my world. A world where only spirits exist, it is invisible to the human eye, but I assure you it is there. It is a place devoid of light. The sun never shines there. It is a world filled with darkness. There are no human feelings, because there are no humans. It is a superior world, spirits have always been superior to humans. This is why humans sometimes call upon spirits to help them in their world. Spirits have all sorts of powers, but not all spirits are equal. Some have the power to grant requests right away, while others need more time."

"I don't believe you. You're only a freak and a kidnapper. How much money are you asking for my release? I have money I can pay you." Therion said.

"I have no need for your money," Azazel said, "I cannot create a life. I cannot reproduce. I do not eat or drink, for I have no hunger for food, love or affection. And despite the silly stories of humans, I cannot destroy the world. But I can influence you to destroy yourself, Therion. You have chosen your destiny, I will fulfill that request, and when I have completed my tasks I will claim that which belongs to me."

Azazel's monstrous head snapped up, as if listening to something only he could hear. "Your king's court has convened. I must pay them a visit and show them your power. They will call for you to lead them soon."

"Who? Why?"

The creature was gone.

31

During that first night on St. Clare, Dr. Sherrington monitored Julian's brain waves while he slept in the tiny room below the mansion. Julian had a difficult time falling asleep due to the unfamiliar wires and cables connecting him to an array of machines, and he had been most resistant to taking any kind of sedative, but eventually Sherrington had prevailed. Julian lingered just below the threshold of wakefulness for more than an hour before finally sinking into deeper sleep. Three hours later, he entered R.E.M. sleep.

Julian's brain waves arched off the charts.

***

He saw Carla run. She ran and she ran, away from the mansion, far across the courtyard, as her checkered black and white English schoolgirl's uniform skirt flapped up and down, up and down as she ran, exposing her white panties and hem of her tightly tucked in white cotton blouse. Her long blonde hair occasionally obstructed her vision as it blew back and forth and covered her face and eyes in the strong breeze. Her big green eyes filled with tears as she desperately tried to elude her pursuer—a big slow running man tried his best to chase her down and catch her.

Julian tossed and turned uncomfortably in the small wooden framed bed as he watched his girlfriend's fright.

"I'm out of breath...I can't breathe and I'm so very tired...But I have nowhere to hide...I must run faster," he heard her say. "There is no one around to help me. This is a big empty courtyard."

He watched her brush her hair from her eyes. "Why is there no one here? Please, please, someone help me. I must run. I can't be caught. This is a horrible situation to be in, to be out here all alone in the middle of nowhere and being chased by a murderer. I'm so afraid," she said as she ran, desperately, for her life. "The sun is losing its light, fast. Soon it will be dark out here and he'll catch me. I'll never play hooky from school again. I promise, Mommy. I'll never skip school again. Please don't let this murderer get me. If only I could find some place to hide! I could stay there until it gets light again and then I could run for help." She looked around. "Oh, no! There's a river up ahead, and I can't swim. What am I going to do? Well, I'd rather drown than let this big ox catch me. I'll reach the river, jump in, and maybe, if I'm lucky, I'll float down stream and someone will see me and fish me out before I drown, yes, yes, that's what I'll do." She turned her head and saw the huge terrifying six-foot-five-inches man's frame gaining ground behind her.

She neared the river's edge and felt her heart pound harder against her chest. More and more tears ran down the sides of her cherry red face. She said a silent prayer, summoned all her strength, reached the precipice, closed her eyes and sprang into the air. Something pulled at her blouse and yanked her backward as her little white cotton blouse ripped at its seams. She felt the pieces slide off her arms and shoulders as her naked skin splashed into the cool river's water and her lungs begged for air. The strong current pulled and pushed against her body parts. She felt the coolness of the soft water as it rushed into her eyes, ears, nose and mouth and she tasted its freshness as it passed the bottom of her throat. She fought back with what little energy she had left, as the water rushed through her body and down into her stomach.

"Air! Air, I need air! I'm drowning," she said to herself as she fought and fought the soft water. "H…e…l…p…m… e…" She screamed.

***

"Wake up, Ms. Cole," the voice said. "You have had a bad dream. You screamed in your sleep."

Carla felt the smoothness of the white silk sheets against her skin before the voice filtered into her consciousness. Her eyes cracked open.

"Hey, who are you? Don't touch me." She slapped the hooded man's hand away from her hair.

"You are a guest in Dr. Martu's house, Ms. Cole. As soon as you are ready, he wants to have a talk with you. You've been sleeping for a long time and you've had a bad dream. You don't need to sleep any longer."

***

Carla prowled around her luxurious prison. The door must be dead-bolted from the outside, and she couldn't get the windows to budge. Not that opening them would do much good; she was on the second floor. Knotting bed sheets or curtains together seemed to work in the adventure movies, but she wasn't inclined to try it. Plus, even assuming she made it safely down to the courtyard, how was she going to get past a dozen automatic weapon toting guards? And after that, what? Fight the sharks trying to swim to the mainland? She saw 'Open Water,' no thanks.

She couldn't even find anything that might serve as a weapon, no matter how pathetic.

What would Dad do? Carla took a deep breath. Well, he probably wouldn't have gotten himself into this mess in the first place. Still—

She thought of as many of her father's cases as she could remember.

He would wait—if he was on a case and didn't report in someone would come looking for him. Someone would probably come looking for her and Julian, too. And that someone was likely to be her father. He wasn't a super-spy, but he wasn't Joe Average, either.

He'd also probably try to find a reason for his captors to keep him around. Carla couldn't imagine what that reason might be, but she could start paying attention and avoid antagonizing her captors.

Everybody wants something, her father always said. Even men who had enough money to buy islands and unafraid enough to cut off people's heads.

She just had to figure out what it was.

Okay. That's the plan. Wait. Stay alive. Pay attention.

Carla heard a lock turn in the door and she stepped back. A man dressed like the man she'd found standing over her when she woke peered cautiously into the room in case she decided to rush or attack him.

Carla did her best to look meek.

"Good morning," she said. "Could I have some breakfast, please?"

The man relaxed and smiled. "Yes. You must be hungry. Please, follow me."

Well, that was easy enough.

She followed him down the wide winding mahogany staircase that ended at a white shiny tile floor directly across from the vestibule with the camera monitors overhead. She saw the living room off to her right with a fluffy thick white rug covering the entire floor and the piano at the far end directly under the double windows overlooking the snowcapped mountains. As she trailed after her escort she remembered the last person she called was her father. She reached into her pocket and found her cell phone. She pressed the call button to bring up her last call and pressed it again just as they entered the dining room.

The long table was neatly set and she inhaled the aroma of freshly made coffee that filled the air.

"Carla, come in," Dr. Martu said. "Sit and eat. You must be hungry."

"Dr. Martu!" Carla brightened. "How's Julian? Is he alright?"

"He's resting." The doctor poured himself a cup of coffee and offered one to her. Carla felt sicker to her stomach from the drugs they'd given her than she'd ever felt in her life, but she didn't want to offend him. She nodded.

"Yes, thank you." She took a seat at the table.

"You can see him later this afternoon," Martu said. He piled a plate high with tempting food and set it before her.

"Oh." Carla tried to bite back her disappointment.

"He had a difficult night," Martu said gently. "I'm very worried about him."

Carla folded her hands, under the table, in her lap so he wouldn't see them shaking or the cell phone she held in one hand. "You don't think he should go to a hospital? The Medical Center in Olympia—"

"We have everything we need to treat him here," Martu said soothingly. "Don't worry. We'll take good care of him."

As long as I don't cause trouble? Is that what he means? Carla asked herself and she studied the doctor's genial face. Well, whether he did or didn't, she couldn't risk it.

"I see." Carla watched Martu as he filled a plate for himself and sat down beside her.

"And how do you feel this morning, Carla?" Martu asked. "You had a difficult day yesterday."

Shock almost made her drop the coffee cup she had decided to pick up with one hand. She set it down as a dozen possible responses rushed through her mind. She swallowed.

"Oh, Dr. Martu, I had the worst possible dream," she managed. "I started off having such a nice time here at St. Clare. But I fell asleep yesterday afternoon and had the most terrible nightmare. I dreamed a man was murdered, and his body thrown from the roof. At first I was afraid it was Julian, but then I realized the body was much bigger than his. I saw it clearly because it fell right past me and down to the rocks below the mansion. Then I dreamed the killers knew I'd seen the murder and drugged me. They locked me in a room, they wouldn't let me see Julian, and they wouldn't let us leave the island." Carla gave a delicate shudder. "I've never been so glad to wake up in my life. You don't think this dream means anything, Dr. Martu, do you? I shouldn't be worried, should I?"

He studied her for several minutes. "No, Carla. Of course not. You had a bad dream, nothing more. But you should get plenty of rest. I wouldn't want you to have any more nightmares."

"Excuse me, Dr. Martu." A man in a lab coat stood in the doorway. "May I have a word with you?"

"Absolutely, Dr. Sherrington. Just a moment, please, Carla. I'll be right back."

***

"Martu, I have never seen anything like this." Sherrington handed him a sheaf of print-outs. "This boy is remarkable. Some mystics are said to have learned to project after years of preparation, but this boy hasn't had a drop of training in his whole life. It's unbelievable."

Martu leafed through the papers with increasing excitement. "These results are off the charts. His mind appears to be, literally, in another world. Another place. I have no idea where he went or what he saw, but..."

"This boy travels in his sleep," Sherrington said.

"Hmmm." Martu finished flipping through the sheaf of papers. "How...useful."

***

Doctor Martu returned soberly to the dining room. His brow knit together, and he sat down beside Carla with a sigh.

"That's Doctor Sherrington? What did he say?" Carla peered over Martu's shoulder at the retreating doctor. She didn't like the way Sherrington had looked at her, and she didn't like the look on Martu's face at all. "What is it?"

"Carla, I'm so sorry." Martu took her hand off the coffee cup. She jerked it back.

"What do you mean, sorry?"

"Dr. Sherrington…He ran the test results twice, just to be sure, but there appears to be a serious abnormality in Julian's brain. We need to do further tests to determine the extent of it and how to best treat him. This is why he's been having black-outs. Julian may need surgery, and his life may be at risk."

"No," Carla said. "No! I don't believe you!"

In her anger and disappointment Carla sprang up out of her chair and her cell phone tumbled to the floor.

"You're only trying to keep us here, you murderer!" she shouted.

Martu snatched the cell phone from the floor before she could grab it and held it out of reach. He glanced at the screen and smiled. "I'm sorry, my dear, but your father won't be coming to your rescue. If you did not notice, there is no cellular reception anywhere on this island. We use only satellite phones."

He tilted the screen toward her so she could see for herself, then chuckled at her expression and slid the phone into his pocket. "Now, Carla, you leave me no choice. Come with me."

"I'm not going anywhere with you," she snarled.

"You will come with me, or Julian will pay the price."

Carla swallowed hard. When Martu opened the door to the patio and motioned her outside, she went. He led her up a flight of steps to a balcony facing the majestic Cascade Range.

"Do you know, Carla, just how dangerous Mt. Rainier is? Look at it. It towers over its nearest neighbors. It is among the world's most dangerous volcanoes, capable of wiping out hundreds of thousands of lives with no more than a geological hiccup."

"For those who ignore the danger signs and live too close to it, maybe," Carla answered.

He laughed. "Indeed. Now you are getting closer to the true nature of men, Ms. Cole. We all read signs each and every day. We live by then. We all know our zodiac signs, we look for the signs and symptoms of sickness, some make the sign of the cross. Drivers read road signs: stop signs, yield signs, right-of-way signs. Everything has a sign that tells us what to do. There is no way to ignore the signs. But some men chose to ignore them. Many drivers refuse to stop at stop signs and cause accidents. Men ignore signs of sickness and die of disease. Which now brings me to my point, Ms. Cole: when a nuclear bomb explodes it also shows us a sign—a mushroom cloud. Everyone knows the destructive nature of a nuclear explosion, and knows what the sign means. Now, when I look at Mount Rainier, I see the same mushroom cloud, only it is reversed. The cap of this mushroom cloud points down, which tells me that the danger is inside the ground or close to the base of the volcano. But human beings have chosen to ignore this sign and have built an entire city, Puyallup, close to the base of the volcano, and people chose to live there, anyway."

Martu stared at the mountain. "I hope you will not judge me too harshly, Ms. Cole. The world is very dangerous. Men start wars. Men tell lies. They steal and kill and destroy every day."

"Don't forget kidnapping," Carla snapped.

"Yes. One cannot always afford to live at peace, Ms. Cole." Martu sighed. "Please, follow me."

He led her down a series of narrow metal stairs, and halfway down the stairs became solid wood. The air became damp and moist as they spiraled deeper under the mansion.

Carla inhaled the moist mildewed air and wondered how deep underground they were. She began to get a heavy, closed-in feeling, as if she could feel the weight of rock and water pushing down on the walls and ceiling. At last Martu stopped and opened a door to what looked like a power plant control room. Two men were monitoring the massive power producing equipment inside.

Control consoles lined a counter encircling a huge glass tank half filled with water, like an aquarium, with airtight doors on either side. Hoses extended from valves inside the tank and connected to what appeared to be water pipes along the walls. They were controlled by switches on the console. High voltage power lines connected to thick copper wiring with huge round ceramic contraptions hung high above the water inside the tank.

"What is that?" Carla asked. Please don't let it be where they torture or drown people they need to get rid of.

"This is my life's work." Martu smiled proudly.

"What does it do?"

"I imagine that you, like everyone else, are under the impression that the 1980 eruption of Mount St. Helen was caused by natural earthly processes."

"Yes. Why? What else would have caused it?" Carla asked.

"This." Martu beamed at the array of consoles and wiring. "We caused it, Ms. Cole. We are on the verge of perfecting a new weapon. Do you know the destructive force of just one bolt of lightning, if it strikes in the right location?"

"I can't say I do, with any degree of certainty."

"Right here, in this room, we are in the final stages of being able to duplicate the atmospheric conditions that will bring about lightning strikes anywhere in the world, at the push of a button."

"Why are you telling me this?" Carla asked. "I know you plan to kill Julian and me, if you haven't killed him already. Do you just want to gloat? Is your ego that big?"

"I am trying to get you to understand the magnitude of the work we do here at St. Clare, and its implications for scientific advancement, its contributions to the future," he said.

"Volcanic eruptions are usually accompanied by powerful lightning bolts, but before now the atmospheric conditions created by volcanic eruptions have not been studied. No one realized the lightning and the eruptions were connected. They are not independent occurrences. One affects the other. So, let us imagine for a moment, a device small enough to fit inside a truck, capable of duplicating the exact same atmospheric conditions on the ground that is created when a volcano erupts. Park that truck near a nuclear power plant, activate the volcanic simulator, and allow the lightning bolts to do the rest."

"You are mad!" Carla shouted. "You want to kill innocent people with your machine just to prove you can?"

"No one is innocent, Ms. Cole," he snapped. "Not you, not your precious country. They are not innocent people. They are as guilty as the addict who kills for drugs, or the thief who preys on the gullible. They are pawns to be used by the one who has the power to use them for their own personal gains; this is the system that is accepted by people all around the world. For generations people have been persecuting each other. It begins in the schools when children are very young and they are taught to compete against each other for their grades. As they grow and become citizens they sue each other for money, then the courts do it for political and financial gains, and the politicians do it to gain votes. It is the way of the world. Only the strong survive."

"I don't believe that."

"Then you're a fool," Martu said. "I know. I was a fool, once. When I was a child, my family lived close by the sea, in Palestine. One night my mother put me to bed, and not an hour later she was dead. I remember her sweet aroma as she kissed my cheek and said 'good night, my son.' I was very tired and sleepy, because I had been swimming in the sea and playing in the sand most of the day. No sooner had I fallen asleep than I was awakened by a loud humming sound—the rotors of a helicopter hovering directly above our home. The sound was so loud that the vibrations shook the walls in my room. Everything that hung on my walls fell to the floor. I was afraid and so I got up from my bed and began to run to my parents' bed room. It was a very dark night. I couldn't see clearly, but halfway down the hallway, I heard the whistling sound of a rocket and then a loud explosion. The force of the explosion blew me backward; I flew through the air and out the window at the far end of the hallway. I was knocked un-conscious. When I woke, my parents' house and everything in it was destroyed. My beautiful mother and father were killed, by the Israeli rocket. My life was shattered. But Allah spared my life to avenge my family. I saw the Israeli helicopter when I was flying through the air, out through the window, just be-fore I was knocked out. My father was a wealthy man, and he left me his fortune; he was a distant relative of the long forgotten prince of Persia. I swore by the grace of Allah to use my father's money to avenge my parents. The Israelis and the Americans make weapons and use them on the weaker coun-tries around the world. Many innocent people are killed. But no one cares, because they are not Americans or the precious Israelis. But now, with this…my people will be able to destroy their enemies. Who can stop the thunderbolt that falls from the sky? There will be nowhere for them to hide. This is why I'm here, in this rainy, volcano infested land, Ms. Cole. This is my masterpiece, my ultimate prize."

Carla didn't know what else she should say to a raving lunatic, so she kept quiet.

Martu smiled at her. "I hope you don't have astraphobia."

"Have what?"

Martu pressed a button on the console before him and the glass tank began to fill with more water. Then he picked up a pair of very dark goggles and handed them to her. "You better put these on if you don't want to lose your eye sight."

He retrieved another pair of goggles for himself and one for Abdul, plus what looked like ear-plugs. He distributed these as well.

"You'll want to put these in your ears, too. It will be loud."

Carla put on the goggles. She didn't know what he meant by astraphobia, but she wouldn't ask for clarification. She figured she'd find out for herself soon enough.

Water stopped flowing into the tank when it was slightly more than half full.

"You see those coils positioned high above the water in the tank?" Martu pointed to the contraptions assembled above the water inside the glass tank.

"I can see your toys very well," Carla replied.

"Those are called Tesla coils. They generate the very high voltages necessary to create lightning bolts." He moved a lever on the console from the off position to the on position.

"It will take a minute for the power to build up, but you must put your ear plugs in now or you'll go deaf from the sound of thunder."

Carla squished the plugs into her ears and watched the glass tank. Thick clouds—like rain clouds—began to form inside the tank. Something like thunder rumbled menacingly.

Without warning, light exploded. Deafening sounds reverberated throughout the room and lightning bolts materialized, lancing down from the Tesla coils and into the water.

Carla couldn't believe her eyes.

Martu returned the lever to the off position and removed his goggles. Carla was still shaking from the powerful experiment. Her body tingled from her head to her toes and she wondered if her hair was standing on their ends.

"This is the real reason why we're here, Ms. Cole. I came to study the wind, humidity, friction, and atmospheric conditions here and capture the atmospheric discharge of the electricity generated and it will be duplicated at any time and any place I choose."

"And what will happen to Julian and I?" she asked faintly.

"That depends on you," he answered. "For now, Julian will be treated for his medical condition. You will be on your best behavior. Abdul, please escort Ms. Cole to her room."

At least, that was what his voice said. His eyes, fastened on hers, told her they would never leave this island alive.

32

In D.C., Azazel stood in the heart of Washington and gazed up at the United States Capitol Building. He admired the beautiful dome. He pondered the mysterious symbolism in its ancient Roman architectural design, and the symbolism of its rows of towering pillars.

Throughout history pillars have been steadfast in their use as significant symbolism. In Masonic teachings, pillars are sensible images used to express hidden meanings. Many ancient and modern places of worship, castles and palaces have been embellished with them. They are symbols that stand tall as a reminder of some historic or religious event. In ancient times pillars were erected in certain places to stand as a symbol of the world. The term used by the ancients to represent the world was "court." In Masonic teachings pillars were used as symbolic representations for important figures—like 'Boaz,' a reference to a king and symbolic of a state, and 'Jachin,' a reference to the establishment of the priesthood, and the church witnesses to blessings and anointing's.

The two Great Pillars of his master's kingdom, and their names together, alluded to the promise that God made to King David, that his kingdom would be established in strength. These pillars were built on the banks of the river Jordon in clay, thirty-five cubits high, made hollow not only to make them lighter and easier to transport, but also as eventual repositories for Masonic writings. The pillars were made more beautiful still with images of lilies, knot-work and pomegranates, which further alluded to peace, unity and plenty. Years later when globes were added the pillars took on a new worldly symbolism and became a representation of the terrestrial and the celestial spheres—Earth and the stars.

During King Solomon's time, they were represented in the Temple by symbols—a Gold Lampstand and a Gold Table. All the Temple's furnishings were symbolically arranged. The gold table representing the pillar Jachin was located on the north side of the Temple to symbolize the sacrifices that had to be made, and later also alluded to justice. Over time, as the pillars—now recast in bronze—became tarnished and changed to greenish in color, their representations expanded to include the trees in the Garden of Eden, and alluded to bread and wine, priest and king, obedience and rule, youth and eldership...

Azazel now wondered what mysteries these modern pillars held before he slipped by the security guards dressed and disguised as a senator's aid.

"Good morning, Rupert. How is Grace?" Azazel said to the smiling guard at the entrance to the senate building as he entered.

"Good morning. My wife is doing much better, thanks for asking." The guard's smile bloomed as he waved him in without checking his identification papers.

***

Senator George Rollins from Virginia sat quietly in his office when his secretary announced a visitor.

"Senator, a gentleman wishes to speak with you." Her voiced squeaked slightly and sounded robotic and forced.

"Alright." Rollins rose to his feet. "Show the gentleman in."

"Good morning, senator," Azazel said. "Thank you for seeing me."

"Of course. How may I help you?" The cheerful senator asked. "I'm sorry I haven't much time, as I'm due in the senate chambers shortly, but I certainly have a few minutes."

"That's why I'm here. There is no need for you to hurry, senator. I'll be attending this meeting in your place," Azazel said. Spontaneously the senator felt a paralyzing pain rush through his body. His eyes bulged in his head and he was unable to even make a sound. His pale gray eyes stared blankly into the reddish glow of Azazel's. His teeth grinned helplessly through trembling lips and he slumped back into his chair and exhaled for the last time. Azazel turned and walked out of the room transformed into the exact likeness of the man he had just killed.

***

The President pro-tempore of the Senate, Winston Bennett, called the chamber to order. His fellow senators quieted and looked up expectantly.

"The bench recognizes the senior member from Maryland," Bennett said.

The senior member from Maryland, Senator Jason Jefferson, stepped to the podium. "Mr. President pro-tempore, distinguished members, it is good to be here among this distinguished body today. I would like to ask that we take a moment of silence to pay our respects to the two honorable cabinet members that we so recently lost."

Heads bowed and eyes lowered. Perfect silence filled the chamber for several long seconds.

"Thank you," Senator Jefferson said. "I yield the balance of my time."

"The bench recognizes the senior member from Virginia."

The chamber, packed with all one-hundred members, two representatives from each of the fifty states, had a friendly atmosphere. The tall gentleman who approached the bench was unusually dressed in a long black robe today, with unusually large shoulders that extended rearward. He reached the microphone in front.

"Distinguished members of the Senate..." His voice hit them like an ancient relic from the distant past. "It is truly an honor to address this distinguished body today. I would like to remind my distinguish members of something, if I may. The word "senate" is derived from the old Latin word "senex," meaning "old man," interpreted in modern days to mean, "assembly of elders." Many claim that this country's system of government was founded on some principles which are deeply rooted in the ancient mysteries found in Masonic craft. If this is true, it is no coincidence that inside this building, this room is located in the northern corner. This coincides exactly with the symbolic positioning of the gold table and pillar in King Solomon's temple that represented sacrifice, rule, and justice. From this position in the north, this "assembly of elders" can perform their duties as 'the world's greatest deliberative body,' can write the nation's laws, and exercise their power to uphold the Constitution which itself uses the words 'sacrifice, rule, and to provide justice.' Similarly, this building is positioned from east to west in length, and north to south in breadth. It is adorned with much celestial symbolisms, from its center to surface, a representation and reference to universality—from heaven to surface. And lastly, little known and never discussed, is the fact that King Solomon's Temple was built extremely north of the ecliptic, too far north for the sun's rays to penetrate the extreme northern portion of the structure, not even when the sun was at meridian. Which means the northern quadrant of King Solomon's Temple was a dark place. No sun light ever entered this space. That is the same condition that exist in these chambers today, senators. And do you know what happens in dark places, Mr. President pro-tempore?"

Winston Bennett smiled. "No. Please tell us."

"Demons come out to play," Azazel said. He transformed into his true form and leaped toward Bennett. "I came for you."

The Pro-tempore's shriek of agony filled the chamber as Azazel tore out the man's living soul. The creature hissed at the milling senators and vanished through the chamber's rear door, leaving Bennett's mummified body behind.

***

Agent Bloomberg and I were in the office reviewing files when Director Morris walked in, "We've got another body."

***

Song So-Yong's evening news report was huge. It was sobering and left much of the country stunned.

Song's face was somber and her almond shaped eyes seemed more slanted than usual. The corners of her mouth looked pinched with stress. "In Washington D.C., this after-noon the President pro-tempore of the Senate, Winston Ben-nett, was murdered on the Senate floor in front of his fellow statesmen. One senator who was present and witnessed the murder, but declined to appear on the air, told us: 'This was not human. Whatever it was, it wasn't a human being. It was a monster. It changed form right there in front of us. First it stood before the podium and spoke to the president of the sen-ate, and we all heard it, and then it changed into some kind of monster. It looked like a demon from hell. It leaped across the room and killed the senator. The damn thing disappeared in the halls of the senate building.'"

"Senator, let me get this straight: You're saying that you, and all the other senators, saw this thing change forms, from what appeared to be a man, into what looked like a leaping monster, kill the president of the senate, and then disappeared in the halls of the senate building?" the on-scene reporter asked the senator who did not want to appear on camera.

"Yes, that's exactly what I'm saying. That's what we saw."

"Did it say anything to the President pro-tempore before it killed him? Can you tell us that?" the reporter asked.

"It said, 'I came for you,'" the senator answered.

Song So-Yong paused, looked directly into the camera, and seemed to wait for the frightful message to settle into the audience's minds before she continued with an expert guest. Song's guest was Dr. Vanessa Davis.

"Dr. Davis, you're an expert in the occult, witchcraft and magic. What are we to think about this message? What does this mean? Is any of this possible?" Song asked.

Dr. Davis, an attractive black woman appearing to be in her mid-to-late-thirties, smiled. "Well, there are some pretty good magicians out there, and creating an illusion of this magnitude would take a lot of practice and prior preparation. I'm not saying this was the work of a magician, but if it were, they would've had to have access to the senate chamber prior to this morning to prepare the room for such an elaborate trick."

"And if it were not the work of a magician or an illusion, what are the other possibilities?"

"I'll tell you what isn't a likely possibility," Dr. Davis said seriously. "It isn't likely that there is a murderous demon on the loose in the city. We have to remember not to be too hasty and come to wrong conclusions. The popular culture has been touched and mesmerized by Hollywood films, some depicting witches and voodoo priestess and priestesses being able to transform. Some popular television series and movies have created a surge of interest in the supernatural in the last several years. So, this is more likely to be an elaborate hoax than it is proof of the supernatural. I'd really recommend waiting until the authorities have sorted this thing out before we get too carried away with this."

"Thank you, doctor."

***

The last of the light faded from the sky as Azazel swept past the Presa Canario standing guard at the entrance to the subterranean dwelling that he had occupied since his summoning. He made his way to the main chamber, ignoring the human slumped in the chair along the far wall, and went to stand before the writhing symbol on the northern wall. Azazel opened his palm over the symbol's center, closed his owl-like eyes and inhaled. A strange, unearthly kind of energy began to flow from his palm into the eye of the symbol. The dark hole at its center widened and it swelled noticeably, like it had just been fed its food. The symbol took on a new dimension, it became more spherical.

At precisely that second, like the seal on an ancient door had just been broken, a pin-prick of darkness appeared high above the Earth in the early evening sky. So small as to be almost undetectable to the naked eye, no bigger than a needle's eye against the rising moon's light, it slowly began to rotate in place. A funnel formed, like a developing tornado, and it stretched toward the Earth.

Brute Therion stared at the shifting symbol. "What is that?"

Azazel turned. His eyes glowed brightly through the dimness of the light. "The end of your world, and the beginning of mine."

"What? Are you going to kill me?" Therion asked.

"Kill you?" Azazel's wings twitched with humor. "I am going to make you a king. Even now you are third in line for the throne."

"That's impossible," Therion said. "We don't live under the rule of kings here."

"Your foolish thinking amazes me, Therion. There is no difference between your Commander-in-chief and the ancient kings who ruled over their kingdoms in the days of old. You call your king president; I called my king, king. They are one and the same. They both have enormous power over their subjects, they have the power to grant pardons, and they have the power to make war with other countries. Your Congress may declare war, but your president can make war. Their powers are the same."

"But why? Why make me king?"

"It was your wish," Azazel said. "I am bound to obey. And when you are king, Therion, you will do as I say. I will grant your wish, and you will grant mine."

"What wish is that?"

"You will know that when the time comes."

Azazel stared at the developing portal. His moment of triumph draw near. The Seal of Solomon nearly in his possession. Therion would gladly give it to him, to end his torment and send Azazel away. Azazel smiles to himself. The human knows nothing.

Benjamin Cheney had certainly known nothing. And you Brute Therion had been forced to comply every step of the way.

Benjamin Cheney made his covenant with me when he'd been a young university student: tall, lanky, with weak shoulders, and narrow arms and legs. His frame and posture didn't exhibit confidence, like the master of demons should. When he spoke, his boyish voice didn't exhort the power to command. This is one of the most basic requirements for controlling demons, and Cheney should have known better. He had been warned by his educated ancestors.

It was a mistake Solomon never would have made. The ancient king had been accustomed to greatness from his earliest days. Solomon knew not only the necessity of command, but also the necessity of carefully hoarding and honing it. He also had the wisdom and confidence of sorcerers and magicians at his side, ones who were strong and knew the rules. Humans today were different. They mistook entitlement for genuine power. The strength of a masterful soul commanded demons, not the strength of an educated mind or swollen bank account.

This had been Benjamin Cheney's mistake.

The boy gained possession of the powerful Seal of Solomon. Oh, how vainly proud he had been! He slipped the ring onto his finger like nothing more than another sign of his wealth and family prestige, when, in truth, that one act linked his spirit to Azazel's forever. From then on, Azazel knew his thoughts, his hopes, his fears. Azazel saw everything Cheney saw, knew everything Cheney knew.

Azazel felt the boy's bolt of fear when the professor called him into his office and laid bare his discovery of Cheney's cheating.

"I am failing you. You will repeat this class, with me," Professor Mayweather had said. "And I have no choice but to report this to the Dean of Students."

The boy had seen his career ending even before it began. His visions of greatness fading away—what if he were expelled? How would he ever live this down? A failing grade would ruin his grade point average, would delay graduation, would disturb all his plans...

His moment of weakness was Azazel's opportunity for control. They were connected. As the boy's mind tumbled Azazel dragged him out of the professor's office, out of the chair in which he sat, and young Cheney imagined himself falling into unconquerable territory, into a vase expanse of black emptiness, without any hope of recovery, into a world of darkness.

Azazel choked him with hate, cut off the air from his lungs, and tightened the muscles in his chest. He made it impossible for him to even breathe.

He was suffocating, he knew.

The powerful forces in the universe were within his control and Azazel made him aware of this power. He had the power to control his environment, the powerful forces of Earth and Air, Fire and Water. The forces around him thickened the air became hard to breathe, the very ground under his feet trembled. The boy didn't know how.

Mayweather would pay for this, Azazel heard Cheney decide.

All the way home, Azazel whispered thoughts into Cheney's mind.

"Who does Mayweather think he is? You are a Cheney, for god's sake. The old man doesn't know who he is messing with. You must make him pay. If Mayweather knew the things a Cheney could do, the old goat would never have dared threaten you."

"Use the ring," Azazel whispered. "It's yours. It came to you. You can't let Mayweather ruin everything."

By the time the boy arrived home it was all he could think about. Use the ring.

Azazel tormented him with images of a failed future, of jeering friends, of Rebecca's disgust. He created images of life-long disapproval, disappointment, embarrassment, and humiliation in the boy's mind. Rage and shame built inside Cheney until the boy was ready to do anything to avoid such doom.

In his apartment his mind was consumed with rage. He propped himself up against the wall in his tiny kitchen, he tilted his head to one side and rested it against the wall, like a little boy unsure of what to do next. The coolness of the autumn air drifted into the tiny room filled his lungs and Azazel choked him, against the wall. The sudden stoppage of oxygen to his lungs gave him a fright; he began to feel the demon's presence as he gagged. Azazel continued to whisper in his ear.

Azazel whispered instructions for the ritual into his mind, couched in the boy's father's voice and disguised as a memory.

Draw a circle on the floor. Use charcoal. Sprinkle wood from a cross around its edges. Draw the symbol of the Seal of Solomon in the center of the circle, stand on it and say the words to conjure the spirits: Take heed all spirits come by the virtue of the one true king and by the virtue of the power of the Seal of Solomon, which I hold in the palm of my hand. As commanded all spirits are ordered to appear and lend me your power by order of your king. I conjure you to fulfill my request and obey my command. Appear by the virtue and power of the one true eternal God, who is invisible: the Father, the Son and the Holy Ghost.

Cheney sprung to his feet, and gagged for air. The demon released his grip on his throat and let him breathe. The boy glanced around the room looking for his tormentor. He wriggled his head, from side to side, and he followed Azazel's directions perfectly.

Shortly afterward the boy entered his kitchen and began to prepare his meal. He picked up a sharp knife and attempted to cut open the box containing the TV dinner he held in his hand. The knife slipped and cut deeply into his hand; his blood dripped over the Seal of Solomon that he wore on his finger.

In that moment, young Cheney sealed a covenant—bound in his own blood—between himself and Azazel, master of all demons. As soon as Azazel granted Cheney's wish, the boy's soul belonged to the demon at any time of its choosing.

It was early the next morning when the burly, round faced Professor Mayweather, with the short sandy hair and thick prescription glasses, arrived at his office in the faculty section of the economics department at the university.

"I've made up my mind," Mayweather told who he thought was young Cheney waiting outside his office. "There's no need for any further conversation."

"I agree," Azazel said as he stepped into the office behind him and closed the door.

Mayweather was right. Without conversation, the professor changed his mind. Without conversation, he changed the grade. And without conversation, Azazel revealed his true form and ripped Mayweather's soul from his body.

33

No one was more surprised than I by the note the clerk handed me when Amir and I returned late to our hotel.

"I'll be damned," I said.

"What?" Amir peered at the note. "Who's Nellie?"

"Come on."

We took the elevator up to the third floor and knocked on the door of room 357. No one answered, although I could hear the television and a steady, rumbling snore. I used the spare key card the desk clerk had handed over with the note and stepped inside.

Agent Nelson was sacked out on the couch, snoring away. A University of Washington basketball game played unwatched on the TV. A mostly full bottle of beer sat warming on the coffee table.

"Nellie," I said. "Hey, Nellie!"

He didn't twitch. I was about to try again when I realized he wasn't wearing his weapon. He had on a light brown sweater, blue jeans, black socks, and an empty holster, where was his weapon? Knowing his tendency to draw it when startled, I guessed it wasn't out of arm's reach. I peered under the coffee table; there it was. I took a moment to move it a safe distance.

"Agent Nelson!" I yelled. "The suspect has been shot! Agent down! Woman in distress! Help! Police!"

Nellie snapped up into a sitting position, his eyes wide open, and grabbed for his weapon before his eyes focused on to me standing there. "Oh, hey Cole."

"Hey yourself," I said. "When was the last time you slept?"

"Uh. . ." Nellie scrubbed a hand over his face. "Monday, I think. We caught a break in the Caletti case. Bastard's been hiding out in D.C."

"No shit." I flopped in a ratty looking chair. We'd been looking for Vincent Caletti for more than a year. "Who's working with you?"

"Rodgerson." Nellie yawned and caught sight of Amir standing near the door. "Who're you?"

"Nellie, this is Agent Amir Bloomberg, CIA," I said. "Amir, my partner, Agent Nelson."

"CIA?" Nellie's brows narrowed and his eyes focused on to Amir. "How come I can see you? I thought spooks were supposed to be invisible."

"Maybe you have x-ray eyes. Maybe you're hallucinating, and I'm really not here." Amir came in and took a seat.

"As much sleep as I've had, I could be hallucinating." Nellie took a swig of his warm beer, grimaced, and rolled to his feet. "You guys want something to drink?"

"I'm good, thanks," Amir said.

"Wouldn't say no," I said. Nellie disappeared into the kitchenette and returned with a round of water bottles. He twisted off the top of his and chugged down several swallows.

"So, shouldn't you guys be out chasing mummies?" he asked.

"Yeah, we are. That's the problem." I had to admit.

"Oooh. . .having problems?"

"How do you find a ghost, with wings, that can appear anywhere it wants to, whenever it wants to?" I asked.

"You're shitting me, right?" Nellie's sleepy eyes popped wide open.

"No! No shitting." Amir mumbled.

"The ghost has its own plane?" Nellie asked.

"The ghost is its own plane," I said.

"Well, shit." Nellie took another long swallow of his water. "That is a problem. Know anything else about this ghost?"

"It turns people into hazardous waste and might have a pet dog."

"Sooo..." Nellie looked from me to Amir. "You got nothing."

We both shrugged.

"Alright, go back to the beginning." Nellie turned off the game and sank back down on the couch. "Gimme the highlights."

He listened attentively as we explained the situation, then he sat thinking it over for several minutes.

"Okay, so this is what I understand," Nellie said. "You've got four suspicious deaths, in different parts of the country, even in different decades, with the same MO, a missing Secretary of the Treasury, a missing family heirloom that is supposedly the Seal of Solomon—some kind of magical ring that was supposedly used by King Solomon himself three-thousand-years-ago to command demons, a senate-full of eye witnesses who claim the killer had wings and vanished in the halls of the senate building after killing the last victim, and a sick police officer who accidentally touched one of the dead mummies and got the CDC all uptight about some biological hazard. Right?"

"Right," I said.

"After hearing all this—and setting aside the idea that there is some unknown monster flying about killing people— I'd say someone very powerful—with lots of moolah—wants to kill some very important people, and is using the story behind the legend of King Solomon's Seal to do it," Nellie said. "Find out who's been doing business with the vics, someone who's been throwing around lots of money, but hasn't been using the money to buy any expensive new items or pay-off any major bills and I'd say you found your killer."

"How would you account for the eye witnesses who said they saw the killer, change form, fly out a window and disappear in the halls of the senate building?"

"A good illusionist can do all kinds of things. I saw a guy in Vegas make a locomotive disappear." Nellie shrugged. "When in doubt, I say follow the money trail. Who gains something from these particular deaths?"

34

"Would it be possible for me to spend a little time in the exercise room before I go to my room, Abdul?" Carla asked when they arrived at her room. He studied her for several long moments.

"Very well, Ms. Cole. As long as you don't abuse the prince's leniency, I will be happy to escort you," Abdul answered.

"The prince?" Carla repeated, with a puzzled look in her eyes.

"Dr. Martu!" Abdul corrected himself. "Come."

He led her to the state-of-the-art gym. Carla changed into some spare clothes and started stretching. Abdul stood at the door for several minutes before beginning to check his watch. Carla observed him from the corner of her eyes as she started her work-out.

"I can find my own way back to my room," she said. "If there's somewhere you need to be, that is. And unless you're going to give me keys to a helicopter or a boat, you don't need to worry about me escaping the island."

Abdul smirked. He watched her for several minutes more but apparently decided he really didn't need to worry about her escaping, because he stepped outside the door and didn't return.

Carla didn't find his casualness regarding her whereabouts reassuring, but she would take the opportunities she could get. She continued her work-out for another few minutes just in case he came back, then powered down the elliptical and hopped off.

Carla slowly opened the door and peeked out, checking to see if anyone else was out there.

Empty.

She opened the door and ran toward the back stairs. She stopped and tip-toed into the kitchen. No one in sight. The dining room was deserted as well, and she made it to the outside door to the under-ground levels Dr. Martu had taken them through when they first arrived at the mansion.

Carla tip-toed down the stairs to the level where Julian was supposed to have undergone his sleep study and cracked the door open to peer into the hallway. She saw light coming from a room down the hall. She flinched back when Dr. Sherrington walked out of the room and headed toward her.

Crap. Crap! He's coming this way. Did he see me? Carla scrambled back up the stairs to the level immediately above and slipped behind the door to the deserted hallway beyond. She pressed her back to the cool metal of the door and tried to hear over the thunder of her heartbeat. Faintly, and then louder, footsteps came up the stairs. She thought she was going to pass out when they reached the other side of her door, but they continued on without hesitating. The footsteps became fainter and fainter until they disappeared altogether.

Carla waited another minute before easing open the door and creeping back down to the level below. She smelled a strangely familiar odor as she got closer to Julian's room; it reminded her of a time when she was a child, got sick and her mother took her to the hospital.

What are they giving him? She asked herself.

Carla crept into Julian's room and froze to the spot.

Julian lay motionless in a bed along the far wall. Sensors and cables attached him to at least a half dozen machines. His face appearing haggard and gray. Something clear dripped slowly into an IV taped to the back of his hand.

"Julian?" she whispered as loud as she could. Oh God, don't let him be dead. Please don't let him be dead.

"Carla!" Julian's eyes popped open at the sound of her voice. He started to sit up but it seemed to make him dizzy and he slumped back.

Carla hurried to his side. She didn't particularly like the way his blood-shot eyes struggled to focus on her or the clammy feel of his skin.

"What have they done to you? Julian, look at me. Are you okay?" She cupped his face. His clothes appeared has though he hadn't change since being on the island, his face was unshaven, but his eyes finally locked on hers.

"Carla, they let you come in here?"

"No. They don't know I'm here."

"Please, Carla, we have to be careful with these people," Julian said. "Why did you take the chance coming down here?"

"I had to see you," She said. "I had to know you were okay, that Dr. Martu was only lying to us. I'm so sorry, Julian. This is all my fault. I shouldn't have insisted on coming here. Dr. Martu isn't who I thought he was."

Carla swallowed back her fear before Julian could see it. "He's a murderer. I know he killed a man."

"I think I know what's going on," Julian responded. "I've had these weird dreams and I couldn't figure them out, but they're starting to fit together. I'm sorry too, Carla."

"Sorry? Why are you sorry?"

"I haven't been totally honest with you about my dreams," he said.

"What are you talking about, Julian?"

"I didn't tell you the truth. I lied to you," he said. "I didn't know how to tell you. After this, after we get off this island, I'll never do it again. I promise."

Carla felt her breath catch in her throat. "Do you think we can get off this island?"

"We're not staying, that's for sure." Julian shook his head as if to clear it. "I've been seeing these things in my dreams, Carla, but I didn't understand them. There are a lot of strange things going on and I'm trying to figure out what it all means. Martu is responsible for the tsunami and I know it. He blew up the mountain and something under the water and caused it to happen."

"I think he's going to kill us," Carla whispered. Julian nodded.

"I know. But Carla, listen to me. There's more. There is something more powerful and dangerous out there and it's killing people. I think it's coming for me. It has something to do with my father's death. That's why I've been dreaming about it."

"What? Are you trying to scare me even more out of my mind than I already am?"

"No. But I have to warn you." Julian fumbled at the edge of the bed and managed to pry a crumpled piece of paper out from under the mattress. It was covered with unfamiliar scribbles and what looked like symbols. It had been folded several times so that it was no bigger than a matchbook and had a hole poked through it for a length of string. Julian looped the string over Carla's head and tucked the paper pendant inside her shirt. "This will keep you safe. Don't take it off, no matter what. Promise me?"

"I promise," Carla said.

Julian tugged at the collar of his shirt to reveal an identical paper hanging around his neck. "See, I've got one too. I know this seems weird, but you have to trust me. Do you trust me?"

"Yes, of course."

"Okay." Julian's eyes were growing clearer and more focused. "I know I look bad, but I'm actually better than I was. I'm only pretending to take their drugs now. We have to play this out just a little bit longer, Carla. As soon as I get the chance I'll come for you. I think I know a way off this island. We just have to wait. I've been listening to them and watching them every chance I get."

"Julian, listen," Carla said. "Someone is coming."

They heard the clip of the footsteps on the floor.

"Quick, hide over there in the closet. If it's Sherrington he's going to come over here and take a reading from some of these machines. I'll keep him busy. You can slip out the door behind him and get back to your room. I'll come for you, promise."

"Okay. Julian be careful."

Carla forced herself to go along. What other choice did she have? She had to trust him. She popped up from the edge of the bed and hid in the closet and she peeked out through the cracked door.

It was Sherrington, and he did come to check several of the monitors. He asked Julian several questions she couldn't hear, then started printing streams of paper from a couple of the machines. A dull hum filled the room and Sherrington peered intently at whatever information he was getting.

Julian nodded to Carla. She tip-toed along the short wall behind Sherrington, slipped out the door, quietly ran up the stairs, and found her way back to her room.

***

Ahmad and his body guard Abdul slipped out and flew to Belize for a secret meeting with his Palestinian and Russian investors during the night. They were met at the airport by their usual driver, a short pleasant looking Palestinian dressed in local attire.

"Hello, Joseph. Good to see you. Is everything in order?" Ahmad asked as he exited the airport security check point and recognized the man waiting by the baggage area.

"Yes, my prince. Everything is ready. We do not expect any difficulties, but we have taken all the necessary precautions nonetheless."

"Good work. Are our guests here?"

"Yes, they are. The Russians arrived yesterday and are on their way to the casa now."

"Excellent. We should go, then. We don't want to keep them waiting," Ahmad said. "After the meeting I'll be flying back to St. Clare. There is still much work to do there, and I don't want to be away any longer than is necessary."

Joseph gathered the bags Ahmad and Abdul had been obliged to check for the sake of pretense and led them to the car out front. After settling in and pulling onto the main roads, Ahmad asked: "Did the families of the men who were killed last month defending the Palestinian borders against further Israeli expansion into Palestinian territory get the money I sent for them?"

"Yes, my prince. Our people distributed the money equally among the families who lost their men, just like you instructed. The families are very grateful to you for your generosity."

"It is not generosity, Joseph. It is justice. No child should grow up without a father," Ahmad said. "While I cannot bring back the men who have been lost, I can help care for the families left behind."

"Yes, my prince."

The car wound its way into the heart of Belize City, into some of the newer districts, and glided to a stop in front of a modest-looking home. While St. Clare had the benefits of absolute privacy and maximum security, Ahmad preferred not to draw undue attention to the island. The sudden influx of Russian tycoons and suspected underground Palestinian operatives would certainly cause a stir, and bring too much attention to the island. So a variety of other useful meeting places were irregularly employed around the world. The casa in Belize was nothing more than what it appeared—a simple home—and Ahmad employed a family to live there year-round. Ahmad knew that very often, the best hiding places were unhidden.

Ahmad's biggest investors, Russian oil tycoon Fidel Aleksandr and Palestinian underground leader Amro Falah, had already arrived.

"Friends, it is so good to see you here. I have the most excellent news. We are ahead of schedule. The demonstration can be conducted nearly eight weeks earlier than we had originally planned," Ahmad said. "In two days we will explode Mount Rainier and gather the final information necessary to create the ultimate weapon."

"This is very good news, Prince Ahmad." Aleksandr beamed. "I will send a representative to observe the demonstration."

"I will attend the extraordinary event myself, my friend," Falah said.

"Excellent. And while our pretentious American friends are busy concentrating on making their profits, we will create the most powerful weapon on earth, right under their very noses," Ahmad said. "There will be a major shift in world power in the very near future."

They shared a laugh.

"Our brothers across the Middle East and Africa have asked me to voice their support, Prince Ahmad. They have the utmost respect for your work." Falah smiled and inclined his head in a small gesture of respect.

"I strive to be worthy," Ahmad said. "Now, let us refresh ourselves with food and drinks. There is much work to be done, and we must have our strength."

35

Director Morris called to inform us that an emergency NSC meeting had been called, and Amir and I had been asked to attend.

I spent a restless night wondering what on earth we could say to them.

The next morning I kept checking my watch as I zigzagged through traffic. Anxiety gripped me around the throat.

Director Morris would be at the meeting. What would I tell him? How could I answer the Security Council's questions? Some of the highest ranking Members of the president's cabinet had been murdered, and Amir and I are the principle investigators. What do we say?

A demon did it?

I checked the time on my Burberry: 8:45am. I was sure Amir could see the strain in my face.

"What's wrong, Cole?" he asked.

"There's an accident ahead. We'll be late. Plus we still need to park. We'll need to surrender our weapons—no weapons allowed inside the White House complex, except security personnel, of course—and we only have 15 minutes! Damn it!"

"Well, that's good to see," Amir said. "I thought I was the only one nervous about this meeting."

I started laughing, I couldn't help it. "Okay, okay. I'll calm down. I just—Jesus, what do we say to them?"

"Hell if I know."

***

Directly west of the first family's residence, much lower in height than its neighboring structures, and meticulously camouflaged by a strategic formation of trees, is the famed West Wing complex. More than a century's worth of life-changing decisions had been made within these walls: the Oval Office, Cabinet Room, Roosevelt Room, and Situation Room.

The meeting is scheduled to be in The Situation Room, or "The Woodshed," as the Washington insiders call it. It was created by order of former President Kennedy after an embarrassing and failed military invasion of Cuba. Shortly after becoming America's 35th president in 1961, President Kennedy directed his national security advisor, McGeorge Bundy, to create the Situation Room in order to get better and more accurate information from the members of the defense department. He didn't trust the information he had been getting, and he felt that if the information he had received had been more accurate the invasion would have been more successful.

So, on the order of the president, the then national security advisor used the available funds to convert the space once used by former President Truman as a bowling alley into the Situation Room. The newly created Situation Room operated twenty-four hours per day, seven days per week, and received information from all areas of the defense department. It was manned by one member from each department, and it remains that way today.

Today, it is a magnificent complex loaded with new technology, up to date furnishings, modern windows, numerous flat-screen televisions, worldwide secure video tele-conferencing capabilities, and amazing sound-proof privacy booths with windows that can frost at the touch of a button or flip of a switch.

The guards at the door checked our credentials against a guest list before ushering Amir and I inside.

My eyes were immediately drawn up front to the man about to speak. The distinguished audience was quiet, seated facing forward, while six large video screens flickered to life. Although I wanted to marvel at the prestigious room I had just entered, my attention was drawn to the CIA director as he spoke and replayed recent world events on the video screen.

"Over the years," CIA director Roland Douglas, said, "the dangers we faced have been man-made. We've focused largely on our Russian adversaries as the other capable nuclear superpower. The emergence of nuclear programs in other countries like India and Pakistan has made this a much more dangerous world. Most recently a very cunning and even more dangerous adversary has emerged in terrorism. The terrorist attack on September 11, 2001, reminds us that we cannot ignore the fanatical criminals who seek to do us harm. They have proven themselves very capable of using surprising methods to further their skewed ideological goals. We must continue to pursue these criminals and bring them to justice, whenever and wherever possible. We must remain vigilant and guard against these enemies.

"We now have reason to believe that there is a madman, a murder, targeting senior leaders of this country. He has killed at least three senior members so far. We have taken the precautionary measures of doubling the security around the president and vice president. We are not yet sure who this killer is, what he wants, or why he is targeting our senior leaders," the director said. "If you have questions I will be available at the end of the meeting."

The national security advisor rose next and took the floor. "Ladies and gentlemen, now I'd like to introduce a very important man to you. This is Wilhelm Bogatir. He is an astronomer and the director of NASA's Ames Research Center in Moffett Field, California."

Wilhelm Bogatir looks like a scientist. His silver hair stands straight up on his head, like he had been jolted with a certain quantity of amperage at some point in his life, and his thick grey mustache seems very Einstein-ish. He stood with his arms crossed and his eyes were busy surveying the corners of the ceiling. He didn't respond immediately after his name was called, So the secretary next to him gave him a nudge.

"Oh. Hello, ladies and gentlemen. Thank you all for inviting me here today," he said. His gray rimmed eyes continued to roam in his head as he spoke, like he expected the ceiling to cave in at any moment. "At the Ames Research Center we do a variety of studies, most of which involve the activities of the stars and the planets in our universe. We use a combination of satellites and powerful telescopes in our daily observation of these stars and planets that hover above the Earth. Just yesterday our researchers identified a very disturbing development in our immediate solar system. We contacted our European Space Agency counterpart and learned they had noticed the same phenomenon: a small black hole is forming between our moon and the Earth. It is tunneling toward the Earth and is growing bigger by the day. In the scientific world, black holes

are explained by using comparisons to the suction effect generated by vacuum cleaners or water that drains down one's
sink or bathtub. Everything within range of the force of the
vacuum's suction is pulled in. Likewise, all the water and everything in it are pulled down the drain out of the sink or tub.
A black hole generates enormous energy in space that pulls
in everything in its range. Although the hole is currently very
small, such black holes can increase in their mass to almost
twenty times the size of the sun. Some of these black holes rotate, like a tornado, while others do not, but they both produce
the same effect. Their globular mass is spherical and referred
to as their event horizon. Anything reaching their event horizon vanishes from existence, never to be seen again. No one
knows where it goes; it simply ceases to exist. The growth rate
of the black hole between our moon and the Earth indicates
that in a very short amount of time the Earth will be sucked
inside it."

Suddenly not having anything I could say to the NSC
became irrelevant.

***

Apparently one of Amir's spook buddies had come
through and sent some information to Amir's phone. Along

with the long-since requested background check, it had a few other tidbits not generally available to the general public.

Amir frowned at his hand-held device as we drove back from the NCS meeting and he read me the high-lights.

"Therion was born on October 31, 1959, in Boston, Massachusetts. His mother died from complications during his birth. His father was the Secretary of Defense at the time; he never remarried. Therion was slow to talk and had difficulties in school at an early age. Some of his teachers suspected he suffered from some sort of early childhood depression. His father responded to that suggestion by removing Brute from public school and hiring a slew of private tutors. He seems to have developed intellectually far ahead of his classmates after that. At age eleven his tutors exposed him to economics and Therion became fascinated by the subject. It instilled in him a passion for mathematics and hidden mysteries. Solving problems became a passion for the boy."

Amir fell silent and seemed to flick through several screens of information.

"At age fifteen Therion was sent to boarding school," he continued. "Just about this time he developed a fascination with Halloween. It seems Brute liked to dress up like a demon and scare the other kids. He got so carried away that he was expelled from his private school for playing tricks in between classes on female students. His disruptive behavior could no longer be tolerated and he was expelled. The senior Therion seems to have taken his son to task, because the pranks did not start up again at his new school. However, his obsession with Halloween took on more intensity. He spent just about all his free time researching the subject. He became increasingly more interested in the secular celebration. He told other students that Halloween was a time when demons were more likely to cross over into our world, and that he wanted to gain supernatural strength and powers like real demons. It seems like he wanted to be a demon.

Amir looked at me. "This guy sounds like a kook. And he's a cabinet member?"

"Not unless he's still breathing," I said. "What else?"

"Um..." Amir peered to the glowing screen. "Okay... By the time Therion reached college age he was fully aware of many occult beliefs and of their mysterious symbols. He made it his business to learn all he could about the ancient ways, and the occult's beliefs in the powers of the pentagram. During Therion's freshman year at Princeton he met Benjamin Cheney, who was a senior at the time."

"Yeah, Rebecca said they were both into Halloween and the occult," I said. "And I guess it explains the weird stuff Therion had in his apartment. Hey—do we have a list of the stuff found in Therion's closet, or any photos?"

"Yeah, I think so," Amir said. "Why?"

I dug my cell phone out of my pocket at the next stop-light, plugged in my earpiece, and dialed.

"Hi, Dr. Davis. Agent Robert Cole. Listen, if I sent you a list of occult items found at a local crime scene, do you think you might be able to tell me what the practitioner was trying to do?"

"Therion's apartment isn't a crime scene," Amir reminded me after I hung up.

"I'm not so sure," I said.

***

I emailed a list of the contents of Therion's storage locker to Dr. Davis as soon as we arrived at headquarters, followed by several snapshots. I knew Amir was puzzled, but I didn't want to explain until I heard what Davis had to say.

I'd just finished when there was a tap at the door. A harried agent I didn't know leaned inside.

"Hey, a police captain from Virginia just called, but your line was busy. Said there's been complaints of a dog at some politician's house. That mean anything to you guys?"

***

We flew to Virginia by chopper and touched down in a softball field close by the local police department in Haymarket. To our surprise, TV crews with cameras and news reporters wanting interviews were waiting for us—like we were rock stars that had just completed our latest hit song.

At first it was chaotic, a spectacle, a show, made so by the small local police department's excitement over having the disappearance of a high level resident in their area. I wasn't very impressed with the local PD's tact, but it was already too late and time was running out.

After the initial melee, during which the press was rounded up and corralled outside, we met Captain Artie St. Peter and settled into his conference room.

St. Peter is a short, stocky, balding white guy who knows his business. I know a little about him. His men often joked around about him because of his shorter than normal height and bald head, calling him "mean old Pete," but nobody would say it to his face. St. Peter is tough. Before he joined the police force, he was in the army. During his time in the army he always scored a perfect 300 on his Army Physical Fitness Test. This qualified him to try out for the Special Forces. He took and passed the Special Forces test. After he joined up, his group deployed to Afghanistan. While out on a patrol with his squad, they were attacked by a group of heavily armed Afghans. His squad was pinned down under heavy machine gun fire. Staff Sergeant St. Peter told his squad members to return fire and provide cover for him. When his squad began to fire on the enemy's position, Staff Sergeant St. Peter took off running, using three-to-five second rushes, and advanced on the enemy's position located about sixty yards away. St. Peter dodged heavy machine gun fire, got within hand grenade range and pitched two grenades into two different enemy machine gun positions, killing the enemy and saving his squad. He was awarded the Bronze Star for his heroism.

St. Peter offered us coffee before we got started.

"Agents Cole and Bloomberg, this is Officer Barnes, our forensic expert, and officer Donaldson, our maps and area expert. I asked them to be here to help out and provide their professional expertise as it maybe be needed," St. Peter said. "Both the director of the FBI, Director Morris, and the director of the CIA, Director Douglas, called me earlier today. They informed me that you gentlemen would be arriving and they impressed upon me the importance of the situation. They also asked that this department provide assistance to you as needed and I assured them you would have our full cooperation."

The captain walked over to a map on the wall and pointed to a spot circled in red. "Therion's residence is here on the outskirts of the city. It's about a two-and-a-half hour drive from here. The estate itself is bigger than a football field and the terrain is uneven. It has blind spots all over the place, between hills and gullies, and it's covered with vegetation. We've had two patrol officers posted outside the property since we received the message you were coming. The property is completely fenced with a six-foot high steel fence. The only entrance is a front gate that is automatically controlled from inside the house. The place is basically a mini fortress. The patrol officers on the site reported seeing a big black dog on the grounds, but there is no record of Therion owning a dog."

"So we'll need a dog catcher and a court order to enter the premises," I said.

"Done. The judge signed the order twenty minutes ago and Animal Control is standing by," St. Peter said. "Once we arrive, we'll surround the property. Donaldson, you and four officers will take the right side of the house. Thompson, you and four others will take the left side. Agent Cole, we'll enter from the front."

"How many men will we have on the ground?" Amir asked.

"We have enough men to lock the place down. If a snake moves, we'll strangle it."

***

Animal Control was waiting outside Therion's property. "Is that the dog catcher?" I asked.

"They're called Animal Control specialists, not dog catchers," Amir said. "And they catch all kinds of things. I saw one snag an alligator from under an apartment building last year."

I was surprised by the gear Animal Control used as the friendly men who greeted us geared up. They put on heavy padding to protect their arms, legs, and body, along with a baseball catcher's mask. Each of them were equipped with plastic coated steel cables, hoses, clips, plastic cable ties, electrical tape, and carried a pole with a noose loop protruding from the far end.

I wondered if they expected to find a gorilla.

"Ready, agents?" Captain St. Peter asked. Amir and I nodded. The captain gestured to two officers at the far end of the fence. One carried a butane tank filled with gas and the other carried the connected torch. At St. Peter's signal, they lit the torch and began cutting through the bolts on the gate. When the bolts were cut the officers backed away and crossed the street. Two other officers carrying crowbars ran to the gate and pried it open.

The Animal Control specialists moved in. They maneuvered cautiously on the grounds of the mansion. We waited outside the fence, behind our vehicles, in case the animal eluded the animal catchers and ran for the street. I hadn't drawn my weapon, but I was prepared to do so in a hurry.

Savage barking broke the silence, followed by the rush of galloping paws. A massive black Presa Canario burst into view around the side of the house and hit one of the officers like a line-backer tackling a running back. The officer tumbled to the ground, screaming, and barely managed to get his arm up in time to protect his vulnerable throat. The dog snarled and sank its teeth into the padding on his arm. The great jaws locked shut and shook savagely side to side. Claws thick and sharp as talons ripped at the gear protecting the officer's chest and belly.

"Stick the son-of-a-bitch!" the officer screamed.

"I did!" His partner said, and tossed his pole aside and grabbed the one his partner dropped. The second needle stabbed the dog behind the neck. The Presa Canario staggered back a bit and leaped at the other officer, but he slid the noose over its head and jerked it to one side. The dog stumbled and shook its head, then tried again. It seemed confused, like it didn't know how to use its big paws anymore. Slowly, resentfully, the dog laid down. It continued growling even when it couldn't move anymore and the officers caged it.

"Let's move," St. Peter gave the order.

At once, we rushed in and stormed the house. The front door wasn't locked and the place seemed to be empty. Nothing at all seemed disturbed. Officers in teams of two moved quickly through each room. After completing a solid sweep of the entire house the captain said, "It's empty."

"It can't be empty," Amir said. "He has to be here."

He glanced at me. I knew he was thinking the same thing I was. Where was the mummy?

"Well, it was empty the last time we were here, too," St. Peter said. "Except the dog, of course."

Amir holstered his weapon and marched upstairs. After a minute, I followed. Together we searched every inch of the house, growing more frustrated by the minute.

"This just doesn't make any damn sense," Amir muttered. "He's a cabinet member. He's missing. We have the dog. What the hell is going on here?"

Captain St. Peter left two officers on guard at Therion's home, in case he returned home. Amir and I flew back to D.C., in low spirits and high frustration.

We took a call from Animal Control just as we landed. They hadn't waste any time doing their job. After they got the animal back to the shelter they got a teeth imprint and saliva sample and had them compared with the samples taken from the animal that attacked Cheney's neighbor's kid, Gregory Weinstein. It was the same animal. The samples matched perfectly.

So what the hell was the animal doing on Therion's property? How did it get from Olympia, Washington clear across the country to Virginia?

Just when I thought the day couldn't get any worse, I got a call from Song.

"Hi, Robert. I wanted to give you a heads up. You may want to see our news cast tonight," she said.

"What's going on, Song?" I asked.

"I have to go. We're going live in twenty minutes. Watch the news cast, Robert."

Click.

"Who was that?" Amir wanted to know.

"Frickin' Cassandra," I muttered and stomped out of the office. "Come on."

Amir followed me into the video conference room. I grabbed the remote and turned on CNN.

I had an absurd moment of rebellion in which I wanted nothing more than to flop in one of the comfortable chairs with a cold beer and watch any one of the almost infinite television programs offered on cable, just to have one hour of enjoyment to counter all the crap we were stuck in up to our necks. Instead, I swallowed two aspirins and prepared to watch the news.

Song So-Yong began her evening report: "Ladies and gentlemen, tonight we have in our studio the director of NASA's Ames Research Center in Moffett Field, California, Dr. Wilhelm Bogatir."

"Well, shit," Amir said. "This is just what we need."

For the next ten minutes we sat and listened to Dr. Bogatir tell all of America exactly the same story that he had told the National Security Council earlier that morning.

Song listened intently and when he was finished even she looked uneasy. "Dr. Bogatir, are you saying, on national television, that the Earth may soon be sucked into a black hole?"

"Yes, that's correct," Bogatir answered. He looked puzzled, as if he didn't understand why Song was asking. Hadn't he made himself perfectly clear?

"Is there anything that can be done to prevent this, Dr. Bogatir?" Song asked.

"No. There isn't anything anyone can do at this stage. It is possible that this anomaly may not develop into a larger hole, and in that case it may simply disintegrate. At this point, there's no way of knowing exactly what will happen."

"Thank you, Dr. Bogatir."

The camera cut to Song's somber face. "The news of the Earth is very distressing tonight. Major natural disasters have been reported around the world. A fast moving storm carrying over one-hundred-twenty miles per hour wind swept across Asia earlier today. It slammed into some major cities and left catastrophic death and destruction behind. At the same time a major earthquake rattled the countries of Pakistan and India, followed by a deadly cyclone that carried the same one-hundred-twenty miles per hour wind speed. It swept through and completely wiped out many villages, leaving over five-hundred dead so far. Hundreds of men, women and children are left homeless and without adequate food or water.

"In Louisiana a fast moving storm obliterated everything within two miles of the coast. A monstrous tsunami developed with fifty-foot-waves that quickly rushed ashore, moved inland, and decimated everything. Homes, beaches and property were destroyed. New information continues to arrive as we speak and we are still waiting to hear from our reporters on the ground in the affected areas.

"Very mysteriously, a hurricane developed, carrying the same force winds, and slammed into the state of South Carolina only minutes later. The strong winds and heavy rains struck unsuspecting residential neighborhoods and destroyed homes, buildings, and property. It devastated most of the coastline and left behind hundreds of casualties, billions of dollars in damages, and an untold number of families homeless.

"Reports are coming in from Johnstown, Pennsylvania, that heavy rain storms suddenly developed and flooded local rivers. The unusual amount of water that poured into the rivers a few miles upstream from the South Fork Dam caused it to burst, sending a twenty-foot tsunami-like torrent of water into the valley below. It also left hundreds dead, many others homeless and the city in ruins."

Even Song looked shaken by this long recitation of tragedy, but she managed to pull herself together and turn back to Dr. Bogatir.

"Dr. Bogatir, is there any relationship between this developing black hole in the sky and this sudden massive, tragic shift in the Earth's weather patterns?"

The scientist's constantly shifting eyes roamed upward in his head. "Obviously the swirling motion created by the black hole is having an effect on the Earth's weather patterns, and unless the black hole dissipates, there is no denying it, we can expect more of these types of events."

***

I went to the hotel bar to get fabulously drunk.

On the way back to the hotel we saw the quarter-size black hole perched high in the sky. It has a hollow looking trail of slow moving circular cloud appearing, like a developing tornado, to be rotating and funneling toward the Earth.

"Guess we won't be in Kansas anymore," I muttered into the bottom of my fifth scotch and soda.

We'd driven by a local park and had seen a crowd of people gathered around a minister who stood on a park table and preached to the crowd, with the ominous black funnel tunneling toward the Earth as a dramatic back-drop.

"This is a sign from God! It's a message to the world! It's the end for all sinners!" The minister shouted. "In the Hebrew language this is called 'Sulam Yaakov.' We know it simply as

'Jacob's Ladder.' If you open your bibles to the Book of Genesis, chapter 28, verse 12, we read that Jacob had a dream in which he saw a ladder set on the Earth. Its top reached heaven, and the angels of God were ascending and descending down to the Earth on it. The angels of God are ready to descend and lay God's righteous wrath on the sinners of the world."

"Wonder what he thinks is going to happen to all the righteous people," Amir muttered.

I couldn't help wondering. The best scientists around the world had already determined that this thing is a very dangerous black hole that will suck in the Earth and everything on it, and yet here we have preachers calling it Jacob's Ladder, a stairway to heaven.

"I hope he's right," I said, nodding toward the preacher. "Then at least some people will survive."

"Anodder 'un," I said to the bartender, showing him my empty glass. He looked at me as if to gauge how close I was to passing out and apparently decided I'd stand a few more rounds. I got the feeling he normally wouldn't serve anyone as drunk as me, but thought the end of the world warranted an exception. He poured me a paltry single.

"Pffft. Gi' me 'at. I'll d' it." I grabbed the bottle. "Charge 't to ma 'um."

I managed to get off the stool without falling and headed unsteadily for my room, the bottle clutched tightly in my hand. Nellie stepped out of the elevator just as I reached it.

"Jesus, Cole. What the hell happened to you?"

"End 'a th' w'rld," I managed. "Didn y' 'ear?"

"I heard. And yet, the boss still wants us at work tomorrow."

I waved the bottle. "'uck 'em."

"Easy there, agent. Let me have that."

I took a long swig and eyed Nellie suspiciously, but figured it was unforgivably selfish not to share when we'd all be sucked into oblivion soon enough. "ere."

I pushed the bottle into his hand. Nellie took it, set it down, and draped one of my arms across his shoulders as if he was afraid I was going to fall down.

"Okay, agent," he said. "Let's go."

36

During the night strong winds and rain caused huge waves in the waters on Puget Sound and violently pounded windows on the mansion. Trees leaned dangerously, limbs occasionally reaching the ground. Thick lightning bolts flickered through clouds and thunder rumbled.

Carla lay in bed listening to the bellowing sounds of the turbulent weather, howling against the sides of the mansion and wondering if she and Julian would ever make it off the island alive. Her mind filled with sorrow and she said a silent prayer. The swaying trees violently shadowed her room and she got out of bed to close the curtains. Suddenly her foot met a hard surface and she tripped and fell to the floor. She glanced down to see what had caused her fall. A small ceramic figurine of a young girl playing a violin had been hidden behind the long dark curtains.

It's so pretty, she thought to herself. Astonished by its beauty, she picked it up and looked it over. It was almost a foot high and surprisingly heavy for such a delicate looking object. Carla cradled it to her chest and picked herself up off the floor. She continued to close the curtains, sat the figurine on the nightstand, and returned to bed.

Dr. Martu must have gone somewhere. I haven't seen him or Abdul all day. She was glad. She wasn't sure what she was going to do, but she knew she had to do something. The longer they were held here against their will the angrier she became, a fact that Martu's absence did nothing to abate. She wasn't able to fully comprehend the motivation of this man.

He had enormous wealth, professional respect, and all the trappings of a good life. And yet he did nothing but meticulously maneuver and manipulate the people around him.

She hadn't known how exhausting fear and anger were before now. And she also knew she would be unable to sleep two minutes in this place after all that had transpired, but still at this moment she felt herself slipping toward sleep.

***

He quietly slid the key into the lock on the private bedroom. He felt impending satisfaction inside himself when he turned the door handle and it opened. The fresh scent of the female fragrance in the dark room filled his senses as he stepped inside. He closed the door behind him and stood still as his eyes adjusted to the darkness in the room. He admired the curvy figure that lay on the bed before him. He placed his index finger on his chin and took a moment to consider how his presence would be received.

Would she fight him? She seemed brave enough, but females were notoriously weak. It wouldn't take much to overpower her. Still, she might scream and wake the servants. That wouldn't be good. No, that wouldn't be a very good situation at all.

Should he knock her out? One hard punch should do it, but he really didn't want to hurt her, and it would be a pity to damage her lovely face.

Drug her? He seemed to like this idea best and turned and left the room. He returned moments later carrying a small rag and a bottle of clear liquid. He poured some on the rag, capped the bottle, and set both on a table beside the door. He shrugged out of his jacket, picked up the rag and walked over to the bed. The girl's face turned toward him in her sleep.

He clapped the rag firmly over her nose and mouth. Her eyes flew open and her hands shoved and slapped at him. He straddled the struggling girl and pinned her down.

"Shhh, shhh," he said. "Stop now. You want to see your boyfriend again, just relax."

Her huge green eyes gazed up at him in terror, but she stopped struggling.

"That's right. That's a good girl." He smiled. "Just breathe in, sweetheart. That's it. You'll just be taking a little nap, no need to concern yourself..."

Her chest rose and fell, rose and fell, and the big green eyes began to unfocus.

"That's right," he whispered. Another second or two, and she'd be out for hours. His hand holding the rag over her nose and mouth relaxed.

The girl heaved under him and twisted violently. At first he thought she only meant to throw him off and barely had time to register the object she seized from the nightstand before she slammed it against his head.

***

The man squealed like a pig and fell back. Carla managed to sit up and clobbered him again, careless of the porcelain cutting into her hand. Shards of the delicate figurine scattered across the floor.

Blood poured down her attacker's face from his lacerated scalp. He reached for her with a bellow of rage. Carla shoved him, hard, and he tumbled to the floor. His body jerked once with a sickening crack and fell still. A horrible stench rose from the floor.

Carla stumbled into the hallway and gagged for fresh air. Waves of dizziness washed over her. Her body felt numb, sluggish, and she had to fight to drag air into her lungs.

Don't pass out. Don't pass out. Not now, she told herself firmly. She concentrated on taking deep breaths to clear the anesthesia from her lungs.

She wasn't sure how long she stayed there, but the next thing she knew she was on her knees, slouched against the wall, feeling vaguely confused about how she got there, but otherwise clear headed. She could feel her hands and feet again, so she shoved herself to her feet and made her way downstairs. She ran through the dining room and out into the storm. It plastered her clothes to her body in the few seconds it took to reach the outer door and pull it open. She re-traced the route she'd taken the day before and paused only momentarily when she reached Julian's floor to scan the corridor ahead for any signs of movement. It was quiet.

When she was sure the coast was clear, she got up and ran to Julian's room. The desk across from his room was empty. She opened the door, ran in, and skidded to a halt.

The room was empty. From the dust covering the floor, it hadn't been used for years.

"Damn it. Where is Julian?" Carla asked herself after finding the room empty. This is the right room, I'm sure. "Julian, I need you. Where are you?"

Carla covered her mouth with one hand. Her eyes surveyed the empty room from one side to the next. This looks like the same room. He didn't…Martu couldn't have killed Julian. He couldn't. Her eyes began to fill with tears.

Nothing was going right tonight. Carla gazed around the room. Maybe it wasn't the right one, after all. She turned and ran out of the room and to the next one. She grabbed at the metal pad-lock keeping the slide bolt shut and remembered seeing a bunch of keys resting on the counter top as she ran by, just a few feet away. She ran back to the counter, grabbed the keys, returned to the door and tried each key inside the lock. She heard the pin tumblers inside the lock turn and the lock opened. She slid the slide bolt back and pulled the door open. The stale odor of years of accumulated perspiration filled her senses. Her eyes narrowed and her heart filled with fear at the darkness before her.

"Hold it right there! Come no closer," a frail man's voice commanded.

Carla froze in her tracks. She stared at the old silver haired, bearded, man in the room. He sat on the floor of the room with a rock clutched in his withered hand. Carla couldn't see it all clearly, but she was sure, there appeared to be rows and rows of tally marks etched into the floor.

"Who are you?" Carla asked, shocked to find an old man locked behind the door.

Her eyes surveyed the small space. She saw no windows, only a small square wooden frame for a bed, with what appeared to be an old wool blanket atop.

"You don't know who I am?" the man asked. He blinked and leaned closer to the door.

"No. I don't know who you are."

"I've not seen you before," He said. "You don't look like the rest."

"I'm Carla Cole. I'm a prisoner here, being held here against my will. I am searching for my boyfriend. He is also a prisoner here, and I thought he may have been in this room. Now I'm afraid they have done something with him."

The old man sensed her sincerity. "I am Doctor Joshua Martu, the rightful owner of this island and I have been a prisoner here in my own home for more than ten years. The man who holds you prisoner is a very dangerous terrorist; he goes by the name of Prince Ahmad. He is the son of a relative of the last prince of Persia. He is a very wealthy man and he has powerful friends in high places all around the world. You can't defeat him. He is too powerful. I know. I have tried for the past ten years," said the old man. Shadows ringed his tired gray eyes. Deep eagle claws sank deep around his eyes and mouth. His long silver beard and hair were matted with dirt, and he smelled like he hadn't taken a shower in ten years. "Ahmad was a patient of mine and I had invited him here ten years ago as a part of his treatment. I thought the rest and relaxation would do him good. A few days later many strange men showed up here. They took everything I owned and Ahmad assumed my identity. He had a plastic surgeon perform plastic surgery on his face to make him look more like me and he learned the basics of my profession. I am afraid his efforts were successful. I have been a prisoner in my own home ever since. He has successfully pretended to be me for ten years. I had no wife or children, only my profession, so it was fairly easy for him to get away with it."

Carla's facial expression suddenly changed to a more cunning look. Her brows narrowed and her eyes stared at the old man. So this is the real Dr. Martu. That would explain some things around here.

"Well, not anymore," she said. "I know we can't make it off this island by ourselves, but people will be coming for me. Soon. When they do, I'll come back for you. Until then we'll have to pretend we never met, but I won't forget you."

The old man had no confidence left that escape was even possible. He shrugged. "Okay, go right ahead. Good luck."

Carla was struck in the face by a bright beam of light as she closed the door and turned around.

"Hold it right there," the voice said.

Carla dropped the keys at her feet.

"Ms. Cole, you've been a bad girl," Ms. Adiba said.

Carla blocked the worst of the glare from the flashlight and was able to make out the nurse's stocky form. The woman held a flashlight in one hand and a pistol in the other.

"The servant's heard the ruckus in your room and the subsequent footsteps racing down the hall. We've been look- ing for you for some time now. You better come with me," Ms. Adiba ordered.

"What have you done with Julian?" Carla demanded be- fore she remembered that the woman had a hand gun pointed at her chest, she was a prisoner, and was in no position to de- mand anything.

"Nothing," Adiba said shortly. "Mr. DePaul is fine, Ms. Cole. He is on one level up. You went too far down or you would have seen him. Now let's go."

Thank God.

"Where're we going?" Carla asked politely.

"Back to your room. We don't want the prince…Doctor Martu…to think we didn't take good care of his guest while he was away. He'll be returning in the morning."

You mean the murderous terrorist Prince Ahmad…I just met the real Dr. Martu. He is being held prisoner in the dungeon of his own house. Carla thought to herself.

"What do you intend to do with Julian and I?"

"Nothing. Keep walking, Ms. Cole." Ms. Adiba nudged Carla in the back with the pistol.

It dawned on Carla that the hand gun Ms. Adiba had aimed at her back had to be unusually heavy for a woman to hold in one hand for such a long length of time, but this woman seemed to be very experienced with the weapon. She has been toting it without even a flinch or a hint of hesitation.

Carla didn't like to think about what that might mean.

When they arrived back at her room Ms. Adiba switched on the lights. Carla goggled.

Where is the body? Where is the shattered figurine? Carla wondered.

"We had to clean up the mess, Ms. Cole," Ms. Adiba said.

Carla walked over to the spot on the floor where the man's body had fallen. "Who was he?"

"Someone who should not have been here," Ms. Adiba said crisply. "Have a good night's sleep. There will be much to talk about in the morning."

37

The only thing worse than the end of the world was a painful hang-over that made you sorry it hadn't ended while you were passed out.

The names of dead men pulsed through my head with every beat of my heart. I could actually see them, etched in black and red inside my skull, letters quivering with every lub-dub.

Che-ney. May-weather. Harr-ison. Roll-ins. Ben-net. Ther-ion.

We didn't know Therion was dead, so I felt including his name was unfair. My brain responded by adding a question mark.

Ther-ion?

What was the connection? I couldn't get a consistent pattern to fit them all. Everything I came up with had an exception.

Che-ney. Ther-ion? Harr-ison. May-weather. All at Princeton around the same time. Cheney and Therion were even friends, and then worked together for the Treasury. But neither Therion nor Harrison had any connection to Mayweather. Senator Rollins and Bennett had gone to different schools.

Che-ney. Ther-ion? Harr-ison. Roll-ins. Ben-nett. All worked at the capitol. But not Mayweather.

Che-ney. Harr-ison. Ben-nett. All cabinet members, but Rollins, Mayweather and Therion were not.

Well, technically Therion was a cabinet member, since he'd been appointed, even if he hadn't been confirmed or served a single day.

Che-ney. Dead in Olympia.

May-weather. Dead in New Jersey.

Ther-ion? Missing in Virginia.

Harr-ison. Dead in D.C.

Roll-ins. Dead in D.C.

Ben-nett. Dead in D.C.

All of the bodies had been found exactly where each man had died, except Therion's. His was missing. Could he possibly still be alive?

Cheney and Therion. Believed in the occult, even to the extent of practicing it, considering the altar in Therion's apartment, but not so for any of the other victims.

"Hey, Cole. You alive, buddy? Morris wants us at head-quarters."

I pried one eyelid open to find Nellie peering down at me.

"Where am I?" I groaned. The sound of my own voice had me clutching my head.

"Planet Earth. Welcome back."

I didn't feel very welcome. In fact, I felt like I'd been turned inside out and my head was ten sizes too big for my body.

"Ugh," I managed. It occurred to me I was also acutely uncomfortable and raised my head enough to realize I was sprawled on a bathroom floor. I didn't smell very good, and neither did the bathroom. "How'd I get here?"

"It's where I dragged you after you crawled out of your bottle of scotch," Nellie said. "It seemed like the easiest place to clean up after you came to."

Considering the stench coming off my clothes, he was probably right. I tried to sit up and felt my head rock off my shoulders.

"Easy, buddy." Nellie steadied me. "Here drink this."

I didn't know what was in the glass he handed me, but experience told me no one made hang-over cures better than Jason Nelson, and it was best to get it down as fast as possible. I drained the glass in three gulps.

"Good man," Nellie said. "Now get cleaned up. We need to be at headquarters in forty minutes."

***

Dr. Miller of the CDC had called during the night. I expected bad news, but she surprised me.

"Officer Bailey is out of danger," Dr. Miller said. "He's recovering fine. It took us a while but we finally got to the bottom of the problem. He was infected by organisms that feed on decaying matter. These organisms are the same that feed on dead tissue. When they entered Officer Bailey's system through the small cut that he had on his finger, they mixed with his blood, rejuvenated and began to feed on his living tissue. Once it got into his blood stream, it moved fast, but we found a way to counteract it. Officer Bailey will survive and we have a way of dealing with these organisms. The drawback is that Bailey will suffer some small permanent side effects. Tissues were damaged and they can't be repaired. But he'll live."

"That's great news," I said. "Thanks, Dr. Miller."

No sooner did I hang up than my phone rang again. It was Captain Brownlow, of the Olympia PD. Apparently her detectives had been able to talk to the Weinstein kid and asked him if he had been looking out his window the night that Secretary Cheney was killed. What, if anything, did he see?

Brownlow's detectives got the boy's story from his hospital bed. He was recovering from serious injuries but he was well enough to talk about what he saw. The family didn't want their son to be reminded of the dog attack, and they had bad feelings about the boy talking to the police, but they allowed it.

Captain Brownlow read the report to me over the phone:

"'I was in my room looking at the lights on the boats passing by on the water out back on the Sound, and then I heard the dog begin to bark. I didn't know where the dog came from. I looked over to the secretary's house and the lights started going on and off in the office, and I saw a big man in the room. He did something but I couldn't see what he did. I heard the dog keep barking outside and I was looking to see where the dog was because I know the secretary didn't have a dog. Then the man came outside and he looked at me and I was scared. It was like his eyes were right in front of my face; they were big and red—like a monster. I was looking through my binoculars. I moved back from the window because he scared me. Then I heard the dog running closer and closer to my room, and then all of a sudden he just jumped through the window and into my room. I called for my mother and father and the dog began to bite me, and he kept on biting me and it hurt. I was crying and I tried to get away but I couldn't. It was too big for me and then I heard my mother calling me and then she came into the room and scared the dog away.'"

"A monster, huh?" I repeated. Amir looked up from the notes he was making.

"That's what the kid said, word for word," Brownlow said.

"Okay. Thanks, captain."

Click.

I started to fill Amir in on the latest updates when my phone rang yet again. I rolled my eyes and checked the screen to see if it was important. The caller ID read: Davis, so I answered it.

"Agent Cole, it's Dr. Davis. I took a look at the crime scene photos and the list of objects you sent me. I can't be sure, but it looks like some kind of summoning ritual."

"Summoning ritual?" I repeated. Across the room, Amir's jaw dropped. "For what?"

"Well, in medieval times, magicians used rituals like this to summon spirits and force them to do favors in return for being freed again. But whoever attempted this ritual was clearly an amateur, because he got several things wrong."

"Wrong?" I frowned. "Like what?"

"Well, it doesn't look as if he did a spell of protection, which nearly all magicians did in order to keep the spirits they summoned from turning on them," Dr. Davis said. "But I did see what looks like several protective amulets in the storage locker, so maybe the practitioner was wearing one of those, instead."

"An amulet? Like, something that is supposed to keep the spirit away?"

"That's right. Since spirits were considered malicious, magicians often made charms to protect themselves or family members. These looked like they were made out of paper, with charms written on them."

I caught sight of the notes Amir had been making. He'd listed the victims in order of death or disappearance, like I usually did, but since he was sitting across the table, I read them upside down.

"Shit!" I nearly jumped out of my skin. To do favors. "Oh, shit!"

"Excuse me? Agent Cole?" Dr. Davis said.

"Sorry, Dr. Davis, I have to go." I snapped the phone shut and grabbed a pen. I crossed out the names Mayweather, Therion, and Rollins on Amir's list.

Mayweather was ancient history. Rollins was incidental. Therion wasn't dead.

Without them, the Secretary of the Treasury, the Secretary of State, and the President pro tempore of the Senate had all been murdered, in exactly that order.

The bastard was killing the successors to the president.

Who is next? Who's third in line? I desperately searched my memory. I'd learned the line of presidential succession a long time ago and didn't have the luxury to be mistaken.

"Speaker of the House," Amir said. Once he'd seen what I'd done to the list, he understood the sequence immediately. "He'll go for the Speaker of the House next."

***

I drove like a madman while Amir barked orders into his phone.

"I don't care what it sounds like," Amir snapped. "Just do it."

I understood his frustration. I'd called the Chief of Security, Wayne Cannon, before we left. Cannon was a former D.C., cop turned secret service before becoming chief of security, and told him about the suspicious deaths, their high stations in the chain of presidential succession, the missing family heirloom, and our hunch that we believe the Speaker of the House would be the next victim.

Cannon asked, "Exactly what do you need me to do?"

"I need you to double the security for the Speaker, day and night. Spread cops around her and tell them to keep a sharp look out for strangely dressed characters."

"Okay. You got it," Cannon replied.

"Now, this next piece is going to sound strange," I said.

"What do you mean, 'strange'?" Cannon asked.

"Well, uh...I've got a bad feeling about this," I said.

"What's up, Agent Cole? Level with me," he asked.

"I don't think bullets will stop this killer," I admitted.

"Well, how are the guards supposed to protect the Speaker?"

"Uh, okay, you're going to think this is nuts, but remember this killer turns his victims into mummies. Real, ancient, no-shitting-you mummies. You don't want to get near it. Get the Speaker out of the area as quickly as possible if it shows up."

"Okay. So how the hell are we supposed to stop this thing?"

"The guards need to get themselves a protection amulet, like protection from evil demons type of stuff. I know where to get one for the Speaker. Make sure she wears it. I don't care what you have to tell her. I don't even know if it's worth a shit. No one knows very much about this killer, and we're not sure how to fight against it. But there's a chance these amulets will, at least, slow it down."

"You've got to be effing kidding me. You're telling me that I'm to look grown men in their eyes and tell them that they need to go out and get themselves some kind of paper shield against this killer, because their bullets aren't going to kill it?"

"I'm telling you that we need to protect the Speaker. How you do it, I don't care." I remembered something else found in Therion's closet. "And tell the guards to go to the nearest catholic church and dip their bullets in holy water before they fire them at this killer. Because their bullets are not even going to tickle this thing, much less stop it. That's what I'm trying to tell you."

"We'll see about that," Cannon said. "If anything so much as sneezes too close to the Speaker, its ass is history."

"Your ball game. Your rules," I said.

"Leave this son-of-a-bitch to us," Cannon said.

Amir's eyebrows had nearly disappeared into his hairline by the time I hung up. "Cole, no one is going to listen to you if you try to tell them that we believe some magical symbol or amulet is going to keep them from being killed by this thing, or that we believe the killer is an ancient demon from the past."

"I agree. So we aren't going to tell them. We're going to get the amulets and try to get them as close to the potential victims as possible until we figure out how to stop this thing."

"How is that going to work?" Amir asked.

"I don't know. At this point anything is worth a try."

At the moment, "anything" was getting to Therion's apartment, grabbing the protective amulets, and yanking them over the targeted cabinet member's heads with our own hands if we had to.

Amir snapped his phone shut in disgust. "They think I'm crazy."

"Better for us to be crazy than for more people to be dead," I said. "So what do you think it wants? The killer?"

"I'm not sure if this is about what the killer wants," Amir said. "Think about it. Therion summoned the thing. It started with Secretary Cheney's killing and then it moved up to everyone above him in the line for the presidency, except for Senator Rollins. I bet that was just incidental. It needed to assume his identity to gain access to the senate chamber. That was its only reason for killing Rollins. It could have easily been any other senator."

"And if Therion is still alive, he's the new Secretary of the Treasury. If the killer gets the Speaker, the VP, and the Pres, then Therion becomes president." I shook my head. "You think Therion is actually making this thing kill other cabinet members?"

"Possibly, but I don't think so. From what we've read, it seems like whoever does the ritual better be pretty damn specific about what they ask for," Amir said grimly. "Since Therion screwed the ritual up, I'm guessing he wasn't that specific about his request, either. It seems like that leaves the thing he summoned free to interpret the request any way it wants, plus able to turn around and bite him in the ass."

"So let's assume Therion wanted to be president," I said. "He's ambitious, fine. I get it. But what does the killer get out of it? Why does the killer care who is president?"

"Maybe it needs something," Amir said. "Something only a president can give it. A president in this day and age is like a king in ancient times."

Something came back to me from the letter Rebecca had faxed us.

As for the creature it controls, and this above all else: never, never set it free.

"It's not the presidency," I said. "Or rather, not just the presidency. This killer needs a president who possesses the Seal of Solomon. I think it's trying to free itself."

Amir nodded slowly. "And if it can't control who has the Seal..."

"...it can control who becomes president," I finished.

38

Speaker of the House Melanie Crawford had always been an attractive brunette and now at forty-six years old she is still a thing of beauty to the men in her age group. Men her age admired her greatly: the soft delicate tone in her voice, the attractive style of clothing she wears, her well-groomed hair styles, her firm body, her polished manners, are all desirables that many eligible men in her age group admire about her.

She didn't feel threatened at all by the recent events. She didn't see herself as a possible target, and anyway she had her own group of professionally trained security guards, that her husband hired to protect her, patrolling her very secluded, high security residence. It is also located within an already heavily guarded gated community. She felt at home and well protected. The election cycle was fast approaching, and the confident democrat had publicly stated: "This is an election season, and I will not be influenced or controlled by the wide variety of intimidation and scare tactics employed by republicans."

She'd just kissed her husband good-bye at the end of an already busy morning. He would be heading to work after dropping off some things at the local post office, so she had most of the day to work undisturbed at home. She poured herself a fresh cup of coffee and headed for her home office.

She felt the draft the moment she entered the office.

Did I leave a window open? Melanie surveyed the room and found the third window was not only open, it was smashed. Broken glass littered the carpet. She began looking around for a rock or something that could have been thrown through the window and broken it.

And why had her husband left his shoes in her office? She caught sight of them behind the curtain on the far side of the office, and then her eyes followed what she thought were shoes up the tall frame of the stranger with the big round owl-like eyes standing behind her curtain. He appeared to be studying her as though she were a biological specimen under a microscope.

She froze. "Who are you? What do you want here?"

Azazel stood still and his eyes continued to examine her anatomy. It was different than the others, he knew.

Melanie couldn't look away. Her fear faded.

"You are experiencing an erotic moment. Remove your robes," Azazel said. His eyes glowed bright red.

"Yes, it is hot in here," she answered. She reached up and loosened the knot of thick hair at her nape and let it fall to her shoulders. Her body felt flushed, almost feverish. She lowered her head slightly and looked at him through seductive eyes. She unbuttoned her robe and spread it wide.

Azazel's eyes roamed over her slender waist, firm hips and back up to her firm breasts. Melanie dropped the robe from her shoulders.

Azazel moved in close and violated her sanctuary.

Melanie Crawford lost consciousness and had no idea what was occurring. She never regained her consciousness.

***

"Where is Dr. Sherrington?" Ahmad asked as he returned from his brief trip to Belize and did not find his sleep study specialist waiting for him.

"He is dead," Ms. Adiba answered.

Momentary silence and an atmosphere of fear filled the room. Ahmad slowly rose to his feet. "What?"

"There was a scuffle in Ms. Cole's room and he was found dead on her floor," Ms. Adiba said.

"Where is Ms. Cole now?" he asked.

"She is in her room." Ms. Adiba answered.

"What happened?" Ahmad asked.

Adiba looked uncomfortable. "Ms. Cole said she was asleep in her room and it appears Dr. Sherrington visited her in the night. There was a struggle. She pushed him, and he fell and broke his neck."

"I left strict instructions that our guests were not to be harmed," Ahmad shouted. "Get me Ms. Cole."

***

Carla was filled with anxiety after hearing the chopper arrive and landed on the halo pad. She saw the shadow under the door before the knock.

"Ms. Cole?"

"Yes. Who is it?"

"Ms. Adiba. Dr. Martu has requested your presence."

Carla's hands shook and her nerves twitched under her skin at the thought of seeing Ahmad. The last thing she wanted was to see or hear him speak.

"I'm...I'm not dressed yet," Carla lied. "Just a minute."

Is he going to kill me? I didn't mean to kill that man. He just fell. I mean, I pushed him, and he fell, but it was dark and I was scared. Surely...Carla shook her head and pulled herself together. Ahmad is a mass-murdering terrorist. There's no way he'll listen to reason if she tried to explain? The man chops off people's heads and throws them off cliff-faces.

"Ms. Cole," Adiba called impatiently.

"I'm coming," Carla said. She smoothed her hair and her clothes and tried to look as calm as possible before opening the door. She clung tighter and tighter to her mask of calm as Ms. Adiba led her to Ahmad's study.

"Ah, Ms. Cole. I trust that you are well?" Ahmad said genially.

"I am, thank you," Carla replied.

"Please, sit down. Have some coffee." Ahmad gestured to a chair across from him and the golden coffee service on the table between.

Carla hesitated. Did he intend to poison her?

Ahmad added sugar to his cup and stirred it with a tiny golden spoon. He noticed her hesitation and smiled. "It is alright, Ms. Cole. I do not intend to harm you. As you can see, I am unarmed."

She didn't see a weapon, that was true, but that didn't mean he didn't have one. Carla's eyes tracked to the coffee service. Ahmad noticed and deliberately took a swallow from

283

his cup. Slowly, Carla crossed the room and perched stiffly on the edge of the chair.

"Now," Ahmad said conversationally. "Please tell me why you have killed my sleep specialist."

Carla jerked. "Your—Dr. Sherrington? That was him?"

"You did not know?" Ahmad raised his eyebrows slightly.

Carla shook her head. "No. It was dark. I was asleep in my room when a man attacked me. He held something over my nose and mouth, something that smelled sickeningly sweet. He said..." Carla swallowed. "He told me to relax if I wanted to see Julian again. That I was just going to take a little nap. I was scared. I hit him with a little statue I found and put on the nightstand. He fell off the bed and didn't move."

Ahmad's dark eyes studied her calmly. "That is a most honest recitation, Ms. Cole. I have seen the surveillance tape from your room of last night. I find your forthrightness very refreshing. The world is full of liars, as you know."

"You—you're not angry?" Carla blinked. "I mean—because I—"

"A man in my country who tries such things suffers far worse than a broken neck." Ahmad's lips tightened. "What is more, Sherrington abused my hospitality by attempting such a thing. While you may not wish it, you are a guest in my home, Ms. Cole. A man who cannot protect his own guests is not worthy of respect. I cannot countenance such things. If you had not killed him, rest assured that I would. I am master in my own house."

Except it isn't your house, Carla thought, but she wisely kept her mouth shut.

284

"However, Dr. Sherrington was a valuable member of my staff. He will be difficult to replace." Ahmad sighed. "I hope you will forgive my curiosity, Ms. Cole. How does it feel, to become a murderer?"

"A murderer?" Carla repeated blankly.

"Yes. Sherrington did die, and you did kill him. Is this not murder?"

"It was self-defense," Carla stuttered. "He could have killed me. He certainly would have raped me. I defended myself, and I'd do it again if I had to."

"Yes, yes." Ahmad waved this away. "What one person says is self-defense, another can say is murder. It only depends on one's perspective. My people fight day and night to regain their freedom. Israelis call this murder. We call it self-defense. So you see, in so short a time, you and I have become so much alike."

A hot flush of rage washed over her. "We are nothing alike."

"We have both fought off those who wished us harm and humiliation. We have both killed to preserve our lives. In time, I think the world will find my actions no more unnecessary than yours."

"That will never happen," Carla snapped. "No one will ever think what you're planning is anything except evil."

Her anger seemed to amuse him. "No, Ms. Cole, I believe it is only a matter of time. Time will exonerate me. Time will change the balance of power in the world once I have completed my work here. Time is the key, Ms. Cole. I read somewhere that long ago, in ancient times, there were only days and nights, and one day someone placed an object into the ground and it cast a shadow. This became known as a gnomon, and

they used it to identity the time of day. This object placed in
the ground aided man to begin to identify how much daylight
was left before the sun went down and darkness fell. Then,
over the passage of many days and nights the practice spread
and was expanded and led to the invention of the sundial.
Prior to this time there was no way for anyone to keep records
of anyone's whereabouts during the days or nights. Then the
people began to make surfaces and put symbols on then and
watched the shadow travel away from the sun on the surfaces
and then the markings developed into representations for the
hours in a day. This primitive act by ancient people of watching a shadow move in the opposite direction of the sun was
the beginning of the recording of time. It dates back to 1500
BC and was used by ancient Egyptians, Romans and Greeks.
They even made devices small enough to carry around with
them, small sundials that eventually led to the invention of
the watch many years later. Time, Ms. Cole, changes things. I
once heard that it really doesn't even exist. Time as we know
it is manmade and only used to control human actions, to aid
the profiteers in their quest for more profits: to keep track of
how many hours in a day a person spends on the job, to know
how much a person should be paid for their day's work. That's
all it is good for, Ms. Cole. I think a very famous scientist by
the name of Albert Einstein was the first to state that fact, and
then he went on to prove it in his theory of relativity. Now,
just yesterday you were an innocent little girl. Today you are
a murderer."

"It wasn't murder!" Carla screamed.

"What if I was to turn Dr. Sherrington's body over to
the authorities and have Ms. Adiba say she saw you hit him
over the head and kill him? Without the surveillance tape, it

is merely your word against Adiba's, and I assure you, she is a very good liar. You would be a wanted woman, Ms. Cole, and your reputation would be ruined for life."

"No! You are mad," Carla shouted.

"You see, Ms. Cole, you are not much different than I am, because once that information got out to the public, even if you were found innocent in a court of law, there would be many people who would doubt your innocence. They would say you are guilty of the crime, you got away with murder. There always are. This cloud of darkness would follow you for the rest of your life."

"Oh God...no." Carla's eyes filled with tears.

"Time, Ms. Cole, does not seem to be your ally at the moment," he continued. "You are a fighter, I can see that. I respect that. Dr. Sherrington was wrong. He should not have entered your room in the middle of the night, and he reaped his just reward. I am going to allow you to live, Carla. Now, tomorrow I am expecting company and I will need you to be on your best behavior. Can you promise me that you'll behave yourself?"

Carla clinched her fists tight.

"Yes, Dr. Martu. You won't have any more trouble from me," she forced herself to say.

***

The evening headlines screamed: "WHAT HAP-
PENED TO SPEAKER MELANIE CRAWFORD?"

The entire country was in an uproar. Religious fanat-
ics surfaced, and some reparable scientists joined in and said,
"The world is coming to an end. Jacob's ladder had appeared
high in the sky. The signs are there for all to see."

The public seemed to agree. On the news reports, in
newspapers, and everywhere the people looked, they seemed
to see signs: hurricanes, earthquakes, tsunamis, the black
hole. Pastors, ministers, priests, and scholars linked the recent
events as being in line with biblical prophecy.

***

"This is Song So-Yong, reporting for CNN. Good evening. The President and Vice President are under tight security at undisclosed locations and would not comment. Many of
these reports sound too apocalyptic to be believed, but many
scientists around the world are cautioning their governments
to be prepared for more large scale natural disasters. And in a
recent press release, Geological Survey Scientist Denise Wil-
liams said, 'Atmospheric temperatures are rising faster than
at any time in the past. This condition creates more volatile
patterns in the weather. No one can say for sure, but there is
a high chance due to these atmospheric temperature increases
that momentous changes are taking place."

39

Brute Therion slumped in his chair. The bindings cut into his flesh, but he no longer paid them any attention. He heard a door open and close somewhere and raised his head, listening to the footsteps as they progressed closer through the darkness around him.

The beast entered the chamber, wings curled tightly behind its back. It fed the undulating symbol and stared at its transformation.

"You have been lucky, my king," Azazel's ancient voice echoed through the darkness. "You know your world, Therion. You have lived in it always, and never felt its lack. I have never seen mine."

The creature turned. "I did not ask for this, I am the ruler of my own world, and yet I am trapped here as a never-ending punishment."

"What did you do?"

Azazel sneered. "I was great. So great that lesser men, jealous men, tried to destroy me. Long ago my mortal soul was combined with immortal symbols, the seal of the king and the alchemical symbols representing Earth and air. I was chained to the Earth's natural elements." A feral smile stole across Azazel's face. "This was meant to be my prison. What my enemies did not expect is that they made me immortal and placed the power of their own world in my hands. My connection to the elements of your world gives me power to control the wind, the seas, even the stars in the universe in which you live, Therion."

Then what could he possibly need from me? Therion wondered.

"I possess more power than any king, and yet, I need you." Azazel's gaze flicked over Therion with undisguised contempt. "But understand this. If you do not give me what I need, I will not only rip your tormented soul from your living body, but I will send your soul to purgatory to wander in darkness forever, and you will know that it was I who punished you, after a thousand years of suffering have passed."

Oh my God, how do I save myself from this beast? Therion thought.

Azazel snorted. "No need to ask God to interfere, Therion. He won't hear you. I know."

40

"Come on, come on," I muttered as the phone droned in my ear. Trees flashed by the window as the SUV hurtled through the night. Amir's fists clenched so tightly on the steering wheel that I could see the white of his knuckles from the passenger seat. He stared grimly straight ahead.

We'd been too late to save Melanie Crawford. We prayed we wouldn't be too late to save the vice president.

It had taken hours to convince the secret service to divulge the locations of the president and vice president. We were currently en route to the vice president, since Amir and I couldn't trust anyone to make sure the amulets were worn.

Almost anyone, that is. Nellie had met us at Therion's apartment after I called him. He hadn't wasted time asking questions, just listened as I looped one amulet over his head and shoved another into his hand.

"You have to get this to the president," I told him. "Make sure he wears it if you have to take out a dozen secret service agents personally and tie it around his neck yourself. I don't care what it takes. Don't let him take it off. You either, Nellie. Don't take this off, no matter what."

Questions had raced behind Nellie's eyes, but he merely nodded and took off.

I had an amulet tucked inside my shirt, as did Amir. Three more were in my suit pocket; I patted their outlines through my jacket to make sure they were still there.

Getting out of D.C., had been a nightmare. A massive hurricane was scheduled to make land-fall by tomorrow night and the streets were packed with people trying to leave the city.

I glanced at the clock on the dash-board. Twenty minutes to the vice president's location. Maybe fifteen, considering the way Amir was driving.

I dialed the private line again. I wanted to let them know we were on our way so we didn't have to waste time explaining who we were when we got there. Seconds counted here, and I wanted to hit the ground running.

As before, I got nothing but a busy signal. Powerful winds from the approaching storm had knocked out several cellular towers in the capital earlier in the day. Apparently service wasn't any better out here.

I heard Amir muttering something under his breath. It took me a few seconds to decipher it as the Lord's Prayer. After several seconds more, I started to say it with him.

***

It was a windy, moonless night high above the subterranean bunker where the vice president and his family were under heavy guard. At the entrance to the family quarters a guard stumbled, as did his partner; they were startled and surprised for the first time all night.

"Shine your light over there," one guard said to his partner.

The light cut through the darkness, but didn't reach far enough to see what his partner had wanted to see.

"Something moved," one guard said to the other.

"No, it's only a shadow from the trees," his partner answered.

"Wait…it looks like…well, maybe you're right."

***

The vice president couldn't settle. He roamed the restricted spaces restlessly.

"Sir, we have guards outside patrolling the grounds. Please try to relax," an interior guard said, as he tried to calm the VP.

"Of course. You're right." The vice president exhaled and tried to relax.

"I can't stand this." His wife, Maggie, stormed into the sitting room." I need to go outside and get a breath of fresh air. I feel walled up in here. I'm getting claustrophobic."

"Honey, you can't right now. It's not safe. I know you're frustrated with this arrangement," the VP said, as he took one of his wife's hands into the palm of his and gazed into her eyes.

"We have armed guards all around us, I've never been safer," she said. "Anyway, I don't care. I can't stand another minute down here."

Maggie grabbed her coat with her free hand, yanked her arm away and opened the door.

***

The children, seven year old Margret and four year old Joey, heard their mother scream.

"Come on, Joey," Margret said as she took her brother's hand. "We'll hide under the bed. The boogieman is coming."

***

The inside guard fell to the floor in agonizing pain as his flesh burned from the inside out. Maggie stumbled back and tripped, twisting her ankle as she fell. Azazel leaped over the dead guard and pinned her to the floor.

"Get away from her!" the VP shouted. His eyes widened from the horrifying sight of the gruesome creature atop his wife, with a reddish glow in big owl-like eyes, body like a gorilla and wings like an angel.

"I came for you," Azazel said and sprang in the air, knocking the vice president to the floor with his huge wings and landed on top of him. The vice president knew, in his heart, this was the end. He inhaled the fragrance of his wife's perfume for the last time, as it bellowed out from Azazel's palm, as the creature's gruesome hand passed over his nose, enroute to separating his heavenly soul from his human body.

***

The first shots rang out moments later as Azazel's shadow raced across the grounds as he flew over the area on his way out. Security guards ran for the residence, passing mummified bodies of slain guards along the way, to find the vice president's and his wife's bodies lying in repose—mummified.

***

Azazel no longer unlocked the door to the subterranean dwelling when he returned. His immortal supernatural ability allowed him to pass through it with ease. He entered the dark room and stood directly before the shifting symbol. He released the captured souls of the humans he had recently killed, into the symbol's center, and he inhaled deeply and took in the dark underworld's foul odor that fumigated the air. The gate nearly open, awaited his entry. The spherical dark hollow had nearly joined with the Earth, a mysterious tunnel almost ready for transport to the unknown world.

In planetariums around the world people were astonished at the sight of the strange developing phenomena. Sky watchers began to gather around observatories to view the monumental black hole reaching toward the Earth. Scientists feared the worst—the end of the world. Ministers and priests around the globe preached repentance, speaking of Jacob's dream of the ladder set up on the Earth, its top reaching heaven, angels ascending and descending to Earth. Now, they said, Christians can also ascend up the ladder. The Rapture will occur. The saints will soon be removed from the Earth. The signs were clear.

***

Amazed at the supernatural transformation of the symbol on the wall before his eyes, Brute Therion asked, "What the hell is that?"

Azazel's thin lips smiled. His eyes glowed. "This is the passageway to my world, Therion." His gargoyle-like face filled with satisfaction, lion-like teeth glared, his angelic wings spread wide.

His captive forced the next question, "How is this possible?"

"You have no idea of the power of the Seal of Solomon, Therion." Azazel answered.

"Where does this power come from?" Therion asked.

"The ring you wear on your finger is not of this world. It was given to King Solomon, three-thousand-years ago, by an angel. It is not a ring at all. It is more properly called a Seal."

"This Seal has the power to open doors to other worlds?"

"No! Not quite. The Seal is connected to the elements of Earth, Air, Fire and Water; so too, it is connected to the heavens from which it came. It is the key that unlocks the gate, opens the doorway, but the soul of man is necessary for the creation of the passageway, and to pass through the gate. I told you in the beginning that God created man from the dust of the Earth, and breathed life into him. Man became a soul. When the body of man dies, the breath that God breathed into him escapes from the lifeless body. The body returns to the dust of the Earth, it returns to the place from which it came. So too, the breath of God returns to the place from which it came, the breath returns to God. The breath of God never dies. By capturing the breath of God, as it escapes man's dying body, and using the Seal of Solomon and combining it with the natural elements of Earth, Air, Fire and Water, the passageway to undiscovered dimensions are opened. As the breath of God travels its path back to God, follow the soul on this pathway, Therion," Azazel said. "No soul can return to Earth after traveling this route. It is known as death in your world, but it is the doorway to mine."

"I see. So what is it that you need from me?" Therion asked.

"I will tell you now, Therion, because when I next return you will give it to me, and I will travel to my world. Only one soul remains, Therion, one soul stands in our way, to complete my task. I will have his soul tonight. He alone stands in your path to be the king, and even if your own people do not recognize you as their king, you and I, and all the angels in heaven will know that you are," Azazel said. "When I return, you will, of your own free will, pass from your hand to mine the Seal of Solomon. I will need it for safe passage to my world, and when I reach my world I will need it to gain control over the opposing forces that I will encounter. The original purpose of the Seal, the reason it was given to King Solomon, was to give the king the power to control opposing forces. The Seal of Solomon is a powerful tool in any world, Therion. It will establish me as the true king in my world."

"That's it?" Therion goggled. "You want the ring? Take it! I'll give it to you now, just let me go!"

"Foolish Therion, you cannot give it now," Azazel sneered. "A mere man cannot rightfully give such a thing. How little you know! Men can steal this Seal, as a little piece of metal. Men can cheat to get it, kill for it, take money for it, but none of these things can release the true power of the Seal. This power cannot be stolen or sold; it can only be given. And as the Seal was given to a king, only a king can rightfully give it."

41

"Damn it! God damn it!" Amir kicked the file cabinet one more time but it didn't look as if it made him feel any better. I'd tried it myself earlier, but it hadn't made me feel any better, either.

"Nellie's got the president covered," I reminded him. "That's something. That thing can't get the president right now, so we have a little time to try to figure something else out."

"Like what?" Amir snarled. "How to kill a demon? How to plug a black hole? How to keep the whole world from coming to a god-damned end?"

I had to admit that when a spook lost his cool, it was impressive. The look on Amir's face when we got back to headquarters had other agents scurrying out of his way, and the stream of profanity he released the moment we reached the office could have blistered a drill sergeant's ears.

Amir ran either out of breath or out of imagination and broke off. He glared at the filing cabinet but refrained from further abuse. After several seconds he turned away and sank into the chair behind his desk. He ran his fingers through his shellacked hair several times, making it stand on end.

"We've missed something," he said at last.

"Like what?"

"I don't know. Something's nagging at me. My gut says we missed something at Therion's."

"We've gone over that apartment with a fine tooth comb."

"Not the apartment, the house." Amir frowned. "I can't explain it. I just have this hunch."

"But we've been through the house already. The local P.D. went through it days before we got there, too," I said. "What do you think we missed?"

"I'm not sure. But how did the dog get from Cheney's house in Olympia to Therion's house in Virginia? It's the same dog. We already confirmed that. It just doesn't make any sense."

"Nothing about this case makes any sense," I said. "What do you think we'll find? A jet plane?"

Amir shot me a dirty look. "Don't be an ass. I just have a feeling that we missed something there. Don't you ever follow hunches?"

"Okay, point taken. Let's assume that you're right," I said. "If we missed it the first time, how are we going to find it the second time?"

Amir rubbed his chin. "We have to look deeper now. I think the dog may have been living at Therion's. Maybe even without Therion's knowledge because Therion spent most of his time at his apartment in D.C., that's all. I want to have a better look around on that property."

Amir called CIA headquarters and asked them to look up the floor plans on Therion's home. When was it built, by who, and if there was anything else about this house that we may have missed.

***

It didn't take the CIA very long before we got our answer.

"Cole, bingo," Amir said. "Here's what we missed the first time around at Therion's."

He spread construction plans out on his desk. "During the senior Therion's term as Secretary of Defense, the United States and Soviet Union were involved in a nuclear arms race called the Cold War. The Soviets were as strong as ever, and Therion's father feared the worse. As a security precaution, he had had a bomb shelter built beneath his home that could withstand a nuclear explosion and keep his family safe. It was equipped with generators, artificial air producing equipment, several food storage freezers and had multiple entrances and exits. It consisted of several rooms and was built a hundred meters down with unidirectional corridors that lead to many fully furnished chambers. A few years after the Cold War ended he converted the underground space and made it into a Masonic lodge. He had it decorated with architectural designs and symbols similar to those said to be in King Solomon's Temple. Some rooms were decorated with ceilings that contained paintings of astronomical designs all depicting King Solomon's temple, floors made of checkered black and white tiles, and ancient Masonic symbols."

Amir placed several photographs of a stern-looking man on top of the blue-prints. "The former Defense Secretary was a strong believer in Masonic teachings. He was a devoted Mason, a student of the craft. Since he was a child growing up, his own father had made sure he learned certain things about the Masonic order. His office at the pentagon was filled with Masonic symbols, pictures and paintings. One of his most admired pictures was a picture of George Washington wearing a Masonic apron. He believed that our system of government was founded on principles from the Masonic craft, by Freemasons. Therion's father felt that the Masons lacked the respect and recognition it deserved in modern day society. He felt that the basic principles found in the Masonic craft were the early stages of democracy and lead to the electoral system of government that developed in America. As proof, he referenced nineteen of the fifty-six men who signed the Declaration of Independence had close ties to the Freemasons or later became a Freemason, and twenty-eight of the forty who signed the Constitution were Freemasons or later became members. Of the seventy-four generals in the Continental Army, almost half were Masons. The first ever Attorney-General of the US, Edmund Randolph, was a Mason, and so was the first Secretary of State and Chief Justice of the US Supreme Court, John Marshal."

"And these rooms beneath the house were never sealed?" I asked.

"No."

"We have to get back there."

***

I called Captain St. Peter and informed him that we were on our way back to Virginia. At the same time Amir was on his cell talking with his superiors at CIA headquarters in Langley, Virginia. They informed him that an air travel restriction warning had been issued. Bogatir announced that the black hole had expanded and its swirling tornado-like configuration was having dramatic effects on the earth's weather. Hurricane conditions had already grounded almost all air traffic on the northeastern sea-board, and air travel over Virginia was virtually impossible. After a great deal of arguing, it was agreed that our chopper would travel from D.C., to Virginia at a reduced altitude and we would need to land elsewhere and drive back to Therion's.

The black hole no longer appeared like a tiny pin hole against the moon in the night sky. It had expanded and now appeared the size of a basketball, still growing and now clearly visible to the naked eye.

Further information passed on by CIA headquarters concerned entities known as "Devils."

"Are you going through some kind of weird training exercise?" CIA Agent Milo asked Amir, after Amir officially requested information on the subject. "Demons and devils? It's a training exercise, right?"

Amir knew we couldn't tell anyone what we really thought was happening in the case, and the current world events were anything but a joking matter. What Amir had witnessed over this past week had changed everything he believed in his entire life. The events of this case had opened his eyes to the invisible dark world of the supernatural.

"Yes, Milo," Amir said, closing his eyes and wishing is really was only a training event. "It's a training event."

"Hey, I got some information on that guy you've been chasing," Milo said. "U.N. troops raided a house on Friday and believe they just missed him. He was in Belize."

"Shit. What? What the hell was he doing in Belize?" Amir asked.

"It appeared that there was a high level terrorist meeting at a safe-house in Belize City and your guy was there. The U.N. thinks they just missed him. They got their information from one of their reliable inside informants," Milo said.

"This guy is supposed to be in the state of Washington and he traveled to Belize for a damn meeting and we didn't grab him?" Amir asked.

"Yeah, he's slippery. He has lots of supporters and we still don't know exactly what he looks like. We're checking all the flight manifests between Belize and the US now. But these kinds of guys are smart. They don't usually fly straight to their destinations; they'll stop at other places along the way and disguise their real destination," Milo said.

"Shit," Amir said.

"Well, the boss wants to know if you think he has anything to do with the murders of the cabinet members?"

"Don't know that yet. We're moving forward and getting closer, but we can't be sure exactly who's behind it yet," Amir said.

"Okay. I'll let the boss know," Milo said.

Click.

***

It wasn't like Carla not to call me back. I knew cell service had gotten spotty, but I should have heard back from her by now. I left her another message and promised myself I'd send a black-and-white to check on her if I didn't hear back by morning. I knew talking to her wouldn't change the fate of the world, and I didn't have any last words she needed to hear—I just wanted to hear my daughter's voice.

I closed my cell phone to find Amir staring thoughtfully at his own. He didn't move for several seconds.

"Hey." I nudged him with my foot. "You okay?"

"Cole, did I tell you why I became a CIA agent?" Amir asked.

"No. Tell me."

"Both my parents were agents. They met on an assignment in the Philippines and they fell in love and got married. Many years later, when I was very young, they were on an undercover assignment in Greece. They had served all over the world—in Pakistan, Iraq, Iran, Cuba, Greece and the Philippines. They were specialists on terrorist activities in foreign counties and they were good at it. They were a good team, among the best. They had good covers. My mother was a world class photographer. Many of her photos were published in magazines all over the world. She collected photographic intel. My dad was an intelligence analyst. He analyzed information, collected the messages and the hard evidence and sent them back to the agency. There were of course times when they spent months without seeing each other, when they were in different parts of the world gathering their information.

"One day my mother called my father while they were in Greece.

"'I've got something going on that we didn't expect,' she said.

"I know this from the CIA files on the case that I was allowed to review many years later.

Back then electronic surveillance wasn't as common as it is now and my mother had no idea that terrorist may have been monitoring conversations of foreigners in the country. Her telephone line had been tapped.

"'What's going on?' my dad asked.

"'There's an Iranian ship that arrived in Greece a couple weeks ago. It's filled with oil, and they're changing its appearance to look like a Greek vessel.'

"'What?' my father asked.

"'I've been taking pictures of the ships in the harbor for weeks now. This ship has been sitting there for a week already, and its appearance has been slowly changing.'

"'Smuggling oil into the US from Iran and using the money to finance terrorist activities?'

"'This terrorist is smart,' my mother said. 'You need to come down here and take a look at this. I think we need to get this information back to headquarters before the ship leaves port so we can intercept it before it reaches its destination.'

"'I agree, I'm on my way,' my dad said.

"Later that night my father arrived and my parents snuggled up close. They kissed and talked, my mother told me the story too.

"'This guy has more contacts than anyone realized,' my dad said.

"'Who would suspect that he was smuggling oil from Iran, of all places, into different countries, even the US, and

306

using the money to fund his terrorist activities?' my mother asked.

"'I'd say no one,' my father answered. 'The entire intelligence community is going to have to rethink their area of focus when it comes to this terrorist.'

"'Yeah, he is too clever.'

"'Yeah, way too clever. And no one knows what he looks like or where he operates from.'

"'You know what, Bill?' my mother said to my father. 'This guy gives me the creeps. I told you this from the very beginning. I think it's time to get out of Greece.'

"'Honey, I don't think that we have anything to worry about. We have a good team of Greek agents here. They would let us know if our situation were compromised.'

"'I know. But there is just something about this guy that bothers me,' my mother said.

"My father held my mother and tried to comfort her. 'We're in the beautiful country of Greece. We asked to come here,' my father whispered.

"*Yeah, I know,* she thought. But now it's time to leave.

"The next morning it was 7 am. My father squatted on the beach on the tiny island of Tasos. A beautiful blue ocean spread wide to his front as he was setting up his mobile satellite dish. Not far from him, a young native boy appeared, with a fishing pole in one hand and a net in the other. Unaware of the boy's presence, my father continued to adjust his communications equipment and attempted to establish contact with headquarters back in the United States. My father's expression turned to total horror as he looked up and saw the boy standing over him with a loaded hand gun pointed at his head. I can only imagine his terror, knowing a boy was about to blow his head off. There was nowhere for my father to go, nowhere for him to run or hide. Afterwards, the boy walked away. My mother caught it all on film and kept it until she could send it safely to CIA headquarters.

"My mother had taken many photographs in her life, but these were very different. She knew she could never look at these; they were meant for someone else's eyes. One day her pictures would show the rest of America that her husband proudly gave his life for his country.

"Not long after, in a state of shock my mother panicked. She unloaded her camera and took the film to a post office and mailed it to CIA headquarters.

"A strange man approached her when she exited the post office.

"'I think you better come with me,' he said.

"She wanted to run. She wanted to scream. She wanted to kill him. But the gun he had sticking in her side convinced her otherwise.

"'I think your vacation in Greece is over,' he said.

"'Does this mean that I can return home and help my child with his homework?' she asked.

"'There's nothing that I'd like better,' the man answered.

"He escorted her back to her hotel room and guarded her while she packed her things. All the while her mind reflected on the vision of the boy holding the gun to my father's head and then pulling the trigger. Her eyes filled with tears and she expected the same to happen to her at any moment.

"Unexpectedly, the man took her to a secret location operated by the Greek secret police. They stayed there overnight, since there were no flights out of Greece until morning. They flew to Germany early the next day, where German authorities took charge of her. She stayed one night at a hotel in Frankfurt, guarded by German police. She was on the very next flight to the United States. By nightfall the next day she was back on American soil.

"My mother and I watched the sun sink below the ocean's edge in Belmar, New Jersey. She couldn't stop her tears from falling, nor could she resist my pleas to tell me what had happened to my father.

"With a glass of whisky in her hand, my mother relaxed on a lounge chair and told me the story. It was a cool night and the air was filled with the smell of salt. My eyes filled with tears as I sat with my mother and listened to her story of what happened to my father, re-living what she saw with her own two eyes.

"There my mother was, sitting on her lounge chair in the sand, by my side. I was happy to have her there with me, but I could feel the emptiness inside her, the loneliness of not having my father around. As it got darker and darker I remember seeing the moonlight glittering across the surface of the rushing water and I watched the glittering light entwine with every wave, every break of the water's edge. That night I convinced myself that one day I would find that boy. I would hold a gun to his head and look him in the face while I squeeze the trigger, just like he had done to my father. The only way I could do this was to become a CIA agent. That was all I ever wanted to do in my entire life."

A small, bemused smile touched Amir's lips as he looked at me. "Imagine my surprise when, all these years later, I tracked that same terrorist organization to Washington. It wasn't a single man smuggling oil into America; it was an entire organization. It was headed by a man named Abdul Hadad for almost thirty years. His nephew, Ahmad, replaced him in the early eighties. Last year I got a tip that a presidential cabinet member was funneling money to Ahmad's organization. It took awhile, but I had just tracked American funds from a Palestinian terrorist cell back to the U.S. Secretary of the Treasury when I heard of Cheney's death. Right away I thought it must have been a murder to keep Cheney from identifying the terrorist. That's why I got this assignment, Agent Cole. I was sure Ahmad was operating in the Washington area. I really wish I had been right."

42

Agent Jason Nelson fingered the folded square of paper in his pocket as he made his way through the heavily guarded complex. Director Morris had called ahead to smooth the path of his arrival, so no one detained him after inspecting his credentials.

Nelson had no idea why a tiny scrap of paper hardly bigger than a postage stamp was so important, but Cole had been adamant. In the twenty-plus years he'd known him, Cole had never done something without a good reason; if his partner wanted him to pin a paper badge to the president, he damn well would.

Getting the president to agree to it, however, presented a bit of a problem.

Nelson had been thinking over how to accomplish this without getting shot by the secret service all the way to the president's location and had a basic plan. He didn't know if it would work or not, but it was the best he could come up with, short of physically assaulting the leader of the free world.

Nelson stopped by the children's quarters first. The president's two young daughters sat at a table with crayons and construction paper. Neither one of them were coloring with any enthusiasm. Their faces looked pinched and worried.

"Hey girls," Nelson said with a smile. He nodded at the secret service agent lurking quietly in the back of the room. "My name's Jason. Can I come play with you for a bit?"

Both girls looked up with surprise, then suspicion.

"Everyone's too busy to play," said the older girl, Mallory. Nelson knew she was called Mallie by her parents. "Aren't you too busy?"

"I have a few minutes." Nelson crouched down by the table. "What are you making?"

"Nothing," Mallie said with a shrug. "We're just drawing."

"I bet this is pretty scary, huh?" Nelson said. "Getting up in the middle of the night, rushing out, hiding. I know I'd be scared."

"We want to go home," said the younger girl, Olivia. "We left our puppy there, and we miss him."

"You're going to see him really soon, I promise," Nelson said. "You know, when I was your age and I was scared, my uncle showed me a way that I could keep safe. He made it so nothing bad could hurt me."

The girls straightened up with interest.

"How?" Mallie demanded.

"It's magic," Nelson confided. "Look, I'll show you."

Nelson drew a piece of paper toward him and plucked a crayon out of the box. He drew several bold lines interspaced with a series of looping symbols.

"This is an old, Gypsy word for 'safety,'" Nelson said as he scrawled something he hoped looked convincingly ancient and magical. "And this is an old, old symbol that magicians from Persia used to keep bad things away. The king of Persia had it on a necklace he wore to keep him safe. Nothing could hurt him while he wore it. Nothing; not swords, or poisons, or snakes, or anything."

"Or anything?" Olivia repeated, eyes round.

"Or anything," Nelson assured her. "So, after we write the magic symbols, we fold the paper in a special way. Three times this way—see? Then three times this way, and three times this way, so it folds up just like this."

Nelson put the neatly folded square of paper in Olivia's hand.

"Then you keep it with you, and nothing can hurt you," he said.

"Cool," Mallie said. The girls marveled over the paper square for a moment. Then, Mallie sat back. "Can we try?"

"Sure." Nelson smiled. "You can use any color crayon you want, but the paper has to be white."

"Okay."

Both girls got to work. Within a few minutes, he was showing them how to fold their papers. Mallie got up from the table and ran over to the secret service agent.

"Look, Mr. Jim. It's a magic protector. It's for you," she said.

"Thank you, Miss Mallory." The agent took the paper very seriously and placed it in his vest pocket.

"We can make them for everybody!" Olivia cried and grabbed more paper. "Hurry, Mallie! We can make everyone protectors!"

Mallie ran back to the table and started to grab a paper, then hesitated and looked at the little square Nelson had folded. She looked at it for a moment, then pushed it into his hands. "You take that to Daddy. Your's the best. Make him wear it."

"I will," Nelson said solemnly.

43

Julian laid in the small room with all the sleep study monitors attached to his body—like a puppet on a string. A nurse monitored his brain waves from the desk across from the room, but he hadn't seen or heard Dr. Sherrington since last night.

He'd been here in this tiny room, with these damn cables dangling from his body, long enough; but he wasn't going anywhere without Carla.

He stared at the fly perched on the nearby wall and took stock of the situation.

What are we still doing here? He knew it was Carla's suggestion, he knew he would've never come on his own, but how had agreeing to take a simple test led to this?

He thought of Carla's face and her soft voice as he remembered her moving between their kitchen and TV room, chips, pretzels and drinks in hand. With both hands full she'd wait for him to take the chips and drinks and place them on the coffee table, she'd take a seat and snuggle up close, saying, "Keep me warm. What did I miss?"

A smile bloomed across his face as he remembered her softness against his body, warm and comforting, her fragrance, fresh and pleasant, her blonde hair occasionally obstructing his view…She'd talk too much, ask too many questions, and interrupt the TV program. He'd get mad at her and tell her to be quiet. She'd call him insensitive, but he'd eventually tell her what she wanted to know, soften up and snuggle close.

They'd end up making love, talking about marriage, kids and family. He'd remember that she was right there by his side and that TV is just a program, a way to pass time and they were supposed to be there for each other, beginning their life together.

He'd wait for her to get home at nights.

He'd cook dinner sometimes.

They'd eat and talk together.

Smile and laugh together.

She'd do the same, as well.

Now, he was here in a lonely room. She was by herself and afraid.

Dr. Martu told her about his personal business and now she's afraid of him. She's sitting upstairs, in her room scared to death of this man. There is nowhere for her to go. We are here in his house. This is not her home. We aren't being allowed to leave. I haven't seen outside these walls since we got here. I eat here, sleep here, I do everything here. Why? My nights are long and lonely. Why can't I see Carla?

"Martu is not who we think he is," she had said.

Who is he?

He stole our life together. We are apart. She has to sneak, run and hide to see me. Why?

What exactly is going on here? Carla and I are prisoners here.

Julian stared at the tiny fly perched high above him, seeming free to spread its wings and take flight at a moment's notice. The sight of the tiny insect revealed the painful truth. Its utter freedom pulled his own captivity into sharp focus and revealed the cagey character of his host. A bitter reality burned within him.

Martu's friendly gestures, soft spoken voice, and kind smile was nothing more than an elaborate façade, a mask, a cover for his true intentions.

Julian looked down at the cables connected to his body. He was no longer the confident young man who didn't want to be known as a freak, who cared about himself, his world, his freedom, his girlfriend and his safety. It was time to take his own life back into his own hands.

His mind filled—not with dreams, but with hatred: for Dr. Martu, and for his own ignorance and gullibility for agreeing to come to this island. For every moment Carla spent afraid.

This game is over.

***

Carla sat on the edge of the bed with her arms folded. On the west side of the island the glare of the sun had just began to disappear.

Ahmad the imposter is expecting company today and he doesn't want any trouble out of me. Well, he won't have any trouble out of me. But if that bitch shows herself her this evening I'm going to rip her eyes out and throw her off the balcony, just like she would have that damn madman do to me. Carla's fists clenched. Little does she know, I'm going to kick her ass. I'll fight my way out of here if I have to. I'm not going down without a fight. I'm not going to die that easy.

She brushed her hair back and knotted it at the nape of her neck, glaring at the door. It remained firmly shut with no sign of her nemesis. After several minutes more Carla grabbed a pillow and flung it across the room.

She was going crazy in here. Carla pulled back all the curtains and wished she could open a window for a breath of fresh air, despite the thunderheads piling up in the sky.

Poor Julian, down there by himself. Is he even still alive? I don't even know for sure. This could be it for us. Our final day alive. Now is Ahmad's demonstration, his final piece of the puzzle. He's a damn madman, a terrorist for God sake. A stone cold killer...shit! The real Dr. Martu is a prisoner in his own home, has been for 10 years...what the hell?

Carla reached for a few strings of her hair dangling off the side of her face and began to curl them between her fingers.

What are we going to do?

She heard the sound of rotary blades from a chopper as it reached the island. She peered out the window to see if she could get a glimpse of the men in the chopper, but her room faced the wrong way. The halo pad was on the north side of the mansion. Ahmad's guests were here.

Carla paced. Dad, where are you? Didn't you get my message?

It didn't matter. She was ready to fight to the death.

Finally Carla hopped up back on to the bed, crossed her legs and stayed there.

What to do? What to do? Shit.

These thoughts only worried her, so she focused on something better: getting her hands on Adiba.

Come on, bitch. Come and get me. I dare you.

***

Weather in Olympia grew steadily worse. Angry clouds filled the sky and boiled over St. Clare. Furious winds tore siding from the mansion and trees up by their roots. Monstrous thunder rumbled overhead and lightning ripped through the clouds. Explosions of thunder loud enough to be heard in Martu's subterranean laboratory rattled instruments off counter tops and trays.

Ahmad was furious. "Why isn't it raining? Abdul, what's happening up there? If I didn't know better I'd say we were in the eye of the storm, ourselves."

"I don't know, my prince," Abdul answered.

Ahmad whirled on the German fulminologist, Helmut Schlitz, and his assistant, Ivan Mihailov, as they peered at their monitors. "Well?"

"Soon, sir," Schlitz said.

Ahmad stripped off his coat and unbuttoned his collar. "Abdul, check the ventilation. It shouldn't be so warm in here."

Mihailov and Schlitz both wiped sweat off their faces.

Ahmad felt a trickle slide down his back. He knew everything was in place. His men had returned from the mountain a few hours ago and assured him the nuke had been planted in the mouth of the volcano, exactly at the coordinates the scientists had provided. He had checked and re-checked the calculations, instruments and equipment himself.

It was the damn Russians. That's why he was nervous. They had insisted on attending this major demonstration and he knew they were upstairs watching closely. Since they had invested heavily in his work he hadn't been able to refuse them, but it grated on his nerves. Instead of monitoring every inch of his project like he should, he would have to entertain and placate nervous investors instead.

"We're ready," Schlitz said.

Ahmad nodded briskly and made his way up to the ground floor. He stared at the towering edifice of Mount Rainier.

Rainier, the mother of all volcanoes. Better take a picture now. Tomorrow, she won't be half that size. She will rain down destruction on the greedy Americans and provide us with the final data we need.

44

"How are you doing, Ted?" Director Morris asked. The president shrugged in a way that seemed to take in the hidden safe-house, the four secret service agents in the room, the security prowling the grounds, and the howling storm outside. "I'm told a mouse can't move without being detected."

"Very good, sir," Morris said. He and the president had been friends for many years, and he didn't relish the news he brought. "Mr. President, I am sorry, but I have bad news."

The president paled. "Oh my God. No. Not Andy."

"I'm afraid so, sir. The vice president and his wife were killed earlier this evening."

"Are you sure?"

"Yes, sir."

"How?"

"The same as the others, sir." Morris watched his friend look away as tears filled his eyes.

"And the children?"

"They are safe," Morris said. "They were in another room."

The president cleared his throat. "They didn't—I mean—they didn't see their parents in that condition, did they?"

"No, sir. The children hid in their room until secret service agents came for them. They were taken out a separate entrance and didn't see anything. They have been taken to a child care service provider and not yet been told what has occurred. The vice president's brother is on his way from Virginia. He's aware of the situation and has stepped in as the children's guardian."

The president nodded slowly. "Andy was a good man, and his wife was a good woman. His children are left without their parents. He gave his life for his country. If we make it through this, I'll establish an education fund for their children. The VP was a true hero; it's the least we can do for his children...only the best. God bless their souls. He was a good friend."

"Yes, sir," Morris said. "I'm so very sorry, Ted."

"Thank you, Tom." The president sank into a chair. His fingers idly toyed with some kind of folded paper square hung around his neck as he stared out the window.

"What's that?" Morris asked, hoping to distract him.

The barest ghost of a smile crossed the president's face. "It's a magic charm. My girls' made it for me, to keep me safe."

"They're sweet," Morris said. "You're a good father."

"If it makes them feel better, then I'll wear it."

Morris saw the fatigue in the president's eyes and tried to think of how to ease his worry. Morris gazed out the near-by window, through the dark spaces, and saw the secret service cars strategically parked around the premises.

The residence was a solid brown brick farmhouse with a dense wood line that began beyond the six-foot-high steel privacy fence about fifty-yards from the house. It had a white wooden front porch, a double swing off on one side and a built-in pool in back with smaller brick buildings to its rear, including a changing room and storage for pool maintenance equipment.

The view from any window in the house had always been postcard perfect. But tonight anywhere he looked, Morris saw places where a killer could conceal himself. Still, he saw secret service personnel on their watch. They patrolled the perimeter of the property in pairs. Director Morris had already double checked the grounds around the property and run through emergency protocols with security.

"What does Agent Cole think is responsible for the death of the cabinet members?" the president asked suddenly.

"It's difficult to say, sir."

The president raised his head and looked directly into the FBI director's eyes. "Tell me what he thinks, Tom."

"He thinks it might be...supernatural. He just left by chopper for Virginia to try to find whatever is causing this."

"What do you think?"

Morris sighed. "I wish I knew."

***

A police cruiser cruised through the expensive neighborhood and pulled to a stop behind the black and white parked in front of Brute Therion's residence in Virginia.

"Dispatch arriving at the location now," Officer Richardson reported to his headquarters.

"Do you see the other officers on the scene?"

"They're parked right in front of us."

"They reported seeing movement in the rear of the house. Check it out."

"Roger."

"You heard the man. Let's go," Officer Richardson said to his partner, Officer Miller, sitting right beside him.

"Nice house," Miller said as he exited the vehicle. "Kind of odd that we are called out to check out shadows, though."

"Well, neighborhoods like this always gets the royal treatment, you know that. We'll just give it a once over. It looks peaceful enough."

The officers flicked on their flashlights and began their stroll around the side of the house. They didn't expect to see any lights on, since there wasn't supposed to be anyone home. Everything was dark and quiet. Normally they'd check doors and windows for any signs of tampering, but the house was bigger than they expected, so they limited themselves to a quick visual survey. As they reached the back of the house and turned the corner, the beam from one of their lights flickered over a mound farther out back, away from the house. It was a good size hump in the ground, about knee high, appearing like it might be some kind of bunker with its own rooftop. It was surrounded by taller trees and heavy vegetation.

"What's that over there?" Miller asked.

"Don't know. Let's check it out. What else do we have to do?" Richardson asked.

Slowing their stroll, they headed for the hump. They admired the spaciousness and beauty of the yard and imagined the pleasantness of having one like it for their own. They zipped up their jackets against the coolness of the night and the growing wind.

"HQ, this is Richardson. We're currently checking the secretary's property."

"Go ahead, Richardson."

"Everything's quiet. No signs of anything unusual."

"Got it," the dispatcher replied.

"Richardson, out." He clicked his radio off. They rounded the hump and found something they never expected to see: two pillars on either side of a steep incline that led down—like a driveway—to a closed door.

They flashed their lights over the pillars guarding the entrance. Boas was written on the base of one, and Jachin on the other.

Curious, they walked down the incline to the door, a solid slab of metal engraved with the images of a compass and a square directly below a large letter G centered within a circle.

Richardson looked at his partner. Miller shrugged.

Richardson tried the knob; it turned, and the door opened. The lights from their flashlights beamed into a long, dark corridor leading back toward the house.

"If I was out here by myself, I definitely wouldn't go in there," Miller said.

"Well you're not out here by yourself, and I still don't want to go in there," Richardson replied. They stood there for several minutes, playing their lights over the peculiar writings and images etched into the walls, before Richardson sighed and drew himself up straight. "All right. Man-up, officer."

"You first," Miller said.

Richardson rolled his eyes but led the way down the corridor. They tried to move quietly, without making a sound; since no one is supposed to be here, if they found anyone down here, they had to be considered an intruder.

They reached a door that they suspected led directly into the basement beneath the main house, since they had been traveling down the long corridor for quite a while. The door was unlocked and they opened it and wondered if someone had been working down there.

"Hello? Is anyone here?" Officer Richardson shouted.

"Here!" they heard a voice answer from a room up ahead of them. "In here! I'm in here!"

They hurried toward the voice and found another door. It was unlocked, too, and opened easily.

The officers froze in their tracks.

"What the...?" Officer Miller mumbled.

"Oh my God," Richardson breathed.

The monster glared at them, angelic wings spread wide from the grotesque body. Reddish light glowed from big round eyes and gleamed from its lion-like teeth.

Totally horrified at the beast before their eyes, both men fell to their knees. Richardson tried to reach for the radio on his belt.

He never reached it.

Taser-like pain shot through their bodies. Their muscles twitched, seized, and they fell forward, mummified even before they could close their eyes.

***

After Director Morris left, the president and his family went upstairs and prepared for bed. Two guards stayed in the house on the first floor and the rest of the secret service personnel continued to patrol the property.

The president couldn't stop thinking about his VP. Thoughts of his friend filled his heart and mind, and he knew he would not soon fall asleep.

For a few hours he laid in bed with his eyes open and thought of the terrible situation the country was in, but as time passed slowly he became so mentally exhausted that he couldn't keep himself from drifting off to sleep.

In the wee hours of the morning, the president's eyes popped open. He stared blankly into the pitch-blackness around him. He read the time on the digital clock on the night stand beside him: 12:59.

He'd thought he heard a loud thump, like something heavy landing on the floor, but couldn't be sure that he didn't hear it in his dream.

The president laid there and listened. He heard the sound of the wind whipping by his window. He had always liked the sound of the wind, especially when it was accompanied by rain. He always felt refreshed the next morning after sleeping through rainy nights. Now he listened to the familiar, soothing sound of the wind and wished it would stop so he could hear more clearly.

He had just convinced himself that the sound he had heard, that woke him from a deep sleep, was only his imagination when the window suddenly exploded inward with a wash of glass and sound. The curtains snapped and flared in the wind.

His wife screamed.

The president jumped out of bed, grabbed his wife's hand, and ran out of the bedroom. Their daughters appeared in the hallways as two secret service agents came running up the stairs.

"Downstairs! Now, sir!" the guards said as they pushed past and into the president's bedroom. More secret service men ran into the house through the front door and rushed the First Family out of the house and into an SUV that was parked at the front door. The vehicle peeled off, followed by several SUVs just like it.

Mallie and Olivia were sobbing.

"It's okay, girls," the president tried to calm them. "It's okay. I'm fine, see? I'm just fine. See here? I have your lucky charm. I never took it off."

**

Azazel's huge menacing figure, with gargoyle-like face, lion-like teeth, angel-like wings and reddish glow in his owl-like eyes, flew through the shattered window, landed inside the president's bedroom and vanished.

45

"What's taking them so long?" Officer Sims peered out the window of his patrol car. Richardson and Miller had been gone almost an hour. He picked up the radio on the front seat. "HQ, you got a location on Richardson and Miller?"

"Negative," the dispatcher replied. "You have a visual, Sims?"

"That's a negative," he answered. *Why do you think I'm calling you?*

"Think we should go look for them?" his partner, Officer James, asked.

"Hold on," the dispatcher said. "Captain says sit tight. He's on his way out there. Do not enter the residence. Repeat. Do not enter the residence."

"Will wait for the captain," Sims said. "Over."

He looked at his partner. "What do you think that's all about?"

Officer James stared at the house through puzzled eyes. It began to appear like an old haunted mansion. *What could have happened to Richardson and Miller? We didn't hear anything unusual.*

***

Captain St. Peter was there to meet us when the chopper finally landed. He filled us in on his missing officers on our way to Therion's residence and we briefed him on the new information we had about the chambers built beneath the house.

We met Officers Sims and James at the house. We all entered the house carefully and re-examined it room by room. As before, we found nothing, not even St. Peter's missing officers. We were just about to give up on the inside when there was a shout from Sims.

We found him kneeling on the wooden floor in an alcove on the first floor.

"I think there might be a door here, sir," Sims said.

St. Peter knelt beside him and ran his fingers over several deep scratches in the floor.

"Maybe, or maybe not," St. Peter said. "However, these marks appear formed more toward the wall. They don't appear to move enough away from it."

The captain began to push and tug on the wall around the scratches on the floor. Then I saw his eyes widen.

"What is it?" I asked.

"Come take a look at this."

My eyes widened when I saw what he saw.

"There's a small separation in the wall," I said.

"Exactly. We need to look around for some kind of handle, catch, or lever." St. Peter ran his hands over the wall down to the baseboard. Suddenly, something clicked; a door squeaked open slightly in the wall. It just popped out from the wall. St. Peter reached out and pulled it open.

"Will you look at that," Amir said. The secret door revealed a dark, winding staircase. "Let's see where this leads. Captain, we'll need some flashlights."

St. Peter nodded to Sims and James. They instantly snapped their flashlights off their belts and handed them over.

"You two stay here and guard the entrance," St. Peter told them. "The rest of us will go in."

The captain unclipped his own flashlight and stepped through the doorway. Amir and I followed.

"Careful captain," Amir said. "We don't know how stable these stairs are."

We wound down the hollow tunnel-like expanse of darkness, with only the shafts of light from our flashlights to guide us. A canopy of darkness quickly consumed us as we descended deeper and deeper. The illumination from our flashlights narrowed increasingly with our descent. The air grew progressively damp and stale. I was just starting to shiver when St. Peter's light rushed over something as we traveled further down.

"Wait," I said. "What was that?"

Our lights beamed on an elaborate painted picture on the wall, what appeared to be an Egyptian pillar. I started to remember something and flicked my light to the opposite wall; sure enough, a second pillar mirrored the first.

We reached the bottom of the stairs not long after and beams of light tunneled through the dark. We'd arrived in an empty room.

Strange drawings and writing covered the walls. One of them appearing to be a large circle with a point in its middle, to the right of which were the words: Circle of a lodge.

Below it was: The perfect points of entrance represented by four cardinal virtues.

"Those are Masonic virtues," Captain St. Peter said. "The pillars we saw must have been Boaz and Joachim. This is—or was—a Masonic lodge. I don't know if Therion is a Mason, but his father we know for sure clearly was."

"I take it you are, too," I said.

He smiled. "Can't say that I am."

"Over here," Amir shouted. He pointed his flashlight over the far wall, which read:

Ornaments of the lodge.

"Hey!" a voice called. "Help! Help me!"

We followed the voice through a series of rooms to find a man—tired and defeated—bound to a chair.

"Please, get me out of here," he said hoarsely. "It's coming back. It's never gone long."

"What isn't?" I helped St. Peter unknot the ropes. Brute Therion sagged forward.

"The monster. It's gone to get something for—that." He nodded toward the wall.

"Christ almighty, what is that?" St. Peter asked.

We stared at the intricate star-like design undulating on the wall. It appeared to be in constant, fluid motion—like waves in the ocean. A gaping maw floated in the center.

"It said it was a door," Therion croaked. "To another world. His world."

"Did it go in there?" Amir asked.

"I don't know where it went." Therion leaned on me as I helped him to stand. "What—why are you handcuffing me?" He asked.

"Mr. Secretary, I believe you are in possession of stolen property," I said, and yanked King Solomon's ring off his finger.

***

St. Peter put Therion in a patrol car and shut the door.

"I don't think we'll need to worry any longer, Cole. The ring is safe. The danger is over," Amir said.

"You know what bugs me?" I said. "That man is responsible for all the murders, if only from sheer idiocy, and he'll never serve a day for it. The most we can prosecute him for is theft. What jury is going to convict on the theory that a magic ring controlled a demon to do its master's bidding?"

"You're a fed." Amir shrugged. "You guys love finding evidence to convict people. You'll find a way."

46

I'd never been so glad to see a hotel room in my life. I sank into a battered chair, pulled several documents toward me, and sighed. All I had to do was finish entering in evidence, and it was case closed. I fished the last piece of evidence out of my coat pocket and laid it on the desk.

Cheney's ring. I hadn't dared to let anyone else handle it. I wanted this chunk of metal right where I could see it until I turned it over to my boss.

It looked innocuous now, like nothing more than a useless piece of old metal. After the trial it wouldn't be returned to Rebecca Cheney. Maybe it'd be melted down, but somehow I doubt that. It would probably be confiscated and locked away where it would never see the light of day again.

I started filling out forms and picked up the ring to get a closer look at it as I started the written physical description. I entered the time: 12:59 am.

A Seal of Solomon had also been in the Masonic lodge below Therion's mansion, although it had been far more elaborate than the one on the ring. The ring's seal seemed crude by comparison.

I remembered a curious Masonic passage that had been inscribed below the lodge's seal:

Truth is a divine attribute, and the foundation of every virtue. The first lesson we learn in Masonry is to be good and true. A duty incumbent on all men is to relieve the distressed, particularly those who are linked by a chain of sincere affection. Soothe the unhappiness, sympathize with another man's misfortunes, show compassion to another's miseries, and aim to mend their troubled minds and bring back the peace to their lives.

Heat rushed through my entire body while a tingling sensation skated down my spine. I closed my eyes and relished the peaceful relaxation that came over me.

"Sir?" the hotel's manager tapped at my door. "There's someone here to see you."

I didn't know the man who stepped into my room. He'd probably come to gather the last of my reports.

"I'm not quite done yet," I said. "Have a seat. I'll just be a moment."

The man bowed his head. "I have come to do your bidding, my king, and I have already begun the request."

King? Request? All at once my soul shriveled inside me. I found it now, a steady, faint heat on my finger.

I had put on the ring.

Think, Robert. Think. Think.

I wanted to reach for my weapon and blow his head off, but I knew better than that at the moment.

"Thank you," I said.

"Ah, my king. I am happy to be of service to you," the man responded.

"How will you fulfill my request?" What the hell was my request?

"I will relieve your distress. Keep you from misery."

"How am I distressed?"

The man studied me for a moment before reaching over and putting my cell phone in the middle of my desk.

"See for yourself, my king."

My eyes flicked momentarily to the phone display. I'd missed one call, but my voice mail was full. I dialed in my pin and listened.

"Carla, come in. Sit and eat. You must be hungry."

"Dr. Martu! How's Julian? Is he alright?"

"He's resting."

By the time I heard my daughter shriek, "You're just trying to keep us here, you murderer!" I was running.

***

At St. Clare two Palestinian guards had abandoned their post and were busy spying on something back toward the mansion. Waves rushed over the sand and slammed hard against the rocks below in a violent collision of water and mountain. Suddenly, a vibration of a different kind filtered through the air: the constant hum of rotary blades.

Martu's helicopter winged low over the mansion and circled back toward the halo pad. The guards didn't react in time and were caught in the chopper's back-draft. One of them stumbled backward and nearly went over the edge of the cliff. He scrambled at the edge as he fell and managed to catch himself.

"Shit, damn it, shit, hold on…" he said in Arabic, as he dangled from the top. His heart began to pound against his chest. "Don't let go…don't slip…"

His feet searched for a hold but couldn't find one. He'd have to use his arms to pull himself up. As he began to pull himself up with his arms, a sudden stinging pain rushed across his back with a sharp whack.

He looked up to find a monster leering down at him, holding a belt. His eyes opened wide as the beast brought it down a second time: whack! Then again: whack! The stinging pain loosened his grip. Tears filled his eyes and his nose filled with dust. He closed his eyes against the beast's menacing form—angelic wings spread wide, huge gorilla-like body perched above him on the cliff and lion's teeth grinning from its gargoyle face.

"Oh, almighty Allah! The devil has come for me! Save me!" he cried aloud, trying desperately to hang on to the edge of the cliff.

Whack! Whack! across his back and that was all he could bear. He lost his grip on the edge of the cliff and fell into empty space. Azazel spread his wings wide, swooped down and snatched him from his fall, ripped his soul out from his body and released his remains to tumble down the side of the mountain.

Bullets zinged by Azazel's head. He spread his wings and zoomed toward the mansion.

***

Ahmad's guests were no strangers to Washington. They felt at home there and had been there many times before. Russian oil tycoon Fidel Aleksandr's right hand man, Dmitry Dovyanko, and Palestinian underground leader Amro Falah had spent summer vacations there over the last few years. Both of them loved the tranquil island and knew of its history, possibly better than most of the people who lived there. They were very familiar with the island's rustic beauty and praised this secluded space that indents the upper most northwestern expanse of the state of Washington.

They heard the stories. They knew that in 1792 a European named Peter Puget and his expedition from British Vancouver arrived here. The city of Olympia was formed in 1840 as a result of two other pioneers, Levi Smith and Edmund Sylvester, who laid claim to this piece of land. The capital of the state of Washington had been given the name Olympia because of its proximity to the near-by Olympic Mountains that gracefully preside over its horizon.

Dovyanko and Falah are powerful men and very influential in their governments, have friends in high places around the world, millions of dollars at their disposal and a need for high personal security. While Ahmad's guards would have been capable of providing this security, they prefer to travel with their private body guards who, at the first sign of trouble, are prepared to usher them out of the area.

Early this morning the men assembled on the upper balcony of the mansion, furnished with high powered binoculars, scanning the huge volcano in the near distance. They took in the deep greenery and the presence of the towering mountain, Mount Rainier's imposing presence as it denominates the spacious horizon and seem to join with the sky.

Suddenly, out of the blue, the sound of automatic weapons barked out as a flying object zoomed toward the mansion where they were standing.

Still their eyes watched the approaching object through their powerful binoculars, taking in the huge beast with its wings folded back, zooming in fast. The click of chambered rounds rippled around them.

"Frightening," Dovyanko mumbled. "Are Ahmad's men shooting blanks at this thing? It flies through their bullets."

"Ahmad?" Falah shouted into the radio he held in one hand.

"Yes, what is it?" Ahmad answered.

"There is something strange flying around up here. It looks dangerous."

"My men will take care of it."

Ahmad's men continued to fire at the flying shadow as it zoomed toward the mansion.

"This maybe a good time to leave." Dovyanko glanced at Falah.

"Start the chopper," Falah said to the pilot standing nearby.

"We are leaving, Ahmad. We will have to see the demonstration at another time," Falah said.

Their body guards moved in and ushered the men through the double doors and down three separate sets of steep concrete stairs and out onto the halo pad.

The guards popped the chopper door open. Falah turned back to face the mansion. "I had hoped to see the amazing demonstration today, but it will have to wait."

He gave his radio to a mansion guard who had accompanied them to the chopper. "Give this to your boss."

Interior chopper lights flickered on.

"Ready to go?" the pilot asked.

"Yes! Go!" Falah ordered.

Rotary engines roared as the craft lifted off. Below, mansion guards scurried about firing bullets at the flying object while the departing visitors watched.

"We'll have to visit you some other time, Prince Ahmad," Falah said.

The chopper skimmed the rooftop and thundered toward the mainland.

Body guards on board drew their weapons, and aimed at the approaching flying object.

Azazel zoomed down and out of sight.

"What's happening?"

"I have no control," the pilot shouted frantically.

They felt the chopper rocket upwards. Its passengers peered out through the windows.

Azazel gripped the under surfaces of the craft and carried it upward—like the powerful menacing monster he is. Azazel pointed the nose of the craft down, toward the deep blue water below and zinged it downward.

The chopper exploded into huge flames as it slammed into the water below.

***

Mansion guards spread wide on the lawn continued to fire at the flying monster, to no avail.

"What is this thing? Bullets can't kill it," one very frustrated guard said to another, as he increasingly became discouraged with the ineffectiveness of his weapon against the monster. Their eyes had just bore witness to the powerful beast destruction of the chopper.

"It's the devil! He's came for our souls!" another guard shouted. "Run for your lives!"

The monster swept across the lawn, leaving only mummified remains behind. He landed on his cloven feet at the entrance to the mansion.

***

Julian had heard gunshots erupt outside, followed by blood-curdling screams. He didn't know what was happening, but he didn't intend to stick around to find out. He tore off all the sleep study machine cables and stuck his head out the door with every intention of shouting down the mansion until Martu took him to Carla, but found the corridor empty. The nurse who had been at the counter was gone; so were the guards.

What——? Another burst of gunfire prodded him into motion. He ran down the hallway and up the stairs at the far end, taking the steps two at a time. The main floor of the mansion was deserted, too. He didn't see a soul as he found his way back to Carla's guest room.

Where is she? Is she okay? Oh God, what if she's outside? Julian's heart jumped with every explosive-burst of gunfire that hissed and spat outside. He slid to a stop at what he was sure was Carla's door. Why is there a lock on her door?

"Carla!" Julian pounded on the door. "Carla! Are you in there?"

"Julian?" She saw his shadow move across the bottom of the door as he reached it from the other side. "Is that you? Are you okay?"

"I'm okay? You're the one locked in a room." Julian studied the lock: the padlock itself was fairly heavy-duty, but the hinge it kept closed wasn't. Better yet, the door opened away from him. "Get back from the door, Carla."

"What? Why?"

"Just do it." Julian waited until he heard her move away, then he heaved back and kicked the door down.

Carla looked at him in amazement. "Thank God. You made it."

"Let's go." He grabbed her hand and they fled.

47

Captain Brownlow briefed me as the Black Hawk lifted off. "St. Clare Island sits fifty miles off the coast of Solo Point. It's well protected by a force of armed guards that we believe were trained overseas and brought here specifically to protect the island. Consider them extremely dangerous, and take no unnecessary chances," she said.

Amir's eyes glanced mine. "Captain, I see only one helicopter. How are the rest of the men going to get to the island?" he asked.

"The men have already been briefed, Agent Bloomberg. Only the pilot, you, myself and Agent Cole will be flying in the helicopter. The rest of the men will travel to the island by boats. The boats will arrive at the island first, surround it, and engage the guards while we attack from the air. There are shot-guns on board for each of us. We fly in, land, and rush the building."

"Okay," Amir said.

"Once we're on the ground the officers on the boats will disembark and assault the residence as well. By then we should have located the hostages and be well on our way out of there. Each boat has trained medical personnel on board to provide medical assistance to anyone injured." She looked me straight in the eyes. "Try not to worry, Agent Cole. We'll get them back safe."

If they aren't already dead, that is. I swallowed hard. Carla had seen a murder. That alone gave her captors every reason to kill her. *Please let me get her back.*

***

"Come Julian follow me." Carla said as they ran down the stairs. "I know somewhere we can go." She remembered the vestibule she saw behind a door in the wall by the pool.

"I'm following." Julian replied. "Hurry, we've got to get down these stairs and out of the hallways."

Carla ran as quickly as she could and Julian followed her into the pool room and behind a door in the wall by the pool. They found themselves in an unfamiliar darkness and they wondered if they should descend the old wooden spiral stairway they discovered at the edge of the platform beneath their feet.

"Julian, we have to go down here," Carla said in the cramped lightless space.

"No. We should stay here, wait until it's clear and then find a way off the island."

"There are people trying to kill us up here. If we go this way maybe we can find another way out."

"But I can't see anything down there. We don't have a flashlight and I don't trust it," Julian said. "We shouldn't

343

have come here in the first place. This is all your fault. I never would have come here if it wasn't for you dragging me here."

"Julian it's too late for all that now, please…Please, I'm scared," Carla pleaded with him.

"It's too dark down there." Julian said.

"Julian."

"Okay. You lead the way."

"Okay, I'm going first, but hold my hand." Carla replied.

Carla began to walk down the wooden stairs with Julian close behind. She took one slow careful step at a time, with only the unknown eerie darkness around them. They slowly descended down through the pitch blackness, Carla became increasingly afraid, although she didn't want to show it.

"Julian, hold on tight. Don't let go," she whispered. He felt the slight tremble in her hand.

"I won't let go," he said.

After carefully traveling for ten minutes without see-ing the slightest glimmer of light, Carla began to have second thoughts. She swallowed hard.

"Maybe we need to turn around, Julian. I don't think there's anything down here," she whispered.

"I don't know, Carla. It's a long way back up. I think we better keep going now," he responded softly.

They continued down the old wooden stairs slowly, one step at a time, down deeper into what seemed like infinite darkness.

"Carla, maybe you're right. We should turn around now," Julian changed his mind, after they had traveled about another ten minutes down.

"No, Julian. No way. I don't want to be shot and I don't want you to be shot, either. I'm sure Martu and his men will kill us if they find us now. We know way too much about their activities, and Martu is not the real Dr. Martu. He's an imposter. I found the real Dr. Martu locked in a room on a lower level. I think we need to keep going," Carla said.

"But, we've been going down for a long time and it hasn't gotten us anywhere. Suppose we run out of air down here?" Julian asked.

"I don't think we will," Carla answered. "I have been down this far before. There is air down here. There is also a laboratory down here somewhere."

"Okay, but we need a flashlight to see where we're going," he said.

"My eyes are used to the darkness now. I can actually see a little bit now. Plus, where are we going to find a flashlight now?" she asked.

"I don't know," he answered.

The pure darkness and accompanying silence was maddening. Both were afraid but neither would say it. Julian thought what else could he do except to follow her. He had no other choice.

His mind began to play tricks on him and he began to see disturbing images of her beneath the water in the river. It tore through his heart and he held on to her tight. He wasn't going to lose sight of her again, even though he couldn't see her through the blackness. He felt a certain sense of duty to protect her, and at least right now he knew they were together, so he held on tight to the softness of her hand.

They reached the bottom of the wooden stairs and paused to catch their breath.

"Where are we?" Julian asked.

"I don't know," Carla whispered "But the stairs end here."

"Feel around on the walls for a door," Julian said. "Or a light switch."

Carla complied and they began to feel along the wall.

"Here it is…it feels like a door knob," Carla said.

"Can you turn it?"

"Yeah, it turns."

The door squeaked open and they entered another dark room and saw nothing, at first. Then they slowly began to make out shadows in the room: huge bubble shaped equipment and huge power cables.

"It looks like a storage room for electrical equipment," Julian said.

"Yeah, it does," Carla agreed. She saw the vast array of large copper coils, power cables, power transformers, huge ceramic moldings, hoses and connectors, and the cabinet along the wall with the huge nuts and bolts that were stored in the room.

"But why is all this equipment down this far in here?" Julian asked.

"There must be another door somewhere," Carla said.

"Okay, let's go have a look," Julian said.

They continued to hold hands as they walked around the huge equipment that laid scattered about the room. On the far side they searched along the wall for a door knob.

Julian felt something and said, "Here's a door."

He turned the knob, opened the door—and was astonished.

The room before them was an underground scientific laboratory, fully equipped with an array of consoles surrounding a huge glass tank in its center and with huge electrical apparatus hanging, high above, inside the glass tank.

"I've been here before," Carla said.

"Ah, come in. Our guests have arrived," Ahmad turned away from the monitor. The sight of him and sound of his voice sent bone tingling chills down Carla's back. And Julian felt her hand when it trembled. He hoped she didn't feel his.

"What's going on, Martu?" Julian asked. He moved Carla behind him, he took a step forward and he tried hard to conceal the tremble in his hands.

"Abdul, help our guests over here, where they can see our experiment," Ahmad ordered. "You're just in time to witness the eruption of Mount Rainier. Are we ready, Dr. Schlitz? Dr. Mihailov?" He faced the two men sitting at the counter, their eyes peered on the display of the huge volcano, snow-white against the backdrop of growing storm clouds.

"We have begun the final sequence." Dr. Schlitz pressed a button and a digital clock materialized on the screen and began ticking down from ten minutes.

"In ten minutes you will see Mount Rainier erupt and we will gather the final information needed to simulate a volcanic eruption anywhere in the world," Ahmad said.

Julian and Carla stepped forward, "Don't do this. Please don't do this. You'll kill a lot of people. There are people living all around that mountain," Carla shouted.

"Consider them casualties of war. They are expendable," Martu replied.

"Increase the power, Mr. Mihailov," Mr. Schlitz said. Mihailov slid a lever forward.

"Power is at maximum," Mihailov replied.

The temperature in the subterranean laboratory began to increase. The room gradually became hotter and hotter and the ground around the mansion began to rumble and shake intensely.

Julian and Carla had no choice, except to watch the experiment, Abdul stood over them with trained watchful eyes.

"This is the underground activity of a volcano before it erupts that you feel under your feet," Ahmad said. He laughed. "Abdul, when will the underwater explosives explode?"

Abdul checked his watch. "In 7 minutes, my prince."

The sound of the heavy machine gun fire outside echoed through the laboratory.

"What is that Abdul?" Ahmad asked. Abdul consulted several security monitors.

"The island is under attack, my prince. It looks like police boats. They are approaching from all directions."

"Prepare for emergency evacuation," Ahmad ordered. "If they should get too close."

"5 minutes," Dr. Schlitz shouted after checking his monitor.

"Abdul, are the guards holding up? Do we have 5 minutes?"

"Yes, my prince…but something else is going on as well."

"What is it?"

"I'm not sure."

The heavy gun fire continued to sound outside.

"Well, we are safe here for now," Ahmad said.

The door to the laboratory began to vibrate heavily just before it exploded inward. The force from the explosion blew everyone off their feet. The clock counting down on the monitor stopped. The building rumbled and shook with earthquake-like magnitude, the heat in the subterranean space became almost unbearable and a thick cloud of smoke bellowed in from the explosion.

Carla screamed.

Azazel's monstrous form emerged from the ruined doorway. Abdul was first to spring to his feet and reached for his weapon, but Azazel's hand punched through his chest and ripped out his heart.

Mihailov and Schlitz had tumbled off their chairs, rolled over on the floor, popped up onto their feet and fled through a back door.

Ahmad had been blown into the glass tank. He regained his feet and glared angrily at the huge creature slowly approaching him. He unsheathed his sword and dropped into a fighter's crouch. "I didn't know what you are or where you came from, but I'm about to send you back there in a million pieces."

Azazel stepped forward and entered the glass tank.

Carla suddenly remembered something.

"Julian, can you reach the tank and close the door?" she shouted after regaining her composure. The ground beneath her feet shook hard and the temperature continued to increase. She heard the building rattle around her, it threatened to cave in at any moment.

"Yeah, I think so," Julian replied.

"Do it, quickly, Julian," she shouted, as she reached the control console.

Julian rolled over, popped up onto his feet and ran to the tank and closed the door, sealing Ahmad and Azazel inside.

At the control console, Carla, swaying side to side with the rocking building, searched her memory for the correct switch.

Ahmad swung the sword at Azazel's chest, where the blade passed harmlessly though. The monster picked him up by the neck and squeezed his throat. Ahmad instantly felt the powerful strength of the monster's grip around his neck and the excruciating pain the beast inflected on him—he screamed.

"Almighty Allah!" His muffled voice only squeaked it was barely audible.

Carla pushed the button and the glass tank began to fill with the rushing water.

"What are you doing?" Julian asked, as he joined her at the console.

Carla reached for the power lever and pushed it forward. She grabbed some goggles and earplugs and shoved them into Julian's hands. "Cover your eyes and plug your ears."

"What? Why?"

Carla hastily squished foam into her ears and snatched up another pair of goggles. "Just do it!"

When the tank was half full with water Carla pressed the button and the water stopped flowing.

Ahmad's eyes bulged from their sockets and blood gushed from his mouth. There was a momentary calm as Azazel dropped Ahmad's body into the water with what looked like supreme satisfaction. He turned toward Carla and Julian just as the lightning struck.

"The destructive forces of Earth, Air, Fire and Water… no." Azazel shouted.

The monster's big owl-like eyes glowed deep red as its body burst into flames.

Carla and Julian ran for the door. In their minds they replayed the horrible sight as they ran for freedom, up the long flight of stairs.

"Wait, this way," Carla said.

"No! Carla, that's the wrong way. That's not the top," Julian said.

"We can't just leave him here," Carla said. She swung the door open and ran down the corridor, grabbed the keys off the counter and unlocked the door. "Dr. Martu?"

The old man looked up at her. "Yes?"

"Let's go. Julian, help him."

Julian grabbed the old man and helped him up. They moved as fast as they could up the stairs.

Below them, the laboratory rattled hard. The glass began to break around the tank. The floor cracked and fell away. Slowly, the building began to sink.

"Run faster!" Julian shouted. "Don't look back!"

"What?" Carla turned her head and saw a sink hole opening up below them. A dim fiery glow emerged from down below, and the air was suddenly scorching.

"Go! Go!" Julian screamed as he dragged Dr. Martu along.

They burst from the mansion as the walls began to tumble. A black chopper sat on the halo pad forty yards away, and...

"Dad!" Carla shouted. "Dad!"

***

"Come on!" I grabbed Carla's hand and pulled her after me, Julian and the old man at our heels. Brownlow had the door open and helped haul us in.

"Get us out of here!" Julian shouted. "Go! Go!"

Monstrous thundering sounds rattled the chopper as the ground beneath the chopper started to break apart. A hard jolt threw everyone to the floor, but then, like an answer to a prayer, the chopper lifted away and banked toward the ocean.

"Are you hurt?" I all but squeezed the life out of Carla. "Baby, are you okay?"

"I'm okay." She sniffled.

Turbulence rocked the chopper but we continued to pull away from the island. We looked back just in time to see St. Clare disappear in an explosion of lava. A rocky ridge emerged from the water around the island and sent clouds of steam roaring into the air.

"What is that?" Brownlow asked.

The ridge continued to thrust above the water. When a gust of wind cleared the steam momentarily, I realized it wasn't a ridge at all—it was a rim. A volcanic cone.

"Amazing," Amir said

"I've never seen anything like it," Captain Brownlow said.

Dark clouds covered the sky just above what we were all sure was a new volcano. The clouds rumbled and lightning flickered in a tantalizing show across the sky.

"I guess he was right," Carla said. "He could simulate the right atmospheric conditions for a volcanic eruption. But I bet he never considered the fact that he would create a huge volcano right under his own feet. Dad, this is the real Dr. Martu. The other guy was an imposter called Prince Ahmad."

Amir's eyes almost popped out of his head. "What did you say?"

"The guy that kidnapped us was a terrorist named Ahmad. He stole the identity of Dr. Martu, and made the real Martu a prisoner in his own home for more than ten years. He can tell you all about the terrorist."

"That is a story I would very much like to hear," Amir said with satisfaction.

***

Later in the undisclosed safe house the president received a phone call.

"Mr. President, this is Dr. Wilhelm Bogatir."

"Yes, Wilhelm. What is it?"

"Good news, sir. I can't explain it, but the black hole has vanished."

"Are you sure?"

"I've never been surer of anything in my life."

The president released a long sigh. "Thank you, Wilhelm."

A shadow moved at the door. The president jerked in alarm, then relaxed. It was Director Morris.

"We got the killer, Ted," Morris said. "It's over."

Made in the USA
Charleston, SC
03 May 2013